At the

WOLF'S TABLE

At the
WOLF'S TABLE

Rosella Postorino

Translated from the Italian by Leah Janeczko

FLATIRON
BOOKS
NEW YORK

AT THE WOLF'S TABLE. Copyright © 2018 by Rosella Postorino. Translation copyright © 2019 by Leah Janeczko. All rights reserved. Printed in the United States of America. For information, address Flatiron Books, 175 Fifth Avenue, New York, N.Y. 10010.

www.flatironbooks.com

Library of Congress Cataloging-in-Publication Data

Names: Postorino, Rosella, author. | Janeczko, Leah, translator.
Title: At the wolf's table : a novel / Rosella Postorino ; translated from the Italian by Leah Janeczko.
Other titles: Assaggiatrici. English
Description: First U.S. edition. | New York : Flatiron Books, 2019.
Identifiers: LCCN 2018030162| ISBN 9781250179142 (hardcover) | ISBN 9781250229151 (international, sold outside the U.S., subject to rights availability) | ISBN 9781250179159 (ebook)
Classification: LCC PQ4916.O88 A9413 2019 | DDC 853/.92—dc23
LC record available at https://lccn.loc.gov/2018030162

Our books may be purchased in bulk for promotional, educational, or business use. Please contact your local bookseller or the Macmillan Corporate and Premium Sales Department at 1-800-221-7945, extension 5442, or by email at MacmillanSpecialMarkets@macmillan.com.

Originally published in Italy in 2018 as *Le assaggiatrici* by Feltrinelli

First U.S. Edition: January 2019
First International Edition: January 2019

10 9 8 7 6 5 4 3 2 1

A man can only live by absolutely forgetting he's a man like other folk.

—BERTOLT BRECHT, *THE THREEPENNY OPERA*

Part
ONE

1

We entered one at a time. We had waited for hours outside, lined up in the hallway. The room was large, its walls white. In the center of it, a long wooden table already laid out. They gestured for us to sit.

I sat with my hands clasped on my belly. In front of me, a white ceramic plate. I was hungry.

The other women had taken their places without a sound. There were ten of us. Some sat up straight and poised, their hair pulled into buns. Others glanced around. The girl across from me nibbled at her hangnails, mincing them between her front teeth. She had doughy, blotchy cheeks. She was hungry.

By eleven in the morning we were already hungry. It wasn't because of the country air or the journey by bus—the feeling in our stomachs was fear. For years we had lived with this hunger, this fear, and when the smell of the cooked food was under our noses, our heartbeats throbbed in our temples, our mouths watered. I looked over at the girl with blotchy skin. We shared the same longing.

The string beans were served with melted butter. I hadn't had butter since my wedding day. The aroma of the roasted peppers tickled my nostrils. My plate was piled high. I couldn't stop staring at it. The plate of the girl across from me was filled with rice and peas.

"Eat," they told us from the corner of the room, more an invitation than an order. They could see it, the longing in our eyes.

Mouths sagged open, breathing quickened. We hesitated. No one had wished us *bon appétit,* so maybe there was still time to stand up, say thank you, the hens were generous this morning, an egg will be enough for me today.

Again I counted the women around the table. There were ten of us. It wasn't the Last Supper.

"Eat!" they repeated from the corner, but I was already sucking on a string bean and felt the blood surging up to the roots of my hair and down to the tips of my toes, felt my heartbeat slowing. *What a feast you've prepared for me—*these peppers are so sweet—*what a feast for me, on a wooden table, not even a cloth covering it, ceramic dishes from Aachen, and ten women. If we were wearing veils we would look like nuns, a refectory of nuns who've taken vows of silence.*

At first our bites are modest, as though we're not being forced to eat it all, as though we could refuse this food, this meal that isn't intended for us, that is ours only by chance, of which only by chance we're worthy of partaking. But then it glides down our throats, reaching that pit in our stomachs, and the more it fills that pit, the bigger the pit grows, and the more tightly we clutch our forks. The apple strudel is so good that tears spring to my eyes, so good that I scoop bigger and bigger helpings into my mouth, wolfing them down until I throw back my head and gasp for air, all in the presence of my enemies.

My MOTHER USED to say eating was a way of battling death. She said it even before Hitler, back when I went to elementary school at Braunsteinstraße 10 in Berlin. She would tie a bow on my pinafore and hand me my schoolbag and remind me to be careful not to choke during lunch. At home I had the bad habit of talking nonstop, even with my mouth full. *You talk too much,* she would tell me, and then I actually would choke on my food because it made me laugh, her tragic tone, her attempts to raise me with a fear of dying, as if every act of living exposed us to mortal danger—life was perilous, the whole world lay in ambush.

WHEN THE MEAL was over, two SS guards stepped forward. The woman on my left rose from her chair.

"Sit down! In your place!"

The woman fell back into her seat as though they had shoved her into it. One of the two braids coiled at the sides of her head loosened from its hairpin, dangling slightly.

"None of you have permission to stand up. You will remain here, seated at the table, until further orders. If the food was contaminated, the poison will quickly enter your circulation." The SS guard scrutinized us one by one, examining our reactions. We didn't breathe. Then he turned back to the woman who had stood up. She wore a dirndl, so perhaps she had risen out of deference. "Don't worry, an hour will be enough," he told her. "In an hour's time you'll all be free to go."

"Or dead," remarked his comrade.

I felt my rib cage constrict. The girl with blotchy skin buried her face in her hands, muffling her sobs.

"Stop it," hissed the brunette sitting beside her, but by then the other women were also crying, in tears like sated crocodiles—perhaps an effect of their digestion.

In a low voice I said, "May I ask your name?" The blotchy-faced girl didn't realize I was talking to her. I reached out, touched her wrist. She flinched, looked at me dumbly. All her capillaries had burst. "What's your name?" I whispered again.

Unsure whether she had permission to speak, the girl looked over at the guards in the corner, but they were distracted. It was almost noon and they may have been getting hungry themselves, because they didn't seem to be paying attention to us, so she whispered, "Leni, Leni Winter?" She said it as though it were a question, but that was her name.

"Leni, I'm Rosa," I told her. "We'll be going home soon, you'll see."

Leni was little more than a child—you could tell by her pudgy knuckles. She had the looks of a girl who'd never been touched in a barn, not even during the weary languor after a harvest.

IN '38, AFTER my brother Franz moved away, Gregor brought me here to Gross-Partsch to meet his parents. *They're going to love you,* he told me, proud of the Berliner secretary whose heart he had won and who was now engaged to the boss, like in the movies.

I enjoyed it, that trip east in the sidecar. "Let us ride into the eastern lands," went the song. They would play it over the loudspeakers, and not only on April 20. Every day was Hitler's birthday.

For the first time, I took the ferry and left town with a man. Herta put me up in her son's room and sent him upstairs to sleep in the attic. When his parents had gone to bed, Gregor opened the door and slipped under my covers. *No,* I whispered, *not here. Then come to the barn,* he said. My eyes misted over. *I can't. What if your mother were to discover us?*

We had never made love. I had never made love to anyone.

Gregor slowly stroked my lips, tracing their edges. Then he pressed his fingertip more firmly and more firmly still until he'd bared my teeth, coaxed them open, slipped in two fingers. They felt dry against my tongue. I could have snapped my jaw shut, bitten him. That hadn't even occurred to Gregor. He had always trusted me.

Later that night I couldn't resist. I went up to the attic and this time it was me who opened the door. Gregor was sleeping. I brought my parted lips close to his, let our breaths mingle, and he woke up. *Wanted to find out what I smell like in my sleep, did you?* he asked with a smile. I slid one, then two, then three fingers into his mouth, felt it water up, his saliva wetting my skin. This was love: a mouth that doesn't bite, or the opportunity to unexpectedly attack the other like a dog that turns against its master.

I was wearing a red beaded necklace when, during the ferry ride home, he clasped my neck. It had finally happened not in his parents' barn, but in a windowless ship cabin.

"I NEED TO get out of here," Leni murmured.

"Shh. . . ." I stroked Leni's wrist. This time she didn't flinch. "Only twenty minutes left. It's almost over."

"I need to get out of here," she insisted.

The brunette beside her had angular cheekbones, glossy hair, a harshness in her eye. "You just can't keep quiet, can you?" she said, wrenching Leni's shoulder.

"Leave her alone!" I said, almost shouting.

The SS guards turned toward me. "What's going on?"

All the women turned toward me.

"Please . . . ," Leni said.

One of the guards walked over to her. He clamped his hand on Leni's arm and hissed something into her ear. I couldn't hear what it was but it made her face twist grotesquely.

"Is she ill?" another guard asked.

The woman in the dirndl jumped up from her chair again. "The poison!"

The other women also shot to their feet when Leni began to retch. The SS guard stepped aside just in time as Leni vomited on the floor.

The guards rushed out, screamed for the kitchen staff, interrogated the chef—the Führer was right, the British were trying to poison him!—some of the women clung to one another, others sobbed against the wall, the brunette paced back and forth with her hands on her hips, making a strange sound with her nose. I went over to Leni and held her head.

All the women were clutching their bellies, but not from spasms—they had sated their hunger and weren't used to it.

THEY KEPT US there far longer than an hour. After the floor had been wiped clean with newspapers and a damp cloth, an acrid stench hung in the air. Leni didn't die, she simply stopped trembling. Then she dozed off at the table, her hand in mine and her cheek resting on her arm, a little girl. My stomach tensed and churned, but I was too exhausted to fret about it.

When it was clear there was no longer cause for alarm, the guards woke Leni and led us single-file to the bus that would take us home. My stomach no longer protested; it had allowed itself to be occupied. My body had absorbed the Führer's food, the Führer's food was circulating in my bloodstream.

Hitler was safe.

I was hungry again.

2

We had never been Nazis. As a little girl I hadn't wanted to join the Bund Deutscher Mädel, hadn't liked the black neckerchief that hung down the front of their white shirts. I had never been a good German.

But that day, surrounded by the white walls of the lunchroom, I became one of Hitler's food tasters. It was autumn 1943. I was twenty-five and had fifty hours and seven hundred kilometers of travel weighing on me. To escape the war, a week earlier I had moved from Berlin to East Prussia. I had come to Gross-Partsch, the town where Gregor had been born, though Gregor wasn't here.

They had shown up unexpectedly at the home of my parents-in-law the day before that first meal. *We're looking for Rosa Sauer,* they said. I didn't hear them because I was in the backyard. I hadn't even heard the sound of the jeep coming to a halt out front but had seen the hens scurrying toward the henhouse all at once.

"They're asking for you," Herta said.

"Who is?"

She turned away without replying. I called out for Zart, but he didn't come. In the morning he would go off to wander around town. He was a worldly cat. I followed Herta, thinking, *Who could be looking for me, no one knows me here, I've only just arrived, oh, god, has Gregor come home?*

"Has my husband returned?" I asked breathlessly, but Herta was already in the kitchen, her back turned to the door, blocking the light. Joseph was also on his feet, stooping with one hand resting on the table.

"Heil Hitler!" Two dark silhouettes thrust their right arms in my direction.

I raised my arm in reply as I stepped inside. In the kitchen were two men in gray-green uniforms, pale shadows shrouding their faces. One of them said, "Rosa Sauer."

I nodded.

"The Führer needs you."

He had never seen my face, the Führer. Yet he needed me.

Herta wiped her hands on her apron as the SS officer continued to speak, addressing me, looking only at me, scrutinizing me as if to make an appraisal: a sturdy piece of craftsmanship. Of course, hunger had somewhat debilitated me, the air-raid sirens at night had deprived me of sleep, and the loss of everything, of everyone, had left me weary-eyed, but my face was round, my hair full and blond. . . . Yes, one look says it all: a young Aryan female tamed by war, a one hundred percent genuine national product, a fine acquisition.

The officer walked to the front door.

"May we offer you something?" Herta asked, too late. Country folk didn't know how to receive important guests. Joseph stood up straight.

"We'll return tomorrow morning at eight. Be ready to leave," said the other SS officer, who until then had remained silent. Then he too walked to the front door.

The Schutzstaffel were declining out of politeness, either that or they weren't fond of roasted acorn coffee, though perhaps there was some wine, a bottle saved in the cellar for when Gregor returned. Or they were practicing self-restraint, hardening themselves through abstention, force of will. Whatever the case, they didn't even consider Herta's offer, admittedly tardy.

They shouted, *Heil Hitler!* raising their arms—toward me.

Once they had driven off, I went to the window. The tire tracks in the gravel marked the path to my death sentence. I shot to another window in another room, ricocheting from one side of the house to the other in search of air, in search of a way out. Herta and Joseph followed me. *Please, let me think. Let me breathe.*

———

It was the mayor who had given them my name, according to the SS. The mayor of a small country town knew everyone, even newcomers.

"We'll find a way out." Joseph tugged his beard in his fist as though a solution might slip out. Working for Hitler, sacrificing one's life for him—wasn't that what all Germans were doing? But that I might ingest poisoned food and die, not from a rifle shot, not from an explosion, Joseph couldn't accept it. A life ending with a whimper, perishing out of view. Not a hero's death but a mouse's. Women didn't die as heroes.

"I have to leave." I rested my cheek against the window. Each time I tried to take a deep breath, a stabbing pain by my collarbone cut it short. I changed windows. A stabbing pain by my ribs. My breath couldn't break free. "I came here to live a better life. . . ." I laughed bitterly, a reproach to my parents-in-law, as though they had been the ones to offer my name to the SS.

"You must hide," Joseph said, "seek refuge somewhere."

"In the woods," Herta suggested.

"In the woods where? To die from cold and hunger?"

"We'll bring you food."

"Naturally," Joseph confirmed. "We would never abandon you."

"What if they come searching for me?"

Herta looked at her husband. "Do you think they would?"

"They won't be pleased, that's certain." Joseph wasn't getting his hopes up.

I was a deserter without an army, ridiculous.

"You could go back to Berlin," he said.

"Yes, you could go back home," Herta echoed. "They won't follow you all the way there."

"I don't have a home in Berlin anymore, remember? If I hadn't been forced to, I never would've come here in the first place!"

Herta's features tensed. I had shattered the politeness that had stood between us because of our roles, because of our scarce familiarity with each other.

"I'm sorry. I didn't mean to—"

"Never mind," she said stiffly.

I had been disrespectful to her, but at the same time I had thrown open the door to intimacy between us. She felt so close that I longed to cling to her. *Keep me with you, take care of me.*

"What about you two?" I asked. "If they come and don't find me here, they might take it out on you."

"We'll manage," said Herta. With this, she turned and left.

Joseph let go of his beard. There was no solution to be found there. "What do you want to do?"

I would rather die in a foreign town than in my own city, where I no longer had anyone.

ON MY SECOND day as a food taster I rose at dawn. The cock was crowing and the frogs had suddenly stopped croaking, as though falling into an exhausted sleep all at once. It was then that I felt alone, after an entire night awake. In my reflection in the window I saw the circles around my eyes and recognized myself. They hadn't been caused by insomnia or the war. Those dark furrows had always been there on my face. *Shut those books, look at that face of yours,* my mother would say, and my father would ask, *Do you think she has an iron deficiency, Doctor?* and my brother would rub his forehead against mine because the silky caress would help him fall asleep. In my reflection in the window I saw the same circled eyes that I'd had as a girl and realized they had been an omen.

I went out to look for Zart and found him curled up, snoozing beside the henhouse as though looking after the hens. It wasn't wise to leave the ladies unattended—Zart was an old-fashioned male, so he knew that. Gregor, on the other hand, had gone away. He had wanted to be a good German, not a good husband.

The first time we had gone out together he'd asked me to meet him at a café near the cathedral, and he arrived late. We sat at a table outside, the air chilly despite the sunshine. Enchanted, I heard a musical motif in the chorus of birds, saw in their flight a dance performed just for me, for this moment with him had finally arrived and resembled love as I'd imagined it ever since I was a little girl. A bird broke away from the flock. Proud and solitary, it plunged down almost as if to dive into the Spree, brushed the water with out-stretched wings, and instantly soared up again. It had followed a sudden urge to escape, a reckless act, an impulse driven by euphoria. That same feeling tingled in my calves. Facing my boss, the young engineer sitting before me at the café, I found I was euphoric. Happiness had just begun.

I had ordered a slice of apple pie but hadn't tasted it yet. Gregor pointed this out. *Don't you like it?* he asked. *I don't know,* I said, laughing. I pushed the plate forward, offering it to him, and when I saw him put the first piece into his mouth and chew quickly, with his customary enthusiasm, I wanted to as well. And so I took a bite, and then another, and we found ourselves eating from the same plate, chattering about nothing in particular without looking at each other, as though that were already too intimate, until our forks suddenly touched. When they did we fell silent, looking up. We stared at each other for a long while, as the birds continued to circle overhead or came to rest on branches, on balustrades, lampposts, who knew, perhaps they were diving down to plunge beak-first into the river, never again to emerge. Then Gregor pinned my fork down with his, and it was as if he were touching me.

HERTA CAME OUTSIDE to collect the eggs later than usual. Perhaps she too had spent a sleepless night and was having a hard time waking up that morning. She found me there, sitting on the rusty metal chair, Zart curled up on top of my feet. She sat down beside me, forgetting about breakfast. The door creaked.

"What, are they here already?" Herta asked.

Leaning against the doorframe, Joseph shook his head. "Eggs," he replied, gesturing at the henhouse. Zart scampered after him, and I missed his warmth.

The soft glow of sunrise had withdrawn like the tide, laying the morning sky bare, pale, drained. The hens began to squawk, the birds to twitter, the bees to buzz against that circle of light overhead, but the squeal of a vehicle coming to a halt silenced them.

"Get up, Rosa Sauer!" we heard them shout.

Herta and I leapt to our feet and Joseph returned carrying the eggs. He didn't notice he'd clutched one of them too tightly and had broken its shell, the yolk oozing through his fingers in viscous rivulets of bright orange. I stared at them. They were about to drip from his skin and would hit the ground without making a sound.

"Hurry up, Rosa Sauer!" the SS officers insisted.

Herta touched my back and I moved.

I chose to await Gregor's return. To believe the war would end. I chose to eat.

In the bus, I glanced around and sat in the first empty spot, far from the other women. There were four of them, two sitting next to each other, the others sitting on their own. I couldn't remember their names. I only knew Leni's, and she hadn't been picked up yet.

No one replied when I said good morning. I looked at Herta and Joseph through the window, which was streaked with dried rain. Standing by the doorway, she raised her arm despite her arthritis, he still held a broken egg in his hand. I watched the house as it fell behind—its moss-darkened shingles, the pink paint, the valerian blossoms that grew in clusters from the bare earth—until it disappeared behind the bend. I would watch it every morning as though I were never to see it again. Until one day I no longer felt that longing.

The headquarters were three kilometers from Gross-Partsch, hidden in the forest, invisible from the air. When the workers began to build it, Joseph told me, the locals wondered why there was all that coming and going of vans and trucks. The Soviet military airplanes had never detected it. But we knew Hitler was there, that he slept not far away, and perhaps in summer he would toss and turn in his bed, slapping at the mosquitoes that disturbed his slumber. Perhaps he too would rub the red bites, overcome by the conflicting desires caused by the itch: though you couldn't stand the archipelago of bumps on your skin, part of you didn't want them to heal because the relief of scratching them was so intense.

They called it the Wolfsschanze, the Wolf's Lair. "Wolf" was his nickname. As hapless as Little Red Riding Hood, I had ended up in his belly. A legion of hunters was out looking for him, and to get him in their grips they would gladly slay me as well.

3

ONCE WE ARRIVED IN KRAUSENDORF, THEY LINED US UP AND WALKED US single file to a red-brick schoolhouse that had been set up as military barracks. We crossed the threshold as docile as cows. The SS guards stopped us in the hallway, searched us. It was terrible to feel their hands linger on my sides, under my arms, and not be able to do anything but hold my breath.

We answered the roll call and they marked down attendance in a register. I discovered that the brunette who had wrenched Leni's shoulder was named Elfriede Kuhn.

Two by two, we were made to enter a room that smelled of alcohol while the others waited their turn outside. I rested my elbow on the school desk in front of me. A man in a white coat tied a tourniquet tightly around my arm and tapped on my vein with his pointer and middle fingers. With the drawing of blood samples, we were officially test animals. While the day before might have been seen as an inauguration, a rehearsal, as of this moment our work as food tasters had officially begun.

When the needle pierced my vein I looked away. Elfriede was beside me, staring at the syringe that drew her blood, filling up with a red color that grew darker and darker. I had never been able to stand the sight of my own blood—recognizing the dark liquid as something that came from inside of me made me dizzy—so I looked at her instead, at her posture straight as two Cartesian axes, her indifference. I sensed Elfriede was a woman of beauty, though I still couldn't see it. Her beauty was a mathematical theory I had yet to prove.

Before I knew it, her profile became a face glaring at me sharply. Her nostrils flared, as if lacking air. I opened my mouth to catch my breath and said nothing.

"Keep pressure on this," the man in the white coat told me, pressing a cotton ball against my skin.

I heard Elfriede's tourniquet come off with a snap and her chair scrape the floor. I too stood up.

IN THE LUNCHROOM I waited for the others to sit down before me. Most of the women chose the same place they had sat in the day before. The chair across from Leni was free, and from then on it was mine.

After breakfast—milk and fruit—they served us lunch. On my plate, asparagus pie. With time I would come to learn that giving different food combinations to different groups of us was one of their control procedures.

I studied the lunchroom as one studies a foreign environment— the windows with iron grilles, the French door leading to the courtyard guarded at all times, the pictureless walls. On my first day of school, when my mother had left me in the classroom and walked out, the thought that something bad might happen to me without her knowing about it filled me with sorrow. What affected me wasn't the danger of the world around me but my mother's powerlessness. It seemed intolerable that my life could go on happening with her oblivious to it. Whatever remained concealed, even if not on purpose, was already a betrayal. I had searched the classroom for a crack in the wall, a spiderweb, anything that might be mine, like a secret. My eyes wandered the room, which seemed enormous, and finally noticed a missing fragment of baseboard, which calmed me.

In the lunchroom in Krausendorf the baseboards were all intact. Gregor wasn't there, I was alone. The SS guards' boots dictated the pace of the meal, clicking away the countdown to our potential death. *This asparagus is delicious, but isn't poison bitter?* I swallowed and my heart stopped.

Elfriede was also eating asparagus, staring at me as she did, and I drank one glass of water after another to dilute my anxiety. It might have been my dress that made her so curious. Maybe Herta was right, maybe I was out of place wearing that checkered pattern, it wasn't like I was going to the office, I didn't work in Berlin anymore. *Get rid of those city airs of yours,* my mother-in-law had told me, *otherwise everyone's going to look down on you.* Elfriede wasn't looking down on me, or maybe she was, but I had put on my most comfortable dress, the one most worn—the uniform, Gregor used to call it. It was the one I never had to question, neither if it flattered my figure, nor if it would bring me luck. It offered me shelter, even from Elfriede, who was scrutinizing me with a serious look on her face and didn't even bother to hide it, her eyes scouring the checks on my dress with enough vehemence to make them fly off the fabric, with enough vehemence to unravel the hem, unlace my heeled shoes, make the wave of hair that framed my temple fall flat as I continued to drink water.

Lunch wasn't over yet and I didn't know if we were permitted to leave the table. My bladder ached, like it had in the cellar in Budengasse where Mother and I would seek refuge at night with the building's other tenants when the air-raid sirens went off. But there was no bucket in the corner here, and I couldn't hold it any longer. Without even consciously deciding to, I stood up and asked permission to go to the washroom. The SS guards nodded. As one of them, a very tall man with big feet, escorted me into the hallway, I heard Elfriede's voice. "I need to go too."

The tiles were worn, the grout blackened. Two sinks and four stalls. The SS man stood guard in the hallway, we went in, and I hurried into one of the stalls. I didn't hear another stall door close or a faucet run. Elfriede had disappeared, or was standing there listening. The sound of my stream breaking the silence was humiliating. When I opened the door she blocked it with the tip of her shoe, grabbed me by the shoulder, and shoved me back against the wall. The tiles smelled of disinfectant. She moved her face close to mine, almost sweetly.

"What do you want?" she said.

"Me?"

"Why were you staring at me during the blood sample?"

I tried to break free. She blocked my way.

"A word of advice: mind your own business. In this place, everybody's better off minding their own business."

"I can't stand the sight of my own blood, that's all."

"Oh, but the sight of someone else's blood is okay, is it?"

The scrape of metal against wood made us start. Elfriede pulled away.

"What are you up to in here?" the guard asked, stepping inside. The tiles were cold and damp, or maybe it was the sweat on my back. "Having a little tête-à-tête, are we?" He wore enormous shoes, perfect for crushing the heads of snakes.

"I had a dizzy spell. It must be because of the blood sample," I stammered, touching the red mark over the bulging vein on the inside of my elbow. "She was helping me. I feel better now."

The guard warned that if he caught us like that again, so intimate, he would teach us a lesson. Or better yet, he would take advantage of it. Then he burst out laughing.

We went back to the lunchroom, the Beanpole watching our every step. He was wrong: it hadn't been intimacy between Elfriede and me, it had been fear. We were sizing up each other and our surroundings with the blind terror of someone who's just been born into the world.

That night, in the bathroom of the Sauer home, the scent of asparagus that emanated from my urine made me think of Elfriede. She too, sitting on the commode, probably smelled the same odor. Even Hitler, in his bunker at the Wolfsschanze. That night, Hitler's urine would stink like mine.

4

I was born on December 27, 1917, eleven months before the Great War ended, a Christmas gift to wrap up the holiday celebrations. My mother said Santa Claus had heard me wailing, bundled up beneath so many blankets in the back of his sleigh that he'd completely overlooked me. And so he flew back to Berlin, unwillingly though, because his vacation had just begun and the unscheduled delivery was an inconvenience. *It's a good thing he noticed you,* Father used to say, *because you were our only gift that year.*

My father was a railroad worker, my mother a seamstress. Our living room floor was always covered with spools of thread and balls of yarn in all different colors. My mother would lick the end of a strand to thread the needle more easily, and I would mimic her. Once, without letting her see, I sucked a strand of thread and played with it on my tongue. When it had been reduced to a soggy clump, I couldn't resist the urge to swallow it and discover whether, once inside me, it would kill me. I spent the following minutes wondering what the signs of my imminent death would be, but, given that I didn't die, I soon forgot about it. Then at night I remembered it, certain my time had come. The game of death began at a very early age. I never spoke a word of it to anyone.

At night my father would listen to the radio while my mother would sweep up the threads strewn on the floor and climb into bed to open a copy of *Deutsche Allgemeine Zeitung,* eager to read the latest episode of her favorite serial novel. That was my childhood, the steamed-up windows looking out onto Budengasse, multiplication tables memorized well in advance, the walk to school wearing shoes that were first too big and then too tight, ants decapitated with fingernails, Sundays on which Mother and Father would read from the pulpit—she the psalms, he the Epistles to the Corinthians—and I would listen to them from the pew, either proud or bored, a pfennig coin tucked in my mouth. The metal was salty, it tingled. I would close my eyes in delight, my tongue pushing it to the edge of my throat until it teetered there, ready to slide down, then all at once I would spit it out. My childhood was books beneath my pillow, nursery rhymes sung with my father, blind man's bluff in the square, stollen at Christmas, trips to the Tiergarten, the day I went to Franz's crib, stuck his tiny hand between my teeth, and bit down hard. My brother howled like all newborns howl when they wake up, and no one found out what I had done.

It was a childhood full of sins and secrets, and I was too focused on their safekeeping to notice anyone else. I never wondered where my parents found the milk, which cost hundreds and later thousands of marks, if they held up a grocery store and eluded the police. Not even years later did I wonder if they felt humiliated by the Treaty of Versailles like everyone else, if they too hated the United States, if they felt unjustly treated for being held responsible for a war in which my father had fought. He had spent an entire night in a foxhole with a dead Frenchman and had eventually dozed off beside the corpse.

During that time, when Germany was a gridlock of wounds, my mother would pull back her lips as she slicked down the end of the thread, on her face a turtle expression that made me laugh, my father listening to the radio after work, smoking Juno cigarettes, and Franz napping in his crib, his arm bent and his hand by his ear, his tiny fingers curled over his palm of tender flesh.

In my room I would do an inventory of my sins and my secrets, and would feel no remorse.

5

I can't make heads or tails of this," Leni moaned. We were sitting at the cleared table after dinner with open books and pencils provided by the guards. "There are too many hard words."

"For example?"

"Salivary alym—no, amyl—wait." Leni checked the page. "Salivary amylase, or that other one: peps—err . . . pep-sino-gen."

A week after our first day, the chef had come into the lunchroom and handed out a series of textbooks on nutrition, asking us to read them. Ours was a serious mission, he said, and we should be knowledgeable as we carried it out. He introduced himself as Otto Günther but we all knew the guards called him Krümel, or Crumbs, maybe because he was short and skinny. When we arrived at the barracks in the mornings he and his staff would already be working on breakfast, which we ate immediately, while Hitler ate at around ten, after being briefed on news from the front. Then, at around eleven, we had what he would have for lunch. When the hour-long wait was over they took us home, but at five in the evening they returned to pick us up to taste his dinner.

The morning Krümel gave us the books, one of the women flipped through a few pages and then pushed her book away with a shrug. She had broad, square shoulders disproportionate to her slender ankles, which were left bare under her black skirt. Her name was Augustine. Leni, on the other hand, went ashen, as though they had announced a big exam and she was certain she would fail. As for me, the task was a consolation—not that I thought it was useful to memorize the phases in the digestive process, nor felt the need to make a good impression. In those diagrams, those tables, I recognized my age-old thirst for knowledge so strongly that I could almost make believe I wasn't losing myself.

"I'll never manage to learn this," Leni said. "Do you think they'll quiz us?"

"The guards sitting at the teacher's desk and giving us grades? Don't be silly," I said, smiling at her.

Leni didn't smile back. "Maybe the doctor will ask us something at our next blood exam, surprise us with a question!"

"That would be funny."

"What's so funny about it?"

"It's like we're peeking into Hitler's innards," I said with incomprehensible cheerfulness. "If we make a rough estimate, we can calculate when his sphincter will dilate."

"That's disgusting!"

It wasn't disgusting, it was human. Adolf Hitler was a human being who digested.

"Has the professor finished her lesson? When the lecture's over we can applaud you." It was Augustine, the woman with square shoulders dressed in black. The guards didn't order us to be quiet. At the chef's request, the lunchroom was to be a schoolroom, and his request was to be respected.

"I'm sorry," I said, lowering my head, "I didn't mean to bother you."

"We all know you studied in the city, okay?"

"What do you care what kind of studies she did?" another woman, Ulla, broke in. "In any case, she's here now, eating just like the rest of us. Delicious food, no doubt, dressed with a drizzle of poison." She laughed, but no one joined her.

Narrow of waist, firm of bosom, Ulla was quite a dish—that's what the SS guards said about her. She liked to clip out photographs of actresses from magazines and glue them into a scrapbook. At times she would leaf through them and point them out to us one by one: the porcelain cheeks of Anny Ondra, who had married Max Schmeling, the boxer; Ilse Werner's lips, soft and plump as she pursed them to whistle the refrain of "Sing ein Lied, wenn Du mal traurig bist" on the radio, because all it took to keep from feeling sad and lonely was to sing a song. Especially, Ulla admitted, to German soldiers. But her favorite was Zarah Leander, with her high-arched eyebrows and the little curls framing her face in the movie *La Habanera*.

"Coming here to the barracks wearing elegant clothes is a good idea," she said to me. I wore a wine-colored dress with a French-cut collar and puffed sleeves. My mother had made it for me. "This way, if you die, at least you'll already be in your good dress. They won't even need to prepare your corpse."

"Why do you all keep talking about such horrible things?" Leni protested.

Herta was right: the others noticed my appearance. Not only Elfriede, who had scoured the checks on my dress on our second day there and was now leaning against the wall as she read her book, a pencil between her lips like a burned-out cigarette. It seemed to weigh on her, having to stay seated. She always looked like she was on the verge of leaving.

"So you like this dress, then?"

Ulla hesitated, then answered me. "It's a bit chaste, but the style is almost Parisian. And it's definitely much nicer than the dirndls Frau Goebbels wants to make us wear." She lowered her voice. "And that *she* wears," she added, pointing with her eyes to the woman next to me, the one who had stood up after lunch on the first day. Gertrude didn't hear her.

"Oh, what nonsense." Augustine slammed her palms on the table for emphasis and turned away. Unsure how to conclude her dramatic finale to the conversation, she decided to move closer to Elfriede, though Elfriede didn't take her eyes off her textbook.

"So do you like it or don't you?" I asked again.

Ulla reluctantly admitted: "Yes."

"Fine. You can have it, then."

A thump made me look up. Elfriede had snapped her book shut and folded her arms over her chest, the pencil still in her mouth.

"So what are you going to do, strip down like Saint Francis right here in front of everyone and give it to her?" Augustine snickered, expecting Elfriede to back her up, but she just stood there staring at me, expressionless.

I turned back to Ulla. "I'll bring it to you tomorrow, if you like. No, wait, give me time to wash it."

A murmur spread through the room as Elfriede pulled away from the wall and moved over to sit across from me. She let her textbook thud to the table, rested her hand on it, and began to drum her fingers on the cover, scrutinizing me. Augustine watched her, certain she was about to pass judgment, but Elfriede said nothing. Her fingers fell still.

"She comes here from Berlin to give us handouts," Augustine said, piling it on. "Wants to give us lessons in biology and Christian charity, to prove she's better than us."

"I do want it," Ulla said.

"It's yours," I replied.

Augustine tsked. I would learn she always did that to express her displeasure. "Oh, please. . . ."

"Line up!" the guards ordered. "The hour is over."

We quickly rose to our feet. Augustine's little scene had captivated the other women, but their desire to leave the lunchroom was even stronger. Once again, we were going back home safe and sound.

As I joined the line, Ulla touched my elbow. "Thank you," she whispered, and ran off ahead.

Elfriede was behind me. "This isn't a boarding school for women, Berliner, it's a barracks."

"Mind your own business," I was surprised to hear myself say. The back of my neck instantly flushed. "You're the one who taught me that, remember?" It sounded more like an excuse than a provocation. I wanted to get along with Elfriede rather than clash with her, though I didn't know why.

"In any case," she said, "the kid's right: there's nothing funny about those books, unless you get a kick out of learning the symptoms caused by various forms of poisoning. Do you enjoy preparing for death?"

I kept walking, without replying.

That night I washed the wine-colored dress for Ulla. Giving it to her wasn't an act of generosity or even a ploy to make her like me.

Seeing it on her would be like scattering my life in the capital into Gross-Partsch, dispersing it. It was resignation. Three days later, I gave it to her, dried, ironed, and wrapped in newspaper. I would never see her wear it to the lunchroom.

Herta took my measurements and altered some of her own dresses for me, narrowing the waistline and shortening the back hems slightly, at my insistence. *That's the fashion,* I explained. *Berliner fashion,* she retorted, pins between her lips like my mother and not even one scrap of thread on the floor of her country house.

I kept the checkered dress in the wardrobe that had belonged to Gregor, along with all my work clothes. My shoes were the same— *Where are you going in those heels?* Herta said reproachfully—but only with them on could I recognize my own footsteps, no matter how uncertain they had become. On foggy mornings I would sometimes pull out the checkered dress, gripping the hanger angrily. There was no need for me to blend in with the other tasters, we had nothing in common, why did I care about being accepted by them? But then I would glimpse the dark circles under my eyes and the anger would wither to despondency. Putting the dress back in the darkness of the wardrobe, I would close the door.

They had been a warning, those circles under my eyes, and I hadn't grasped it, hadn't foreseen my fate, blocked its path. Now that death was finally upon me, there was no longer room for the little girl who sang in the school choir, who went roller-skating with friends in the afternoon, who let them copy her geometry homework. Gone was the secretary who had made the boss fall head over heels for her. Instead there was a woman whom the war had suddenly aged. That was the fate written in her blood.

THAT NIGHT OF March '43, the night my fate had taken a sharp turn for the worse, the air-raid siren had gone off with its usual whine, the smallest run-up and then a leap, just long enough for my mother to roll out of bed. "Rosa, get up," she urged me. "They're bombing."

The day my father died, a year and a half after we entered the war, I had begun to sleep in his place beside her. We were two adult women who had both experienced everyday familiarity with the marriage bed, had both lost it, and there was something profane in the similar smell of our two bodies beneath the covers. Still, I wanted to keep her company when she woke during the night, even if the siren wasn't going off. Or maybe I was afraid to sleep all alone. That's why, six months after Gregor had gone off to war, I had rented out our apartment in Altemesseweg and moved back in with my parents. I was still learning the ropes of being a wife and already I had to stop that and become a daughter again.

"Hurry," she said, seeing me search for a dress, any dress, to change into. She threw her coat on over her nightgown and headed down in slippers.

The siren was no different from the previous ones, a long wail that built up as though to last forever, but after eleven seconds it diminished in tone, abated. Then it started up again.

All the ones before it had been false alarms. Each time we had run downstairs with our flashlights on, despite the blackout orders. In the dark we would have tripped over the other tenants, bumped into them as they too headed for the cellar, carrying blankets and children and canteens filled with water, or descended terrified and empty-handed. Each time we had found a tiny patch for ourselves on the floor and sat down beneath a dim, bare lightbulb that dangled from the ceiling. The floor was cold, the people cramped, the dampness sinking into our bones.

Huddled against one another, we who lived at Budengasse 78 wept and prayed and cried for salvation. We urinated in a bucket too close to the eyes of the others, or held our bladders though they were ready to burst. A young boy bit into an apple and another boy stole it out of his hand, taking as many bites as he could before the first boy snatched it back and slapped him. We were hungry and sat there in silence or dozed, and would reach the dawn with haggard faces.

Soon afterward, the promise of a new day would drift down onto the light blue façade of our stately building in the outskirts of Berlin, making it glow. Hidden away in the depths of the building, we couldn't see that light, much less believe it possible.

As I raced down the cellar stairs with my arm around my mother on that March night, I wondered what note it was, the sound of the air-raid siren. As a girl I had sung in the school choir, the teacher had complimented my pitch, the timbre of my voice, but I hadn't studied music, so I couldn't tell the notes apart. And yet, as I nestled down in my spot beside Frau Reinach with her brown kerchief on her head, as I stared at Frau Preiß's black shoes deformed by her bunioned big toe, at the hairs sticking out of Herr Holler's ears, at the Schmidts' son Anton's two tiny front teeth, and as my mother's breath—*Are you cold?* she whispered to me. *Bundle up*—became the only profane yet familiar smell I had to cling to, all that while the only thing that mattered to me was finding out what note corresponded to that long blare of the siren.

The rumble of planes overhead instantly banished the thought. My mother squeezed my hand, her nails piercing my skin. Pauline, who was barely three, stood up. Her mother, Anne Langhans, tried to pull her down, but with all the obstinacy of her scant ninety centimeters the little girl broke free. She tilted back her head and looked straight up, turning around as if to seek the origin of the sound or follow the plane's trajectory.

The ceiling shuddered. Pauline toppled over as the floor lurched, a deafening hiss drowning out every other sound, including our screams, her cries. The lightbulb flickered out. A massive explosion burst into the cellar, caving in the walls, hurling us every which way. The blast sent our bodies flying through the air, slamming into one another, tangling together as the walls spewed plaster.

After the bombing ceased, sobs and shouts reached our injured eardrums, muffled. Someone pushed on the cellar door. It was blocked. The women shrieked, the few men present kicked it again and again until finally it burst open.

We were deaf, blind, the dust had masked our features, made us strangers even to our own parents. We searched for them, calling out, *Mother, Father,* unable to utter any other words. My eyes saw only smoke. And then Pauline: she was bleeding from the temple. I tore the hem off my skirt with my teeth and stanched the wound, tied the strip of fabric around her head, looked for her mother, looked for mine, recognized no one.

The sun arrived by the time everyone had been pulled out. Our building hadn't been leveled but the roof had a gaping hole in it. The roof of the building across from ours was entirely gone. Lined up on the street were the wounded and dead. Survivors leaned back against the wall, gasping for breath, but the fine debris had left throats stinging, noses clogged. Frau Reinach had lost her headkerchief, her hair clumps of smoldering dust that sprouted from her scalp like tumors. Herr Holler was limping. Pauline had stopped bleeding. I was intact, no aches, no pains. My mother was dead.

6

I would give my very life for the Führer," Gertrude said, her eyes half closed to show her solemnity. Her sister Sabine nodded in approval. Because of her receding chin I couldn't tell whether she was younger or older. The table in the lunchroom was bare. Only half an hour to go before we could leave. Standing out against the metal-gray sky framed by the window was another food taster, Theodora.

"I would give my life for him too," Sabine said. "He's like an older brother to me. He's like the brother we lost, Gerti."

"I, on the other hand," Theodora said with a grin, "would have him as a husband."

Sabine frowned, almost as if Theodora had disrespected the Führer.

The window fixtures rattled. Augustine had leaned against them. "Go ahead and keep him, your Great Consoler," she said. "He's the one who sends your brothers, fathers, and husbands out for slaughter in the first place. But then again, if they die, who cares? You can always pretend *he's* your brother, right? Or you can dream he'll marry you." Augustine ran her finger and thumb down the corners of her mouth, wiping away frothy white spittle. "You're ridiculous, all of you."

"You'd better pray you're not overheard!" Gertrude snapped. "Or do you want me to call in the SS?"

"The Führer would have kept us out of war if it had been possible," Theodora said, "but he didn't have a choice."

"I take that back: you're more than ridiculous—you're fanatics."

Though I didn't know it then, from that point on "the Fanatics" would be our name for Gertrude and her little group. Augustine coined it while frothing at the mouth. Her husband had fallen at the front, that was why she always dressed in black. Leni told me that.

The women had grown up in the same town, and those of the same age had gone to school together. They all knew one another, at least by sight. All of them except Elfriede. She wasn't from Gross-Partsch or the surrounding area, and Leni told me she'd never met her before we'd become food tasters. Elfriede too was from out of town, then, but no one was giving her any trouble over it. Augustine didn't bother her. Augustine was nasty to me not so much because I came from the capital but because she saw my need to fit in, and that left me vulnerable. Neither I nor the others had ever asked Elfriede what city she came from, and she had never mentioned it. Her coldness left us apprehensive.

I wondered whether Elfriede had also fled to the countryside in search of peace and had immediately been recruited, just like me. On what basis had they chosen us? The first time I boarded the bus I had expected to find a den of zealous Nazis singing songs and waving flags. Soon I would realize that loyalty to the party hadn't been a criterion in their selection, except perhaps in the case of the Fanatics. Had they enlisted the poorest ones, the neediest? The ones with the most children to feed? The women talked about their children nonstop, except for Leni and Ulla, who were the youngest ones, and Elfriede. They were childless, as was I. But they didn't wear wedding bands, while I had been married for four years.

THE MINUTE I got home that afternoon, Herta asked me to help her fold the sheets. She barely even said hello to me. She seemed impatient, as though she'd been waiting for hours to be able to take care of the laundry and now that I had arrived she wasn't about to wait one second more. "Bring in the basket, please." She would normally ask me about work and then say, *Go rest, lie down for a while,* or she would make me some tea. Her brusque behavior today was making me uncomfortable.

I carried the basket into the kitchen and put it on the table.

"Come on," Herta said, "hurry up."

I pulled on the end of a sheet and tried to untangle it from the others without overturning the basket. Her rushing me made my movements clumsy. When I gave it one last tug to free it completely, a white rectangle fluttered into the air. It looked like a handkerchief. It was going to fall on the floor and my mother-in-law would be displeased. Only when it hit the floor did I realize it wasn't a handkerchief but a sealed envelope. I looked at Herta.

"Finally!" she said, laughing. "I thought you'd never find it!"

I laughed too, with amazement, with gratitude.

"Well? Aren't you going to pick it up?"

As I leaned down she whispered: "Go read it in the other room, if you like. But then come right back here and tell me how my son is."

My dearest Rosa,
At last I can reply to you. We've been traveling a lot,
sleeping in the trucks. We haven't even changed our
uniforms for a week. The more I travel through the streets
and villages of this country, the more I discover there's only
poverty here. Its people have withered, the homes are
hovels—far from a Bolshevik paradise, the workers'
paradise. . . . We've stopped for the time being. Below,
you'll find the new address where you can send me letters.
Thank you for writing so often, and forgive me if I write
less frequently than you, but at the end of the day I'm
exhausted. Yesterday I spent all morning shoveling snow
out of a trench and then last night I stood guard for four
hours (wearing two sweaters under my uniform) while the
trench filled up with snow again.

Afterwards, when I collapsed onto my straw mattress, I
dreamed of you. You were sleeping in our old apartment in
Altemesseweg. That is, I knew it was our apartment though
the room was somewhat different. The strange thing was
that lying on the rug was a dog, like a sheepdog. It too was
asleep. I didn't even wonder what a dog was doing in our
home, whether it was yours. All I knew was that I had to

be careful not to wake it because it was dangerous. I
wanted to lay down beside you, so I tiptoed over to avoid
disturbing the dog, but it awoke and began to growl. You
didn't hear a thing, you kept on sleeping, and I called out to
you, afraid the dog would bite you. Suddenly it barked
fiercely and lunged—and just then I woke up. It left me in
a foul mood for a long time. Maybe I was only worried
about your journey. Now that you're in Gross-Partsch I'm
calmer. My parents will take care of you.

After everything you had been through, the thought of
you all alone in Berlin was a torment to me. I recalled
when we argued three years ago, when I decided to enlist. I
told you we mustn't be selfish or cowardly, that defending
ourselves was a matter of life and death. I remember the
period after the Great War—you don't, you were too young,
but I remember it well. Such misery. Our people were
foolish, they let themselves be humiliated. The time had
come to strengthen our resolve. I had to do my part, even
though that meant leaving you. And yet today I no longer
know what to think.

The following paragraphs were crossed out. The lines covering the
sentences to render them illegible disturbed me. I tried to decipher
the words, but to no avail. *And yet today I no longer know what to think,*
Gregor had written. He usually avoided writing compromising things,
fearing the mail was opened and censored. His letters were brief—so
brief that at times they seemed cold. The dream he'd had must have
made him lose control, later forcing him to cross it out, and violently
so; in some places the lines had torn through the page.

Gregor never dreamed, or so he claimed, and he used to tease me
because of the importance I attributed to my dreams, almost as though
they had revelatory power. He was worried about me, that was why
he had written such a melancholy letter. For a moment I imagined
the front would send me back a different man and I wondered if I
would be able to bear it. I was shut up in the very room where he had
dreamed as a little boy but I didn't know his childhood dreams, and

being surrounded by what had once belonged to him wasn't enough
to make him feel close. It wasn't like when we used to share a bed in
our rented apartment and he would fall asleep on his side, arm outstretched to clasp my wrist. Reading in bed, as always, I would turn
the pages of my book with only one hand so as not to detach myself
from his grasp. At times he flinched in his sleep, his fingers tighten-
ing around my wrist as though some spring mechanism had been triggered, and then relaxing again. Who could he cling to now?

One night my arm grew stiff and I wanted to change positions.
Gently, trying not to wake him, I pulled my hand free. His fingers
curled up around nothing, grasped empty space. At the sight of it, all
the love I felt for him had risen to my throat.

> *It's strange to know you're at my parents' house without me
> there as well. I'm not one to get emotional, yet recently it's
> happened to me when I imagine you wandering the rooms,
> touching the old furniture I grew up with, making jam
> with my mother. (Thank you for sending me some. Give a
> kiss to her for me, and tell my father I say hello.)*
>
> *I need to sign off now. Tomorrow morning I wake at
> five. The Katyusha organ plays around the clock, but we've
> grown used to it. Survival, Rosa, is all a matter of chance.
> Don't worry, though—by now I can tell from the whistle of
> the bullets whether they'll fall close by or far away. Besides,
> there's a superstition that I've learned in Russia: it says
> that as long as your woman is faithful, soldier, you'll never
> be killed. So I suppose I have no choice but to count on you!*
>
> *To make up for my prolonged silence I've written quite
> a bit, so I hope you find no reason for complaint. Tell me
> about your days. I simply can't imagine a woman like you
> living in the countryside! You'll get used to it soon enough.
> You'll like it, you'll see. Tell me about this job of yours, too.
> You said you would describe it to me in person, that it was
> better not to do so by letter. Have I reason to be concerned?*
>
> *I've saved the best for last, a surprise: I'll be coming
> home on leave for Christmas and staying for ten days. We'll*

celebrate together, for the first time, in the place where I
grew up, and I can't wait to kiss you.

The letter in my hands, I rose from the bed and reread it. I wasn't mistaken, he really had written it. Gregor was coming to Gross-Partsch!

> *I look at your photograph every day. Since I always keep*
> *it in my pocket, it's getting awfully worn. It now has a*
> *crease that crosses your cheek like a wrinkle. When I return*
> *you'll have to give me another one, because in this one you*
> *look older. You know what I say, though? You're even*
> *beautiful old.*
>
> *Gregor*

"Herta!" I rushed out of the room, waving the letter in the air. "Read this part here!" I pointed to the lines where Gregor mentioned his leave—only those, as the rest were between me and my husband.

"He'll be here for Christmas . . . ," she said, almost in disbelief. She was eager for Joseph to come home so she could give him the good news.

The uneasiness I had felt just minutes earlier was gone; happiness had drowned out every other possible emotion. I would take care of him. We would share a bed again, and I would hold him so close that he would no longer be afraid of anything.

7

Sitting around the hearth, we daydreamed about Gregor's re-turn. Joseph planned to kill a rooster for our Christmas dinner and I wondered whether I would have to eat at the lunchroom that day. What would Gregor do while I was at the barracks? I was jealous of the time Herta and Joseph would spend with him while I was gone.

"Maybe he could come to Krausendorf. After all, he's a soldier in the Wehrmacht."

"No," Joseph told me, "the SS wouldn't let him in."

We ended up talking about Gregor as a child. We often did. My mother-in-law told me that until he was sixteen he had been a slightly chubby boy.

"He had red cheeks, even when he wasn't running around. It often looked like he'd been drinking."

"Actually," Joseph said, "he did get drunk once."

"Why, that's right!" Herta exclaimed. "Oh, what memories you've made me recall. . . . Listen to this, Rosa. He might've been seven, no older than that. It was summer, we came back from the fields and found him lying right there on that chest." She pointed at the wooden trunk by the wall. "He was so happy. 'Mother,' he says, 'that juice you made is delicious.'"

"On the table was an open bottle of wine," Joseph said, "almost half empty. 'Good god,' I ask him, 'why did you drink that?' And he says, 'Because I was really thirsty.'" Joseph laughed.

So did Herta. She laughed herself to tears. Watching her arthritis-twisted hands wipe her eyes, I thought of all the times they had caressed Gregor when he awoke, had brushed his hair from his fore-head as he ate breakfast—thought of all the times they had scrubbed every last inch of his filthy body when he returned in the evening, exhausted from his fierce battles at the edge of the marsh, a slingshot sticking out of his shorts pocket. All the times she had slapped him and then, sitting in her room, had wanted to cut off the hand that caused such disgrace—the disgrace of striking someone who was once you and was now another human being.

"Then he grew up, grew tall, all at once," Joseph said. "Sprouted up overnight, like he'd soaked his feet in water."

I imagined Gregor as a plant, a towering poplar tree, just like the ones lining the road to Krausendorf—wide, straight trunk; clear bark speckled with lenticels—and longed to embrace him.

From then on I counted the days by crossing them off the calendar with X's, each X shortening the wait by a little bit. To fill the time, I followed a self-imposed routine.

In the afternoons, before getting back on the bus, I would go to the well with Herta to get water, and when I returned I fed the hens. I would leave the feed in the henhouse and they would rush over and peck at it, twitching anxiously. There was always one who couldn't squeeze her way into the group and would lash her head left and right, wondering what to do, or maybe she would only do so in dismay. Her scrawny head was disconcerting to me. Letting out a deep belly-squawk, the hen would scurry around in search of a gap and then thrust herself between two of her companions, shoving one of them out of the way. With this, the balance of power would change again. There was food for all of them, but the hens never believed it.

I would watch one of them laying an egg in her nest and would become hypnotized by her quivering beak, her neck jerking up, down, to one side, then the other. Suddenly the hen's neck seemed to snap beneath a strangled screech that opened wide her beak and her round, emerald eyes. I wondered if she was screaming from pain, if she too had been condemned to painful childbirth, and what sin she might have committed. Or if just the opposite was true and they were cries of triumph. Every day the hens witnessed their own miracle, and I had never had even one.

I once caught the youngest of them pecking an egg she had just laid and I almost kicked her. It was too late, though. She'd already eaten it.

"She ate her own child," I told Herta, shocked.

She explained that it happened from time to time. The hens accidentally broke an egg and instinctively tasted it. Since it was flavorsome, they consumed it all.

In the lunchroom Sabine once told her sister Gertrude and Theodora about when her young son heard Hitler's voice on the radio and was frightened. His chin had begun to quiver, dimples showing, and the boy had burst into tears. *He's our Führer, why are you crying?* his mother had asked him. *Besides, the Führer adores children,* Theodora said.

Germans love children. Hens, at times, eat their young. Living creatures appalled me. I had never been a good German.

ONE SUNDAY I went into the forest with Joseph to gather firewood. Among the trees, a symphony of birdsong. We brought the logs and branches back in a wheelbarrow to store them in the barn, which had once been used for animal feed. Gregor's grandparents had farmed the land and raised cows and bulls, as had his great-grandparents, for that matter. Joseph had sold off everything to pay for Gregor's education and had found a job as a gardener at the von Mildernhagen castle. *Why did you do that?* his son had asked him. *We're old now, anyway,* Joseph replied, *we don't need much to live on.* Gregor had no brothers or sisters. His mother had given birth to two other children but they had both died, and he'd never known them. He arrived by chance, when his parents were already resigned to the thought of growing old alone.

The day Gregor announced he was going to study in Berlin, his father was openly disappointed. Not only had the son who had come to them so unexpectedly grown up all at once, overnight, but now he'd gotten it into his head to abandon them.

"We quarreled," Joseph admitted to me. "I couldn't understand him. I was angry. I swore he would never leave, that I would never let him."

"Then what happened?" Gregor had never told me this story. "He didn't run away from home, did he?"

"He would never have done that." Joseph stopped the wheelbarrow. He twisted his face into a grimace and rubbed his back.

"Are you aching? Here, let me push it."

"I'm old," he retorted, "but not *that* old!" He started moving again. "A teacher came to talk to us. Sat down at the table with Herta and me, said Gregor was a very good student, that he deserved it. The fact that a stranger knew my son better than me sent me into a fury. I was mad at that teacher, treated him rudely. Then, out in the cowshed, Herta made me come to my senses and I felt like a fool."

After the teacher's visit, Joseph made the decision to sell off all the animals except the hens, and Gregor moved to Berlin.

"He studied hard and got what he wanted: an excellent profession."

I pictured Gregor back at his office, sitting at the drafting machine, perched on his stool as he moved the scales over the paper and scratched his neck with a pencil. I liked to spy on him as he worked, spy on him whenever he was doing something and forgetting about what was around him, forgetting about me. Was he still himself when I wasn't there?

"If only he hadn't gone off to war . . ." Joseph stopped again, not to rub his back. He stared into space without speaking, almost as though needing to go back over the events in his mind. He had done what was right for his son, but what was right hadn't been enough.

We stacked the firewood in the barn in silence. It wasn't a sad silence. We often talked about Gregor, he was the only thing we had in common, but after talking about him we had to be quiet for a little while.

When we stepped inside the house, Herta told us we were out of milk. I said I would go get more the next day. I had learned the way.

THE FOLLOWING AFTERNOON, the smell of manure told me I had arrived, well before I spotted the line of women holding empty glass bottles. I had brought a basket full of vegetables to barter.

A loud moo echoed through the countryside like a cry for help, sounding like an air-raid siren, that same desperation. I was the only one startled by it. The other women inched forward, chatting with one another or standing in silence, holding their children by the hand or calling to them if they strayed.

Two young women came out of the dairy. They looked familiar. When they were near I realized they were two of the other food tasters. One had short-cropped hair and dry facial skin, and was called Beate. The other had squeezed her bosom and broad hips into a brown coat and full skirt. Her face was a bas relief, her name Heike. On impulse I moved my arm to wave, but then froze. I didn't know how secret our assignment was, whether we had to deny we knew one another. I wasn't from their town and had never run into them at the dairy. Besides that, we had never had a real conversation in the lunchroom. Maybe saying hello was out of place, maybe they wouldn't say hello back.

They passed by without even looking my way. Beate's eyes were red. Heike was telling her, "We can split this one, and next time you can give me a little of yours."

Eavesdropping on them embarrassed me. Beate couldn't afford milk? We hadn't been given our first payment yet, but we would be paid for our work—that was what the SS guards said, though they hadn't specified how much. For a moment I doubted the two women were tasters, despite having seen them from close up. How could they not have recognized me? I followed them with my eyes, hoping they would turn around. They didn't. They kept walking until they disappeared from sight, and a moment later it was my turn to go in.

On the way home it began to pour. The water made my hair cling to my temples and drenched my coat. I shivered from the cold. Herta had warned me to take a mantle but I had forgotten. With my city shoes on, I risked tumbling into the mud. My view blurred by the lashing water, I could easily take the wrong road. Despite my heels, I began to run. Suddenly, not far from the church, I spotted the silhouette of two women walking arm in arm. I recognized them from Heike's full skirt, or maybe from their backs, which my eyes observed in the lunchroom every day as we stood in line. If they spread out both their mantles all three of us would fit underneath. I called out to them.

A clap of thunder drowned out my voice. I called out again. They didn't look back. Maybe I was wrong, maybe it wasn't them. Slowly I came to a halt and stood there in the rain.

The next day, in the lunchroom, I sneezed.

"Gesundheit," someone to my right said.

It was Heike. I was surprised to recognize her voice, though my view of her was blocked by Ulla, who was sitting between us.

"Did you catch a chill yesterday too?"

They had seen me, then.

"Yes," I replied, "I have a cold."

Hadn't they heard me calling to them?

"Warm milk with honey," Beate said, almost as if she had waited for Heike's approval before speaking to me. "If we had more milk than we knew what to do with, that would be our remedy."

THE WEEKS PASSED and our suspicion of the food faded, as toward a suitor with whom you gradually grow more intimate. We women now feasted avidly, but immediately afterward our bloated bellies would curb our enthusiasm, the weight on our stomachs like a weight on our hearts. The hour following each banquet was filled with desperation.

Each of us still feared we might be poisoned. It happened if a cloud suddenly darkened the high midday sun, it happened during those seconds of confusion that often come right before dusk. And yet none of us could hide the comfort given to us by the Griessnockerlsuppe, with those semolina dumplings that melted in our mouths, or our total devotion to Eintopf, despite the fact that we missed pork and beef and even chicken. But Hitler refused to eat meat, and on the radio he encouraged his citizens to have vegetable stew at least once a week. He thought it was easy to find vegetables in the city during the war. Either that or it was none of his concern; Germans didn't die of hunger, and if they died they were bad Germans.

I thought of Gregor and would touch my belly, now that it was full and there was nothing left to be done. *Spare me until Christmas, at least until Christmas,* I would repeat to myself, my legs trembling, and with my finger I would secretly draw a sign of the cross in the spot where my esophagus ended—or at least where I thought it did, imagining the inside of my body as a cluster of gray puzzle pieces like the ones I had seen depicted in Krümel's books.

From the outside, covered with clothes, my body didn't seem different. But I felt my hips spread out until they brushed against my forearms when I sat down, and when I stood up, my thighs stiffened with the arrogance of new, strengthened muscles. My ribs didn't press against my skin anymore and my round face, Herta said, had regained its color. The Führer's food had changed my appearance, had transformed us all.

Maybe for this reason, the tears gradually started to seem pathetic to everyone, even to Leni. If her panic rose I would squeeze her hand, stroke her blotchy cheeks. Elfriede never cried. During the hour-long wait I would listen to her noisy breathing. When something distracted her, her face would forget its harshness and she became pretty. Beate chewed with the same fervor she would have used to scrub bedsheets. Heike, her next-door neighbor since they'd been little girls—Leni had told me that—was seated across from her, and she cut her trout in butter and parsley with her left hand, raising her elbow until it bumped into Ulla's arm. Not even noticing, Ulla continued to lick the corners of her mouth. It must have been that childish gesture, repeated distractedly, that sent the SS guards into ecstasy.

I would study the food in the others' dishes, and the woman who happened to have been served the same food as me that day would become dearer to me than a close relative. My heart was suddenly touched by the sight of the pimple that had formed on her cheek, by the energy or indolence with which she washed her face in the morning, by the pillings on the old wool stockings she might put on before getting into bed. Her survival was as important to me as my own, because we shared the same fate.

With time even the SS guards relaxed. During lunch, if they were on their good behavior, they would chat among themselves without taking much notice of us and wouldn't even tell us to stop talking. If, on the other hand, they were feeling aroused, they would lock their eyes on us and dissect us. They stared at us like we stared at our food, almost as if they were about to take a bite out of us. They would prowl around our chairs with their weapons in their holsters, badly judging the distance, their guns brushing against our backs, making us flinch. At times they would lean over one of us from behind—normally it was Ulla, their "dish." They would lower their finger to her bosom, murmuring, *You've got food on your shirt,* and all at once Ulla would stop eating. We would all stop.

Leni was their favorite, though, because her green eyes sparkled against her pale skin, which was too thin to mask any uncertainty, any doubt, and because she was so defenseless. One of the guards pinched her cheek, fussing over her in a falsetto voice—*Puppy eyes!*— and Leni smiled, not from embarrassment. She thought the tenderness she brought out in others would protect her. She was willing to pay the price for her fragility, and the SS men sensed it.

In the Krausendorf barracks we risked dying every day, but no more than anyone else alive. *Mother was right about that,* I thought, as the radicchio crunched between my teeth and the cauliflower filled the room with its homey, comforting smell.

8

ONE MORNING KRÜMEL ANNOUNCED HE WAS GOING TO PAMPER US.
That's how he said it—*pamper*—to us, who no longer believed we had
the right to be pampered. He was going to let us taste his zwieback,
he said, he had just baked some as a surprise for his boss. "He loves
it. He even had it made in the trenches during the Great War."

"Sure he did. After all, it's so easy to find the ingredients at the
front," Augustine whispered. "The butter, honey, and yeast he produced himself, by sweating." Fortunately the SS guards didn't hear
her, and Krümel had already disappeared into the kitchen with his
assistant chefs.

A noise escaped Elfriede's nose, a sort of laugh. I had never heard
Elfriede laugh before, and it caught me so off guard that it made me
feel like laughing too. Though I tried to retain my composure, when
I heard another snort I couldn't hold back a titter. "Berliner, can't you
control yourself?" she said, and at that point a mixture of snickers and
grunts fermented in the lunchroom, growing fuller and fuller until
we couldn't hold back any longer. All of us burst out laughing before
the SS guards' astonished eyes.

"What's so funny?" Fingers touching a holster. "What's come over
you?" One of the guards pounded his fist on the table. "Do I have to
beat it out of you?"

With effort, we fell silent. "Order!" the Beanpole said, though our
sense of amusement had already faded.

Still, it had happened: for the first time, we had laughed together.

THE ZWIEBACK WAS crispy and fragrant. I savored the merciless sweetness of my privilege. Krümel was pleased, though with time I would discover he always was. It was a question of pride, pride in his profession.

He too was from Berlin. He had begun his career with Mitropa, the European company that managed railway sleeping and dining cars. In '37 he had been hired by the Führer to *pamper* him during journeys on his special train. The train was armored with light anti-aircraft cannons to respond to low-altitude attacks and was equipped with elegant suites, Krümel said. They were so elegant, in fact, that Hitler jokingly called it "the Hotel of the Frenetic Reich Chancellor." Its name was *Amerika,* or at least it was until America joined the war. Then it was downgraded to *Brandenburg,* which sounded less grand to me, though I didn't say so. Now, lodged in the Wolfsschanze, Krümel cooked over two hundred meals a day for Hitler's staff, also pampering us tasters.

We weren't allowed to enter the kitchen, and he would come out only if he had something to tell us or was summoned by the guards—for example, because Heike reported a strange taste in the water, which Beate consequently noticed. The women leapt to their feet—headache, nausea, stomachs churning from distress. But it was Fachingen spring water, the Führer's favorite! "The water of well-being," they called it, so how could it harm anyone?

One Tuesday, two kitchen helpers didn't show up for work. They had fevers. Krümel came to the lunchroom and asked me to give him a hand. I don't know why he chose me, maybe because I was the only one who had studied his books on nutrition—the other women had soon grown bored with them. Or maybe it was because I was from Berlin, like him.

The Fanatics turned up their noses at his choice. If someone was to have access to the kitchen, it should be them, the perfect homemakers.

One day I had heard Gertrude ask her sister, "Did you read about the young woman who went into a Jew's shop and was kidnapped?"

"No, where did it happen?" Sabine asked, but Gertrude went on: "Just imagine—the back of the shop led to an underground tunnel. Passing through it, with the help of other Jews the shopkeeper took her to the synagogue and they all raped her, all at once."

Sabine covered her eyes as though witnessing the assault. "Really, Gerti?"

"Of course," her sister replied. "They always rape them before offering them in sacrifice."

"Did you read that in *Der Stürmer*?" Theodora asked.

"I just know it happened, and that's that," Gertrude replied. "We housewives aren't safe anymore, not even when we go shopping."

"That's true," said Theodora. "It's a good thing all those shops were closed down."

Theodora would have defended tooth and nail the German ideal of mother-wife-homemaker, and it was precisely because she was its worthy representative that she asked to speak to Krümel. She told him about the restaurant her family had run before the war. She had experience in the kitchen and wanted to prove it. The chef was persuaded.

He handed us each an apron and a crate of vegetables. I rinsed them in the large sink while Theodora cubed some, sliced others. With the exception of scolding me for not rinsing away all the grit or because I had left a puddle on the floor, she didn't speak to me on the first day. Like an apprentice, she spent her time shadowing the assistant chefs, sticking so close behind them that she hindered their movements.

"Out of the way!" Krümel ordered her, when he nearly tripped over her feet.

Theodora apologized, then added, "How better to learn than by watching? I can barely believe I'm working side by side with a chef of your caliber."

"Side by side? Out of the way, I told you!"

Over the following days, though, convinced she was now a full-fledged member of the team, out of professional ethics she decided to take me into her confidence. After all, I was her coworker—or rather, my blatant incompetence made me her underling. And so she told me about her parents' restaurant, a small establishment, not even ten tables.

"It was charming, though. You should have seen it." The war had forced them to close it down. She planned to reopen it, though, when the war was over, and with several more tables. On the outer edges of her eyes, her wrinkles formed tiny flippers, making them look like two little fish. Her restaurateur dreams filling her with enthusiasm, she began to speak excitedly, the flippers on her face moving so quickly I almost expected to see her eyes spring from her face, dive through the air, and plunge into the pot of boiling water in front of her.

"But if the Bolsheviks arrived it would be impossible," she said. "We could never reopen the restaurant. It would be the end of everything." All at once, the flippers went still. Her eyes were no longer swimming. They were age-old fossils. How old was Theodora?

"I hope it's not the end of everything," I dared to say, "because I don't know if we're going to win this war."

"Don't even think that way. If the Russians won, we would be doomed to destruction and slavery, the Führer said so himself. Hordes of men being marched off to the Siberian tundra. Didn't you hear him say so?"

No, I hadn't.

I REMEMBERED GREGOR back in our living room in Altemesseweg. He got up from the armchair we had bought from a secondhand shop and went to the window, sighing. "Russian weather." Soldiers used that expression, he explained to me, because Russians attacked even in the worst conditions. "They can endure anything."

He was on leave and spoke to me about the front—he did that sometimes. He told me about the Morgenkonzert, for example, which was what they called the symphony of explosions the Red Army performed at dawn.

In bed one night, he said, "If the Russians arrive, they'll show no mercy."

"Why do you think that?"

"Because the Germans treat Soviet prisoners differently from the others. The British and French receive aid from the Red Cross, and in the afternoon they even play football, while the Soviets are forced to dig trenches under the surveillance of soldiers from their own army."

"From their own army?"

"Yes, men who are lured into it by the promise of a piece of bread or an extra ladleful of broth," he replied, turning off the light. "If they do to us what we've done to them, it's going to be horrible."

For a long time I tossed and turned in bed, unable to sleep, and all at once Gregor embraced me. "I'm sorry. I shouldn't have told you those things, you shouldn't know about them. What good does knowing do? And for whom?"

I lay awake even after he had fallen fast asleep.

"We'll deserve what they do to us," I said to Theodora.

She glared at me with contempt, then went back to ignoring me. Her hostility darkened my spirits. There was no reason for me to feel that way—she wasn't someone I wanted a connection with. Actually, I had no connection with any of the other women either. Not with Augustine, who needled me—*Made a new friend, have you?*—or with Leni, who heaped praises on the food as though I'd cooked it myself. I had no connection with those women, apart from a job I never would have imagined for myself. *What do you want to be when you grow up? Hitler's food taster.*

Nevertheless, the Fanatic's hostility made me uncomfortable. I wandered through the kitchen more clumsily than usual, and out of distraction burned my wrist. A shriek escaped me.

At the sight of my skin withering around the burn, Theodora suspended her silent treatment, grabbed my arm, and turned on the faucet. "Run cold water over it!" Then she peeled a potato as the chefs continued their work. She patted my wrist dry with a towel and rested a slice of raw potato on the burn. "It'll soothe the irritation, you'll see." Her motherly care touched me.

Standing in a corner as I held the slice of potato on my wrist, I saw Krümel toss something into the soup and chuckle to himself. Noticing I'd spotted him doing it, he raised his finger to his lips. "It's not healthy to go entirely without meat," he said. "You learned that for yourself in those books I gave you, right? That stubborn man can't get it through his head, so I sneak lard into his soup. You can't imagine how angry he gets when he notices! But he almost never notices." Krümel roared with laughter. "And when he's convinced he's gained weight, I can't get him to eat a thing."

Theodora, who was pouring flour into a mixing bowl, moved closer.

"Believe me, not one thing!" the chef said, looking over at her. "Spaghetti with quark? He digests it so well but refuses it. Bavarian apple cake, his favorite—just think, I serve it to him every evening for his nighttime tea, after his last meeting—but I swear, if he's on a diet he won't touch a single slice. In two weeks he can lose as much as seven kilos."

"His nighttime tea?" the Fanatic asked.

"A late-night meeting among friends. The chief drinks either tea or hot chocolate. He's wild about hot chocolate. The others guzzle down as much schnapps as they can. Not that he approves of it. Let's say he tolerates it. Only once has he lost his temper, with Hoffmann, the photographer—the man's a drunkard. Usually, though, the chief doesn't bother noticing. He listens to *Tristan und Isolde* with his eyes closed. He always says, 'If I were about to die, I would want this to be the last thing my ears hear.'"

Theodora was enraptured. I took the potato slice off my wrist. The afflicted area had spread. I wanted to show it to her, expected her to scold me, to come over and put the slice back in its place, *Keep it there and stop making a fuss.* Suddenly I missed my mother. But the Fanatic wasn't paying attention to me anymore—she was hanging on Krümel's every word. From the way the chef spoke about Hitler, the man was obviously dear to his heart, and Krümel took it for granted that Hitler was dear to our hearts too, even mine. But then again, I had declared my willingness to die for the Führer. Every day my plate—our ten aligned plates—conjured his presence as though through transubstantiation. No promise of eternal life; two hundred marks a month, that was our pay.

When they had handed us our first envelope, we stuck it in our pockets or purses—none of us dared open it on the bus. In my room with the door closed, I thumbed through the bills with astonishment. It was more money than my salary in Berlin.

I chucked the potato slice into the trash bin.

"The chief says eating meat and drinking wine makes him sweat, but I tell him he sweats because he's too agitated." When Krümel started talking about him, he couldn't stop. "'Look at horses,' he tells me, 'Look at bulls. Those animals are herbivores, and they're strong and robust. On the other hand, look at dogs. One brief run and their tongues are already hanging out.'"

"It's true," Theodora said. "I've never thought about that. He's right."

"Bah, I don't know about that. In any case, he says he can't stand the cruelty of slaughterhouses." Krümel was talking only to her now.

I picked up a roll from a large basket, separated the crust from the soft insides.

"Once at dinner he told his guests he'd been in a slaughterhouse and still remembered the fresh blood lapping against his galoshes. Just imagine: Dietrich had to push his plate away. . . . Poor fellow is impressionable."

The Fanatic let out a hearty laugh. I balled up the insides of the bread, shaping them into tiny circles and petals. Krümel reproached me for the waste.

"They're for you," I said. "They're like you, Crumbs."

Not listening to me, he stirred the broth and asked Theodora to check on the radishes in the oven.

"Everything here is a waste," I went on. "We women are a waste. No one could ever manage to poison him, not with all the security measures here. It's ridiculous."

"Oh, so you're an expert on security now, are you?" the Fanatic said. "And maybe on military strategy too?"

"Enough," Krümel warned, a father whose daughters were quarreling.

"Well, how did he manage before hiring us?" I asked her defiantly. "Before that, wasn't he afraid they would poison him?"

Just then a guard walked into the kitchen to have us take our places at the table. The clumps of bread lay there to dry on the marble countertop.

The next day, as I made my way around the assistant chefs' perfect coordination and the Fanatic's zeal, Krümel appeared with an unexpected gift: in secret, he gave Theodora and me fruit and cheese. He personally put it in my satchel—the leather bag I used to take to the office in Berlin.

"Why?" I asked.

"You two deserve it," he said.

I took it home. Herta couldn't believe her eyes when I unwrapped the bundles Krümel had given me. It was thanks to me that she had such delicacies for dinner. It was thanks to Hitler.

9

Augustine marched up the aisle of the bus so briskly that the hem of her dark skirt seemed to froth. She rested her hand on the back of our bench, touching Leni's hair, and said, "Let's change spots, okay? Just for today."

It was dark out. Leni looked at me, confused, then got up and plopped into an empty seat. Augustine took her place beside me.

"Your bag's full," she said.

Everyone was staring at us—not just Leni. Even Beate, even Elfriede. The Fanatics weren't. They were sitting way in the front, right behind the driver.

We had spontaneously broken into groups. Not that we expected affection within those groups. More simply, fractures and shifts had occurred with the same inexorability with which the earth's plates move. The need for protection that Leni betrayed with every blink had left me responsible for her. Then there was Elfriede, who had shoved me in the washroom. In that gesture I glimpsed my own fear. It had been an attempt to make contact. Intimate, yes; the Beanpole might have been right about that. Elfriede had been looking for a fight, like little boys who understand who they can trust only after duking it out. The guard had averted the fistfight, which meant we still had a score to settle, she and I, a debt that generated a magnetic field around us.

"It's full, isn't it? Answer me."

Theodora looked over her shoulder, an automatic reaction to Augustine's harsh voice. A few weeks ago Theodora had remarked that the Führer worked on gut reaction, that he was a man of instinct. *Yes,*

yes, he has a brilliant mind, Gertrude had said, two hairpins clasped between her teeth, not realizing she had just contradicted her friend. *But do you know how many things they don't report to him?* she went on, after sticking the hairpins firmly into the braid coiled up on the side of her head. *It's not like he knows everything that happens, it's not always his fault.* Augustine had feigned spitting on her.

Now she sat beside me, cross-legged, one knee pressed against the seat in front of us. "For a few days now the chef's been giving you extra food to take home."

"Yes."

"Good. We want some too."

"We" who? I didn't know what to say. Solidarity among us food tasters was a foreign concept. We were tectonic plates that shifted and collided, floating beside one another or drifting apart.

"You can't be selfish. He likes you. Make him give you more."

"Take what's here." I held my satchel out to her.

"It's not enough. We want milk, at least a couple bottles. We've got children and we have to have milk."

They earned even more than the average laborer, so it wasn't a question of need. *It's a question of fairness,* Augustine would have said if I had pointed that out. *Why on earth should you be given more than us?* To this I could have shot back, *Ask Theodora to do it.* She knew Theodora would refuse. Why did she expect me to agree, though? I wasn't her friend. But she sensed how desperate I was for approval, had sensed it right from the start, even if I couldn't admit it.

How do people become friends? Now that I could recognize their expressions, could even anticipate them, my companions' faces seemed different from the ones I had seen on the first day. That happens at school, or at work, in places where you're forced to spend many hours of your existence. People are forced to become friends.

"All right, Augustine. Tomorrow I'll try asking him."

THE NEXT MORNING, Krümel told the two of us that his helpers had returned, so we were no longer needed. I explained this to Augustine and the other women who had chosen her as their spokesperson, but Heike and Beate were relentless. *It's not fair that you were treated to something extra and we weren't. We have children. Who do you have?*

I didn't have children. Whenever I had spoken to my husband about it he would tell me it wasn't the right time, that he was away at war and I was alone. He had left in '40, a year after our wedding. There I was without Gregor, in our apartment furnished with things from the secondhand shop where we liked to go on Saturday mornings, stopping for breakfast at the nearby bakery, cinnamon Schnecke or poppyseed strudel, which we ate directly out of the bag, one bite each, as we strolled along. There I was, without him and without a child, in an apartment full of junk.

Germans loved children. During parades the Führer always stroked their cheeks and urged women to have lots of them. Gregor wanted to be a good German but wouldn't let himself be influenced. He said putting a person into the world meant condemning them to death. *But the war will end,* I objected. *It's not the war,* he replied, *it's life. Everyone dies all the same.* When I accused him—*You're not well, ever since you left for the front you've been depressed*—he became angry.

Maybe at Christmas, with Herta and Joseph's help, I would manage to persuade him.

If I became pregnant I would be nourishing the child in my womb with food from the lunchroom. A pregnant woman isn't a good guinea pig, since she might muddle the results of the experiment, but the SS wouldn't find out—at least not until the quarterly lab results or my belly gave me away.

I would risk poisoning the baby. We would both die, or we would survive. His mealy bones and tender muscles nurtured by Hitler's food. He would be a child of the Reich even before being my own. But then again, no one is born without sin.

"Steal it," Augustine told me. "Go into the kitchen, chat with the chef to distract him—talk to him about Berlin, about when you used to go to the opera, come up with something—then, the minute he turns the other way, take some milk."

"Are you insane? I can't do that."

"It's not his to begin with. You're not taking it away from him."

"But it's not fair. He doesn't deserve this."

"What, Rosa—do *we* deserve this?"

Light glimmered off the marble countertops, which the kitchen helpers had degreased.

"Sooner or later the Soviets will surrender, you'll see," Krümel said.

We were alone. He had sent his staff to unload the provisions that had arrived by train at the Wolfsschanze station, saying he would catch up with them later, since I had asked him to explain a chapter in the book I was reading, a book he had given me. I hadn't thought of a better excuse to keep him there. After he had explained—Krümel delighted in playing the teacher—I was going to ask him for two bottles of milk, even if he would never give them to me, even if he replied rudely, harshly. It's one thing to be given something as a gift but another thing to demand it. Besides, who was it for? I didn't have children, had never nursed anyone.

Krümel had sat down to talk to me and within minutes was chatting away excitedly, as always. The disaster in Stalingrad that February had demoralized everyone.

"They died so Germany could live on," Krümel said.

"That's what the Führer says."

"Well, I believe him. Don't you?"

I nodded hesitantly.

"We're going to win," he said, "because it's only right."

He told me that in the evenings Hitler ate facing a wall decorated with a Soviet flag that had been seized at the beginning of Operation Barbarossa. In that room he explained to his guests the danger of Bolshevism. The other European nations underestimated it. Didn't they realize the USSR was as dark, eerie, and unfathomable as the ghost ship in Wagner's opera? Only a man as stubborn as himself could sink it, even if it meant chasing after it until Judgment Day.

"Only he can," Krümel said, checking his watch. "Oh, I need to go. Was there anything else you needed?"

I need fresh milk. Milk for children who aren't mine. "No, thank you.

In fact, is there something I can do to repay you? You've been so kind."

"Actually, I could use a favor. We have several kilos of beans to shell. Would you mind starting on them, at least until it's time for you to go back home? I'll tell the guards you need to stay here."

He left me alone in his kitchen. I could have poisoned the supplies, but that didn't even cross Krümel's mind. I was one of Hitler's food tasters, was part of his team, was also from Berlin. He trusted me.

ONCE IN LINE for the bus, my satchel against my belly, I thought I heard the glass bottles rattle together and tried to hold them still with both hands, walking slowly. Not so slow as to make the SS guards suspicious. Elfriede was behind me. She often stood in line behind me. We were always the last ones to move. It wasn't laziness—it was our inability to conform. No matter how willing we may have been to follow the rules, the rules had a hard time fitting us. We were like two pieces of the wrong size, or made of some incompatible material, but that was all you had to build your fortress, so you found a way to adapt.

Her breath tickled my neck. "Berliner, did you let them get you into trouble?"

"Silence," one of the guards said listlessly.

I gripped the bottles through the leather, walked slowly to prevent the least contact between them.

"I thought you'd learned it's best for everyone to mind their own business around here." Elfriede's breath on my neck was torture.

Then the Beanpole came toward us calmly. When he was beside me, he looked me up and down. I continued to follow the other women until he grabbed my arm, pulling it away from the leather. I braced myself to hear the clink of glass against glass, but the bottles didn't wobble. I had done a good job, nestled them snugly into the dark depths of my bag.

"Having another tête-à-tête, you two?"

Elfriede stopped behind me and the guard grabbed her as well. "I warned you that if I caught you again I would take advantage of it."

The cold glass against my hip. All the guard had to do was accidentally touch my satchel and he would catch me. He let go of my arm, clasped my chin between his thumb and forefinger, and leaned down toward me. My chin was trembling. With my eyes I sought Elfriede.

"You stink a bit like broccoli today. It'll have to wait for another time." The Beanpole cackled. "Why that look on your face? I was joking. We even joke with you here. What more could you ask for?"

THE HANDOFF TOOK place back on the bus, hidden from view by the bench seats. Augustine had brought a small cloth sack. My chin was still trembling. Below my cheek, a nervous tic.

"You were great, and generous." Her smile of thanks looked sincere.

How do people become friends?

Us and them. That was what Augustine was proposing. Us, the victims, the young women with no choice. Them, the enemies, the abusers of power. Krümel wasn't one of us—that was what Augustine meant. Krümel was a Nazi. And we had never been Nazis.

The only one who wasn't smiling at me was Elfriede. She was focusing on the expanse of fields and silos that passed by one after the other outside the window. Every day the bus carried me down eight kilometers of road until reaching the bend at Gross-Partsch, my place of banishment.

10

From Gregor's bed I studied the edges of a photograph of him that was stuck into the frame of the mirror above the bedside table. He must have been four, five years old—I couldn't say. He wore snow boots and was squinting in the sunlight.

I couldn't fall asleep. Since I had come to Gross-Partsch I hadn't been able to. Nor had I been able to in Berlin, where we had been barricaded in the cellar with the rats. Herr Holler used to say we would eventually resort to eating those as well, once the cats and sparrows were gone, they too having been massacred, and without the glory of a memorial. Of all people, it had been Holler who said it—Holler, whose anxiety left him with intestinal distress and who, if he withdrew into the corner where we kept the bucket, would leave behind an unbearable stench.

Our suitcases were packed, to make a quick escape if need be.

After the bomb on Budengasse I went up to our apartment. It was flooded. The pipes had been damaged. Up to my knees in water, I opened my suitcase on the mattress and searched through my things for the photo album. It hadn't gotten wet. Then I opened my mother's suitcase and breathed in the scent of her clothes. They had a smell too similar to my own. Now that she was dead and I wasn't, that smell—of which I remained the only heir—seemed even more profane. In her suitcase I found a photo of Franz, sent from America in '38, just months after he'd set sail. We hadn't seen my brother since. Of me, there were no pictures. If she and I had been forced to flee, we would have done so together—that was what my mother believed. Instead she died.

After the bomb, I buried her and went through the abandoned homes on our block. I searched the cupboards and gobbled down what I could, stole tea sets to sell on the black market at Alexanderplatz along with the porcelain dishware Mother kept in the display cabinet.

Anne Langhans let me stay at her place, where we shared a bed, little Pauline between us. Sometimes I pretended she was the daughter I had never had. Her breath consoled me, grew more familiar than my mother's.

I convinced myself that one day Gregor would return from the war. We would fix the pipes in my family home and have a child—or, better, two. In their sleep they would breathe slowly, with their mouths open, like Pauline.

GREGOR WAS SO tall when he walked beside me down Unter den Linden, all the trees gone. The people had to have a clear view of the Führer passing by in the parade—that was why the lindens had been chopped down. I only went up to his shoulders, and along the way he took my hand.

I said, *Isn't it a bit old, this cliché about the secretary and her boss?* He said, *If I fire you will I have the right to kiss you?*

It made me laugh. He stopped, leaned against a shop window, and slowly pulled me against him. I stifled my laughter in his wool sweater, then raised my face and glimpsed the portrait in the window: the halo painted around the Führer's head was yellow and his gaze cross, as though he had just driven the merchants from the temple. We kissed before his eyes. Adolf Hitler blessed our love.

I OPENED THE bedside table drawer, took out all of Gregor's letters, reread them one by one. It was like hearing his voice, pretending he was near. The *X*'s marked in ink on the calendar reminded me that soon he really would be.

THE MORNING HE departed, he found me slumped in the bedroom doorway, my forehead pressed against the frame. *What's wrong?* he asked. I didn't reply.

It felt like I had known happiness only since meeting him. Before then I had never thought I was entitled to it. Those circles around my eyes, like fate. Instead, my happiness was so dazzling and so complete and so mine, the happiness Gregor had given to me as though it were the simplest thing in the world, as though it were his personal vocation.

But then he relinquished that vocation, found a more important one. *I'll be back soon,* he said, stroking my temple, my cheek, my lips, trying to slip his fingers into my mouth in our customary gesture, our silent pact—*Trust me, I do trust you, love me, I do love you, make love to me*—but I clenched my teeth and he withdrew his hand.

I IMAGINED HIM moving swiftly through the trenches, his breath misting in the freezing-cold air. *Only two men have failed to realize Russia is cold,* he wrote to me. *One of them is Napoleon.* Out of caution, he didn't mention the other one. When I asked him about the war, he said he had to respect military secrecy, though it might have been an excuse to avoid frightening me. Maybe just then he was eating by the fire with the other soldiers, mess tins of canned meat on their laps, their uniforms growing baggy because they were losing weight. I knew Gregor would eat without complaining so none of the others would think of him as a burden. He had always needed others to lean on him in order to feel strong.

At first he had written that he was uncomfortable sleeping with strangers around, each with a weapon at his disposal. He could have been shot by anyone at any time, be it because of a squabble over a card game, an overly vivid nightmare, a misunderstanding during their march. He didn't trust them. Gregor trusted only me. Now that he had grown so close to his fellow soldiers he felt ashamed for having thought that way.

There was the painter, who had lost two sections of his fingers in battle and didn't know if he would ever paint again. He hated Nazis and Jews in equal measure. As for the former lawyer, a zealous Nazi, he cared little about the Jews and was convinced that not even Hitler lost any sleep over them. He said Berlin would never be bombed because the Führer wouldn't allow it. When my parents' home had been struck, I wondered if that chipped away at his certainty. Hitler had calculated everything, Gregor's comrade-in-arms said. My husband had let him talk because they were in the same unit and in wartime, he said, they became a single body. They were the body he felt he belonged to, a mirror that infinitely reflected his own. They, not I, were flesh of his flesh.

Then there was Reinhard, who was afraid of everything, even lice, and clung to Gregor like a little boy clings to his father, though he was barely three years younger. "Shitbritches," I called him. In the last letter that had made it through to Berlin, Gregor had written that excrement was proof of God's inexistence. Sometimes he liked to provoke people—everyone at his office knew that—but he had never said anything of the sort before. *We all have diarrhea here,* he wrote, *because of the food, the cold, the fear.* Reinhard had soiled his pants during a mission, a common occurrence among the soldiers, but for him it had been humiliating.

If mankind really was created by God, my husband wrote, *do you think God would invent something as vulgar as shit? Wouldn't He have found some other way, one that didn't involve the repulsive product of one's digestion? Shit is such a perverse invention that either God is perverse or He doesn't exist.*

Even the Führer, for his part, struggled with the product of his digestion. It was a torment for Krümel. Though the diet he had developed was perfectly healthy, his boss was dependent on the antiflatulence pills his personal physician prescribed. The patient swallowed as many as sixteen of them a day. Hitler had designed a complex system to avoid being poisoned by the enemy, yet in the meantime he was poisoning himself.

"You mustn't go around telling all these stories. I'm a gossip," Krümel said, chuckling, "but you'll keep them to yourself, won't you?"

After lunch I was back in the kitchen, almost done shelling the multitude of beans he had assigned to me. Theodora had offered to help—the kitchen was her territory and she hated the idea of my being there without her. I told her there was no need, and Krümel had had too much on his mind to listen to her. He went to the station with his men, leaving me alone again.

I got up from the chair, very slowly so it wouldn't scrape against the floor, tiptoed over—even the least bit of noise might have drawn the attention of the guard posted outside the door—and took two bottles of milk from the refrigerator. My skin tingled as I took them. However, I was so pleased with my courage that I didn't even consider that Krümel might notice that two—no, four—bottles were missing, even believed he wouldn't notice. Every item in the kitchen was bound to be counted, he must keep a list of everything that came in and went out. But why should he suspect me? He had assistant chefs, it might have been them.

LATER, AS I stood in line for the bus, the Beanpole walked over to me and opened my purse. It wasn't a spectacular gesture. The latch simply snapped open and the necks of the bottles peeked out. The Beanpole turned toward Theodora, who said, "There you go."

"I don't want to hear a word out of you!" he snapped, silencing her. My companions had shocked, alarmed looks on their faces.

Someone went to summon Krümel from the Wolfsschanze. They made us stand there in the hallway until he arrived. When he was in front of me he looked even leaner, almost brittle.

"I gave them to her," he said.

A pang in my belly. Not a baby's kick, but God's perversion.

"They're a little compensation for the work she's done in the kitchen. Rosa Sauer isn't paid to do it, she's paid to taste the food, so I felt it was only right to reward her, also because she kept on working even after the assistant chefs had all left. I hope it isn't a problem."

Another pang. No one ever got what they deserved, not even me.

"No problem, if you felt it was appropriate. Just warn us next time."

The Beanpole looked at Theodora again, and she looked at me. She wasn't asking for forgiveness, she was expressing her contempt.

"That's enough," said another guard. What did he mean? *Enough with the lavishing food on Rosa Sauer? Enough with the snitching on Rosa Sauer?* Or, *For god's sake, Rosa Sauer, enough with the trembling?* "Come on, everyone. Walk."

My ears burned and my vision blurred with tears that sprang to the surface like water from drilled earth. If I could avoid blinking they would pool in the basin of my eyes, evaporate. Not even on the bus would I let them fall.

Augustine didn't hand me the cloth sack. The bottles traveled with me all the way to the curve by our house. The moment the bus set off again I poured the milk onto the ground.

It had been intended for their children—no, it had been intended for Hitler. How could I waste such a concentration of calcium, iron, vitamins, protein, sugars, and amino acids? From one of the books Krümel had given me, I had learned that the fat in milk was different from all other fats. It was easier to absorb, and the body used it immediately and efficiently. I could have stored the bottles in the cool cellar, invited Augustine, Heike, and Beate, *Here's the milk for your children—Pete, Ursula, Mathias, and even the twins—they're the last two liters, I'm sorry it didn't last, but it was worth it.* I could have served them tea in Herta's kitchen. How did people become friends? They had asked me to steal for them.

I could have given the bottles to Herta and Joseph, lied about how I had gotten them. *Krümel is so generous, he dotes on me. Here, drink this, it's fresh, nutritious milk, and it's all thanks to me.*

Instead there I was, leaning over, motionless, as I watched the milk splash onto the gravel. I wanted to waste it. No one was to drink it. I wanted to deny it to Heike's and Beate's and Augustine's children, deny it to any child who wasn't my own, without feeling guilty.

Only when the bottles were empty did I look up. Herta was at the window. I wiped my eyes with the back of my hand.

THE NEXT DAY I mustered the courage to open the kitchen door. "I'm here for the beans," I said. I had prepared the greeting, especially the tone, in advance: cheerful but not too much, with an imploring undertone if one listened carefully. My voice, however, came out fake.

Krümel didn't turn around. "Thank you. I don't need your help anymore."

In the corner, the wooden crates were stacked one atop the other, empty. The refrigerator was on the opposite side. I didn't dare look at it. I studied my fingernails. They had yellowed, but now that my work was over they would go back to how they had been before: a secretary's nails.

I stepped over to Krümel. "No, thank *you*. Forgive me." This time my voice wasn't fake. It was broken.

"Don't show your face in my kitchen again," he replied, finally turning to look at me.

I couldn't hold his eyes.

Hanging my head and bobbing it several times to let him know I would do as he said, I walked out, forgetting to salute.

11

I<small>T WAS WELL INTO</small> D<small>ECEMBER</small>. E<small>VER SINCE THE WAR HAD STARTED, ES</small>-pecially after Gregor had left, Christmas had lost its festive spirit for me. But this year I awaited it with the same eagerness I had as a child, because it would bring me the gift of my husband.

In the mornings I would put on one of Herta's knitted woolen caps before I got onto the bus, which would cross the snowy expanse, amid birches and beech trees, and take me to Krausendorf, where I would participate in the liturgy of the lunchroom together with other young German women—an army of worshippers prepared to receive on our tongues a Communion that wouldn't redeem us.

Who could ever have preferred eternal life to their life here on earth? I certainly couldn't. I swallowed each bite that might kill me as though it were an offering—three offerings a day for each day of the Christmas novena. *Offer up to the Lord the effort of your studies, your sadness over your broken skate, or your head cold,* my father would tell me when he would pray with me at bedtime. *Look at this offering, then, look at it: I offer up my fear of dying, my appointment with death which has been put off for months and which I cannot cancel, I offer them up in exchange for his coming, Father, for Gregor's coming. Fear comes to me three times a day, always without knocking. It sits beside me and if I stand up it follows me, by now it's practically a constant companion.*

People can grow accustomed to anything—to digging coal out of the cramped tunnels in mines, rationing the need for oxygen; to walking swiftly across the beams of a construction site suspended high in the sky, facing the dizzying void. People can grow accustomed to the blare of sirens, to sleeping in their clothes so they can evacuate quickly in the event of an air raid. People can grow accustomed to hunger, to thirst. Of course, I had grown accustomed to being paid to eat. It might have seemed like a privilege, but it was a job like any other.

ON THE DAY of Christmas Eve, Joseph took a rooster by the legs, turned it upside down, and with a flick of his wrist broke its neck. A brief, crisp snap. Herta put a pot over the fire and when the water was boiling dunked it in three or four times, holding it first by its head and then by its legs. Finally she plucked it, pulling out the feathers with her hands. All that savagery just for Gregor, who was about to arrive. Fortunately Hitler had left town, so I would be free to eat with my husband and his parents.

The last time Gregor had been back on leave, in Berlin, while he was sitting in the living room in Budengasse and listening to the radio, I had gone to his side and caressed him. He'd accepted my caresses without reacting. His distraction felt like a challenge, but I said nothing, not wanting to ruin the few hours we had left to spend together. He took me as I slept, without saying a word. I awoke to find his body, his fury, on top of me. Only half awake, I neither resisted nor indulged him. Afterward I told myself he needed the darkness, that for him to make love to me he needed for me not to be there. It frightened me.

LATER THAT DAY, the letter arrived. It was brief. Gregor said he had been admitted to a field hospital. He didn't say what had happened to him or what his injuries were. All he said was that we shouldn't worry. We replied at once, begging him for more information.

"If he managed to write to us," Joseph said, "it means it's nothing serious." But Herta sank her face into her arthritic hands and refused to eat the chicken she had prepared.

The night of the twenty-fifth, suffering from my usual insomnia, I couldn't even stay in Gregor's room. The photo of him as a little boy tore me apart. I slipped out of bed and wandered the darkness of the house.

I bumped into someone.

"I'm sorry," I said, recognizing Herta. "I can't fall asleep."

"No, I'm sorry," she replied. "Tonight you and I are bound to be sleepwalkers."

I FOLLOW MY course with the precision and confidence of a sleepwalker, Hitler had said as he occupied the Rhineland.

She's a silly old sleepwalker, my brother would say when I talked in my sleep as a girl.

My mother said, *She's always talking, she never pipes down, not even when she's sleeping.* Franz stood up from the table, his arms extended in front of him and his tongue lolling as he moved like a marionette, grunting. *Cut it out and eat your dinner,* Father said.

I would dream I was flying. A force swept me off the ground and pulled me higher and higher, empty space beneath my feet, a wind that howled and hurled me toward the trees, toward the walls of buildings. I avoided them by a hair's breadth, the noise deafening. I knew it was a dream, knew that if I spoke the spell would be broken and I would be returned to my bed, but I had no voice, just a bubble of breath trapped in my throat—it burst a second before impact, exploding into a shriek: *Franz! Help!*

At first my brother would mutter groggily, *What is it, what'd I do?* Then he would wake up only to snap, *What's the matter with you, anyway?*

I called it the Abduction. Not with Franz or with my parents—I just called it that in my mind, and only once with Gregor, who put his arms around me in bed and found me covered in sweat. Gdańsk had just been occupied. I murmured, *It's the Abduction, it hasn't happened for years.* Instead of asking me to explain, he murmured, *You were only dreaming.*

Three years later, after the bomb that killed my mother, I thought the Abduction had always been a prophetic dream. But at the end of the day every life is a form of compulsion, with a constant risk of crashing.

DECEMBER 27 WAS MY birthday. It had stopped snowing and I yearned for the Abduction to carry me away. It would have been a liberation, a rush of anguish expelled all at once without the responsibility of holding it in to avoid upsetting Herta, who was already in pieces, to avoid worrying Joseph.

The Abduction didn't return. My husband wasn't there and would never write to us again.

Another letter was sent to us two and a half months later from the main offices of the military family notification services. It said that Gregor Sauer—age 34, height 1.82 meters, weight 75 kilograms, chest 101 centimeters, blond hair, average nose and chin, blue eyes, fair complexion, healthy teeth, profession engineer—had been declared missing.

Missing. On the page it wasn't written that Gregor Sauer had lean calves, that his big toe was separated from his pointer toe as though by a gulf, that the insides of his soles always got worn down first, that he loved music but never sang it under his breath—in fact he would plead, *Be quiet, I beg you,* because I sang under my breath nonstop, at least before the war—and he shaved every day, at least in times of peace, and the white of the shaving cream he would spread on with the brush contrasted with his lips, making them redder, and plump, even though they weren't, and he would run his finger across those thin lips when he drove his old NSU, and it bothered me because it looked like a gesture of uncertainty—I didn't love him if he was vulnerable, if he saw the world as a threat, if he didn't want to give me a child—to me it looked like a shield, that finger on his mouth, a distance taken from me. It wasn't written on the page that in the morning he preferred to wake up early and have breakfast alone, take a break from my talking, even though we had been married for barely a year and he had to set off for the front, but if I pretended to be sleeping, right after finishing his tea he would sit on the edge of the bed and kiss my hands with the devotion with which one kisses children.

They thought they were identifying him through that string of numbers, but if they hadn't said it was my husband they might as well have been talking about anyone.

HERTA COLLAPSED INTO a chair. "Herta," I called out. She didn't reply. "Herta!" I shook her. She was stiff and yielding at the same time. I held out some water; she didn't drink it. "Herta, please." She dropped her head back and I pulled the glass away. Her face to the ceiling, she said, "I'll never see him again."

"He isn't dead," I shrieked, and her body slumped back into the chair. Finally, she looked at me. "He isn't dead," I insisted. "He's missing. Right here it says *missing*, understand?"

Slowly her features reemerged, and an instant later they contracted. "Where's Joseph?"

"I'll go get him, okay? But drink something." I held the glass to her lips.

"Where's Joseph?" she repeated.

I ran through town, heading for the von Mildernhagens' castle, where he was working. Scrawny, spindly tree trunks, emaciated branches, roof tiles splotched with mold, geese rambling inside their pens, women at the windows, and a man on a bicycle removing his hat to me in greeting, still pedaling as I ran and ignored him. Atop a utility pole, a nest. The stork raised its bill toward the sky as though in prayer—it wasn't praying for me.

Covered with sweat, I clung to the bars of the gate and called out for Joseph. Had the storks arrived so soon? Not long from now it would be spring, and Gregor wouldn't have returned. He was my husband. He was my happiness. Never again would I play with his earlobes, never again would he press his forehead against my bosom, curling up around me to have me stroke his back. He would never hold his cheek to my swollen belly, I would never have a child from him, he would never hold him in his arms, would never tell him about his hi-jinks as a young country boy, entire days spent among the trees, cannonball dives into the lake, ice-cold water and purple lips. I yearned to slip my fingers into his mouth again and feel safe.

My nose between the bars, I screamed. A man came, asked me who I was, I mumbled that I needed the gardener, *I'm his daughter-in-law*, and before he had even opened the gate entirely I was inside and was running who knew where, then heard Joseph's voice and ran over to him. I handed him the letter. He unfolded it and read it.

"Come home, please. Mutti needs you."

The clatter of footsteps on the stairs made us turn around.

"Joseph." It was a woman with red hair, a round face, and a creamy complexion, holding the hem of her gown as though she had run over to join us. Her coat, draped over her shoulders, had slid down to the side, revealing a burgundy sleeve.

"Baroness." My father-in-law apologized for the disturbance, explained what had happened, and asked permission to leave. She came over and took his hands in hers, supported them as if afraid they might collapse, or at least it seemed that way to me. "I'm so sorry," she told him, her eyes glistening. It was then that Joseph burst into tears.

I had never seen a man, an old man, weep. It was a soundless cry, one that made the joints creak, something more to do with lameness, the loss of muscle control. A senile desperation.

The baroness did her best to console him, then desisted, waited for him to calm down. "You're Rosa, aren't you?" I nodded. What did she know about me? "It's a pity that we should meet on such a sad occasion. And to think I was so eager for us to get to know one another. Joseph has told me all about you." Before I could even wonder why she might want to know me, why he might talk about me, why she—a baroness—would converse with a gardener, my father-in-law detached his gnarled hands from the woman's, dried his sparse eyelashes, and told me we should leave. I don't know how many times he apologized to the baroness, how many times he apologized to me on the way home.

I WAS A widow. No, no, I wasn't. Gregor wasn't dead. We just didn't know where he was or if he would ever return. How many missing soldiers had returned from Russia? I didn't even have a cross to leave fresh flowers on every week. I had the photo of him when he was a child, squinting in the sunshine, not smiling.

I imagined him lying on his side in the middle of the snow, his arm outstretched and my wrist far away, absent. His hand clutched air. I imagined him sleeping. He hadn't been able to overcome the exhaustion, his fellow soldiers hadn't wanted to wait for him, not even Shitbritches—such ingratitude—and Gregor had frozen. When the weather turned warm, the slab of ice that had once been my husband would melt, and perhaps a young woman with cheeks as red as a matryoshka's would awaken him with a kiss. With her he would begin a new life and have children named Yury or Irina, would grow old in a dacha, and from time to time before the fire would have a feeling he couldn't put his finger on. *What are you thinking about?* the matryoshka would ask him. *It's as though I'm forgetting something—no, someone,* he would reply, *but I don't know who.*

Or perhaps years later a letter would arrive from Russia. The body of Gregor Sauer discovered in a mass grave. *How do they know it's him? How do we know they aren't making a mistake?* We would believe it. We would have no choice.

12

When the brakes of the SS bus squealed, I pulled the sheet over my face.

"Get up, Rosa Sauer!" they shouted from outside.

The afternoon before, in Krausendorf, I hadn't said a word about what had happened. I was so stunned by the news that my body had rejected it instead of metabolizing it. Only Elfriede had said something. *Berliner, what is it?* she had asked. *Nothing,* I replied. She grew serious, touched my shoulder. *Rosa, is everything all right?* I moved away. The contact with her hand had brought the dam crashing down.

"Rosa Sauer!" they repeated. I listened to the hum of the engine until it was switched off. I lay there, not moving. The hens weren't squawking, hadn't done so for months. Zart had imposed silence; his presence was enough to calm them. By now they were used to hearing the tires screeching to a halt on the gravel, we were all used to it.

A brief rapping on my bedroom door, Herta's voice calling to me. I didn't answer.

"Joseph, come," she said. Then I heard her walk toward me, push the sheet back, shake me gently. She was making sure I was alive, that it was me. "What are you doing, Rosa?" My body was there, it wasn't missing, but it didn't react.

Joseph went to her side. "What is it?"

Just then, they knocked.

My father-in-law went to the door.

"Don't let them in," I begged.

"What are you talking about?" Herta protested.

"Let them do what they want to me. I don't care. I'm tired."

A crease formed between Herta's eyebrows, a short vertical slit I had never noticed before. It wasn't fear. It was resentment. I was playing dead while her son might actually be dead. I was putting myself in danger, along with the two of them.

"Get up," she said.

It came in handy to her, the two hundred marks I was earning each month.

"Please." She felt around the covers in search of my hand and stroked it through the fabric.

An SS guard burst into the room. "Sauer."

We all cringed.

"Heil Hitler," Herta said mechanically, then added: "Apologies. My daughter-in-law was unwell last night. She'll get dressed now and go."

I didn't get up. It wasn't rebellion, it was lack of strength.

Behind the guard, Joseph stole a concerned glance at me. Herta walked over to the uniformed guest. "Meanwhile, may I offer you something to drink?" This time she remembered to play the hostess. "Come now, Rosa. Hurry up."

I stared at the ceiling.

"Rosa," Herta pleaded.

"I can't. I swear I can't. Joseph, you tell him."

"Rosa," Joseph pleaded.

"I'm tired." I turned my head and looked at the guard. "Especially of all of you."

The man shoved Herta aside, threw back the covers, grabbed me by the arm, yanked me out of bed and across the floor with one hand, the other hand clamped to his holster. Not a peep from the hens, they sensed no danger.

"Put on your shoes," the guard ordered, releasing his grip on my arm, "unless you want to go barefoot."

"Forgive her, she hasn't been well," Joseph hazarded.

"Quiet, or I'll teach all three of you a lesson."

What would he do?

I wanted to die, now that Gregor was gone. *Missing,* I had told Herta, *not dead, do you understand?* But during the night I had convinced myself that he too had abandoned me, like my mother. I hadn't planned to go absent without leave—was that what I was doing? It wasn't like I was a soldier, wasn't like we were an army. *Germany's cannon fodder*, Gregor once said. *I fight for Germany, but no longer because I believe in it, no longer because I love it. I'm shooting because I'm afraid.*

I hadn't imagined the potential consequences: a summary trial, a summary execution? I too wanted to disappear, that was all.

"Please," Herta whimpered, huddling up, "my daughter-in-law is delirious. My son was just declared missing. I'll come in her place today. I'll taste the food for—"

"Quiet, I said!" The guard struck Herta, elbowed her violently, pistol-whipped her, I don't know, I didn't see it—all I saw was my mother-in-law huddling up even more than before. She doubled over, a hand on her rib cage, Joseph supported her, I stifled a scream and grabbed my shoes, trembling, put them on, felt my heartbeat hammering in my throat, got up, was shoved by the guard toward the coat rack, grabbed my jacket, put it on. Herta didn't raise her head. I called to her, wanted to say I was sorry. Joseph silently cradled her in his arms. They were waiting for me to leave before they groaned, fainted from the pain, or went back to bed, changed the lock, never again to open the door to me. *I don't deserve anything except what I do: eating Hitler's food, eating for Germany, not because I love it, or even out of fear. I eat Hitler's food because it's what I deserve, it's what I am.*

"Did the little girl throw a tantrum?" the driver said, smirking, when his colleague shoved me into a seat. Theodora, in the front row as always, didn't say hello. Nor did Beate and Heike dare to, that morning. Then, as the others pretended to be asleep, Augustine called to me in a whisper. She was sitting two rows in front of me on the left. Her nervous, shifting profile was a blurry splotch in my line of vision. I didn't reply.

Leni got on board and headed toward me. She hesitated. The sight of me with my coat over my nightgown must have frightened her. She didn't know my mother had died dressed this way, that to me this clothing signaled the end. I had put my shoes on without stockings, felt a chill on my legs, my toes numb beneath the leather. They were the shoes I used to wear in Berlin, at the office where Gregor was my boss and I his delight, *Where are you going with those heels on?* Herta would say to me, but this morning she had a broken rib, or a fractured one, she couldn't speak, *Where are you going with those heels on,* Leni must have thought, *heels with a nightgown, it's insane.* She blinked her green eyes several times, then sat down beside me.

I would get blisters, would pinch them between my fingernails until they burst, a power wielded over my body by me and me alone. Leni took my hand and just then I realized it had been resting on my thigh. "Rosa, what happened?" she said, and Augustine turned around. A splotch, a blur in my vision. Gregor said, *I see butterflies, gnats buzzing around, spiderwebs*; I told him, *Look at me, my love, concentrate.*

"Rosa." Leni gently held my hand in hers. She looked inquisitively at Augustine, who shook her head. The splotch danced, my sight gave out. I lacked the strength.

A person can cease to exist even when alive. Gregor might have been alive, but he no longer existed, not to me. The Reich carried on fighting, designed Wunderwaffen, believed in miracles, but I had never believed in them. *The war will continue until Göring manages to put on Goebbels's trousers,* Joseph said. It seemed the war would have to last forever, but I decided not to fight anymore, I mutinied, not against the SS—against life. I ceased to exist, sitting there on the bus as it drove me toward the lunchroom table in Krausendorf, the altar of the Kingdom.

THE DRIVER WAS pulling over again. Through the window I saw Elfriede waiting at the side of the road, one hand in her coat pocket, cigarette in the other. Her eyes met mine and her cheekbones flickered beneath her skin. Staring at me steadily, she crushed the cigarette under her shoe, got on board.

She came toward us. I don't know if Leni motioned to her or Augustine told her something or if it was my eyes; she sat down in the seat across the narrow aisle from Leni, said, "Good morning."

Leni sheepishly mumbled hello. It wasn't a good morning, hadn't Elfriede realized that?

"What's with her?"

"I don't know," Leni replied.

"What did they do to her?"

Leni said nothing. But then again, Elfriede wasn't talking to her. She was addressing me, but I no longer existed.

Elfriede cleared her throat. "So, Berliner, I see you gave yourself a 'bomb shelter' hairdo this morning."

The women giggled. Only Leni held back.

I thought, *I can't, Elfriede. I swear, I can't.*

"Ulla, what do you say about her hairstyle? Do you approve?"

"Better than braids," Ulla said shyly.

"Must be the latest trend in Berlin."

"Elfriede," Leni said reproachfully.

"The outfit's pretty daring too, Berliner. Not even Zarah Leander would be so bold."

Augustine let out a few loud coughs. Maybe it was a signal to Elfriede, *Don't push it, don't go too far,* maybe she understood—she, who had lost her husband in the war and had decided to wear mourning clothes forever.

"What would you know, Augustine? You're a country girl. The Berliner here even braves the cold in the name of fashion. Teach her a thing or two, Berliner!"

I stared at the roof of the bus, hoping it would crash down on me.

"Seems we aren't worthy of even a peep from her."

Why was she doing it? Why was she tormenting me? And again all the fuss about my clothes. *A word of advice: mind your own business,* she had said. Why wouldn't she leave me alone today?

"Leni, have you ever read *The Stubbornhead*?"

"Yes . . . as a little girl."

"Nice story, isn't it? I think we'll call Rosa that from now on. The Stubbornhead."

"Cut it out," Leni begged her, squeezing my hand. I pulled it away, dug my fingers into my thigh until it hurt.

"Right. The enemy is listening, like Goebbels always says."

I shot my gaze toward Elfriede. "What is it you want, anyway?"

Leni pinched her nose between her thumb and forefinger, as if about to jump into water. It was how she calmed her nerves.

"Move," I told her.

She let me pass. I got out of my seat, stood in front of Elfriede, leaned over her. "What the hell do you want?"

Elfriede touched my knee. "You have goose bumps."

I slapped her face. She shot to her feet, shoved me, I threw her to the floor and in a flash was on top of her. Thick veins bulged from her neck like taut cords to pluck, to yank out. I didn't know what I wanted to do with the woman. *Hate*, my history teacher at high school had said, *we German women must know how to hate*. Elfriede gritted her teeth, struggled to break free, to flip me over. I breathed raggedly against her breath.

"Have you vented enough?" she suddenly asked. I had loosened my grip without realizing it.

Before I could answer, the guard grabbed me by the collar, dragged me down the aisle of the bus just as he had done to me at home, kicked my sides, my bare legs, over and over again, yanked me to my feet, and forced me into a seat up front, in the spot behind the driver, next to Theodora, in the same row as Gertrude and Sabine. Theodora had plugged her ears. She hadn't expected that the SS would be allowed to beat us—not us, Hitler's food tasters, *Such an important task, a question of life or death, Corporal, sir, a bit of respect*. Or maybe she was used to it, maybe her husband beat her regularly, and not only when he drank too much beer. *The bigger the man, the more insignificant the woman must be, even Hitler says that. And so, Fanatic, get off your high horse, remember your place.*

After me it was Elfriede's turn. I heard the impact of his boot against her bones but not even one whimper.

IN THE LUNCHROOM I could barely get anything down. I forced myself, not because I was afraid of the SS—I was hoping for poison. If I could swallow just one mouthful of it I would be delivered to death without having to seek it myself, would be relieved of at least that task. But the food was safe and I didn't die.

For months my companions hadn't seen their husbands or boyfriends. Though Augustine was the only official widow, we had all been alone for quite a while. I couldn't claim exclusive rights to grief, they wouldn't have allowed me to. Maybe that was why I didn't say anything, not even to Leni, not even to Elfriede, neither of whom had a husband or a boyfriend.

Leni spoke of love with the dreamy naïveté of someone who'd read about it in serial novels but didn't really understand what it was. She hadn't experienced emotional dependence on another human being, one who didn't produce you, one who hadn't been there when you were born. She had never left her father and mother to cleave to a stranger.

One time Augustine had said, *Leni wants the war to end because she's afraid if it doesn't it'll be too late for her to marry. She was searching for true love, was saving herself until she found it.*

Don't make fun of me, Leni had peeped.

But then the war broke out, Augustine went on, *and the men disappeared.*

Leni defended herself: *I'm not the only spinster.*

But you aren't a spinster, I reassured her, *you're so young.*

Elfriede isn't married either, Leni said, *and she's always alone.*

Elfriede heard that. She raised her fist to her mouth as if to block her words. Her lips touched her ring finger.

ALL ALONE IN the world, with no one to wait for, no one to lose, Elfriede ate with her head bowed, one forkful after the other. When she finished, she asked permission to go to the washroom. The Beanpole wasn't there, nor was the one who had beaten us on the bus. As one of the guards turned to escort her, I said, "I need to go too," and just then Elfriede almost stopped in her tracks.

She locked herself in a stall. I went up to her door. "It's all my fault," I said, resting my forehead against the whitewashed wood. "I'm sorry." I didn't hear her tinkling, moving, anything. "Gregor was declared missing. That's what happened. He might be dead, Elfriede."

The lock turned, the door began to open outward. I stepped back and stood there, waiting for it to be completely open. Elfriede came out, her eyes hard, her cheekbones angular. She rushed at me. I didn't move.

She embraced me in a hug. She had never done that before. I clung to her body full of sharp edges. It wasn't waiting for anyone, that body, it could offer refuge to mine. It was so warm, so welcoming, that the sobs welled up in my chest until they overflowed. Since the moment I had received the letter, I hadn't yet wept. It was months since I had last hugged anyone.

HERTA STOPPED BAKING bread, collecting eggs in the morning for breakfast with Joseph, chatting in the evening with us as she knit. She unraveled the scarf she had made for Gregor and threw away the skein. Zart found it in the trash bin in the back room and played with it all through the house, unrolling the yarn, which tangled around the legs of the chairs and table. Wool fibers floated through the air, stuck to everything. Maybe the mischief would have once amused us. Maybe now it reminded Herta of her son's childhood mischief and it was to banish the thought that she sent the cat outside with a feeble kick.

Joseph didn't stop listening to the radio after dinner, or smoking his pipe. In fact, he searched for foreign stations more doggedly than before, almost as if expecting to intercept Gregor's voice: *I'm alive, I'm in Russia, come get me.* But it wasn't a treasure hunt—no map, the only clues the increasingly alarming news reports.

As for me, I stopped making jam with Herta and working in the vegetable garden with Joseph. Before, when picking vegetables I had put on the galoshes Gregor had worn as a boy. His father had found them in the cellar. They were only a little tight on me. My heart had been warmed by the tenderness of my husband's childhood feet, feet I had never seen, never touched. But now they tormented me.

I decided to write to him every day, write what was going through my head, a diary of me missing him. When he returned we would read it together, he would tease me by pointing out the saddest passages or the overly sentimental ones, and I would slap him on the chest, but only in jest. I tried. But I couldn't write anything, there was nothing for me to talk about.

I didn't go into the woods anymore, didn't spot empty stork nests, didn't go all the way to Moy Lake to crouch at the water's edge and sing. I had lost all desire to sing.

Leni awkwardly tried to console me, was the only one to do so. "I'm sure he's still alive," she declared with unbearable optimism. "Maybe he deserted and is on his way home now."

The fact that widowhood—be it actual or potential—was a common condition was no consolation. I had never imagined it could happen to me. Gregor had come into my life to make me happy, that was his role. Anything else was a betrayal, made me feel tricked.

Elfriede might have sensed this. That was why she didn't even try to comfort me. *Want a cigarette?* she asked me once. *You know I don't smoke,* I said. *You see? You're stronger than I am,* she said, smiling. For a second, that smile, of which only I was worthy, reestablished order. For a second, a merciful feeling of half sleep spread through my body. Elfriede hadn't even checked the bruises on her thighs during the days following the beating, had mentally archived them before they even faded, I was sure of it.

Unlike her, I studied mine every morning. When I pressed my finger against them they throbbed, and it was as though Gregor weren't entirely lost. The bruises were a sign of a rebellion still being waged. When that physical pain was gone, never again would my skin present any sign of my husband's presence on earth.

ONE DAY HERTA woke up, her eyes less puffy than usual, and decided Gregor was fine. He would turn up at the door one morning at dawn, identical to how he was when he enlisted, but with a much heartier appetite. Imitating her, I tried to convince myself of it too.

I would seek him out in the last picture in the photo album, the one of him in uniform. I would speak to him, and it was like a bedtime prayer. That he existed was a wager; that I believed it, a habit. The first years of our relationship, my every organ would yield to him, I would succumb like a child. Now at night I tossed and turned, slept in fits and starts. Gregor was missing, perhaps dead, and I continued to love him. It was an adolescent, unequivocal love that needed no reciprocation—only stubbornness, trusting patience.

USING HIS OLD address in America, I wrote Franz a long letter. I so needed to talk to someone from my family, someone who had chased after me on a bicycle, who had taken baths with me before mass on Sundays, someone I had known since his birth, since he had slept in his cradle and wailed until he was blue in the face because I had bitten his hand—my brother.

I wrote to him that I had no longer heard anything from Gregor, just as I hadn't heard from him. It was a nonsensical letter, and only as I was writing it did I realize I could no longer see Franz's features clearly in my mind. I saw his broad back clad in a caban jacket, his bowed legs carrying him off, but I couldn't picture his face. Did he have a mustache now? Did he still get cold sores on his lip? Had he needed to buy glasses? Franz as an adult was unknown to me. When I thought of my brother, when I read the word "brother" in a book or heard it spoken, in my mind I saw his knobby knees covered with abrasions, his legs streaked with scratches—they were what triggered in me the longing to hug him again.

For months I hoped for a reply, but no letter from Franz arrived. No one wrote to me anymore.

Of those months I remember nothing, apart from the day on which the purple clover in the fields, glimpsed from the window of the bus on the way to Krausendorf, awakened me from my monastic everyday existence. Spring had arrived, and a vague feeling of nostalgia swept over me. It wasn't only that I missed Gregor, it was that I missed life.

Part
TWO

13

One afternoon in late April, I was sitting on a bench with Heike and Augustine in the barracks courtyard, which was surrounded by a fence. Since the weather had grown warmer, during the hour-long wait after our meal the SS men would let us go outside under their supervision. One would stand guard by the French door while the other would patrol the yard with his chin held high and his hands behind his back.

Heike was nauseated, but no one thought about poison anymore.

"Maybe you're still hungry," said Elfriede, who was standing in front of us.

"Maybe you're getting your period," said Leni, who spent the hour counting her footsteps on the faded remains of a hopscotch court drawn on the cement in white paint. You could barely make out the squares, which may have been why Leni wasn't hopping—not because she found it over the top. Still, she liked being there, almost as if placing herself within that perimeter protected her from all possible attack. "I just got mine, and everyone knows that when women spend lots of time together their menstrual cycles end up synchronizing."

"Would you listen to yourself?" Augustine tsked to emphasize how preposterous she found Leni's remark.

"It's true." Sitting on the ground, Ulla nodded with such emphasis that her chestnut curls bounced like springs. "I've heard that too."

I was there with them but it was as though I weren't there at all. I had nothing to say. Occasionally the others would try to rouse me from my lethargy, at times quite awkwardly. For the most part they had grown accustomed to my silence.

"Such nonsense," Augustine said. "Women's menstrual cycles synchronizing? Just another superstition, one of the many they use to subjugate us. What are we going to believe in next, magic?"

"I believe in it." Beate stood up from the swing so quickly the seat shot back. Its chains twisted around and instantly untwisted, making the seat twirl.

Since the first day they let us come outside, I had wondered why the SS hadn't torn out the playground equipment. Maybe they hadn't had time, maybe there had been more important things to think about. Maybe they hoped the barracks would one day welcome schoolchildren again, once the East had been defeated, the Communist threat crushed. Maybe the men had kept it there because it reminded them of the children they had left behind somewhere, in some city in the Reich, children who would grow up so much they would be unrecognizable to their fathers returning home on leave.

"I'm a witch, didn't you know?" Beate said. "I can chart horoscopes, read palms, and even read cards."

"It's true," Heike said. "She's read them for me lots of times."

Leni crossed her barrier of faded paint and stopped in front of Beate. "You can predict the future?"

"Sure she can. She even knows precisely when the war's going to end," Augustine said. "Ask her if your husband is still alive, Rosa."

My heartbeat lost its rhythm, went off the tracks.

"Leave her alone," Elfriede snapped. "Why do you always have to be so tactless?"

With this, she walked away. I could have followed her, uttered the thank-you trapped in my throat, but instead I remained in my spot beside Augustine, only because it required no effort.

"You should put a curse on Hitler," Ulla said, to change the subject. The women laughed to ease the tension. I didn't.

"So, Beate," Leni said excitedly, "tell me if I'll find a fiancé once the war's over."

"I can't believe this," Augustine groaned.

"Yes, come on!" Ulla said, clapping her hands.

Beate reached into her pocket, pulled out a black velvet pouch tied with a cord, and opened it to reveal a deck of tarot cards.

"Do you always bring those around with you?" Leni asked.

"What kind of a witch would I be if I didn't?" Beate said. She knelt down and spread out the cards. Then she arranged them slowly, focusing, following a pattern invisible to us. She pulled some out of the stack and laid them down, shuffled the deck, then turned over other cards. Augustine watched her skeptically.

"Well?" Ulla was impatient. Leni didn't dare utter a word. The others were leaning over her in a circle. All except Elfriede, who was walking around, smoking; except the Fanatics, who almost never came outside after lunch, preferring to remain diligently seated at their workstations; and except me, still sitting on the bench.

"Actually, I do see a man. . . ."

"Oh, my god!" Leni covered her face with her hands.

"Good for you, Leni!" The women playfully tugged on her arm and nudged her shoulder. "At least ask her what he's like. Is he handsome?"

It was a means of survival, every ounce of energy being dedicated to this sole purpose. That's what the women were doing. I couldn't bring myself to do the same anymore.

"I can't see whether he's handsome or not," Beate said apologetically, "but I see that he'll arrive soon."

"Why the gloomy tone?" Heike asked.

"He's ugly and she doesn't want to tell me so," Leni whined. Once again, the women burst out laughing.

Not Beate. "And when—"

"To your feet!"

The voice boomed through the courtyard, toward us. It came from a uniformed officer. We had never seen him before. As the women stood up straight and I rose from the bench, Beate gathered her cards and tried to tuck them away, but they caught on the mouth of the velvet pouch and fell to the ground. The man screamed at her, "To your feet, I told you!"

When he reached us, Leni still had her hands on her cheeks.

"What is all this?" The man scrutinized Beate. "And you, show me your face," he said, yanking on Leni's elbow. She crossed her arms over her chest, clasping her shoulders, a means of comfort, or perhaps self-condemnation.

The guards hurried over. "Lieutenant Ziegler, what's going on?"

"Where were you?"

The guards snapped to attention and stole angry glances at us—thanks to us they were in trouble. They didn't reply. It was clear to everyone that it was best to remain silent.

"They're just some stupid cards. Nobody ever said it was forbidden, and we weren't doing anything wrong."

I had been the one to speak.

Looks of astonishment weighed upon me, and not only from the other women. The lieutenant stared at me. He had a small, childish nose. His eyes were somewhat closely set and hazel in color. That was his limitation—his eyes didn't frighten me.

Elfriede was standing against the wall, and the guards didn't call her over. Like us, they waited for the lieutenant to sentence me. At that moment, the courtyard of the former school, the barracks, the rural homes in Krausendorf, the rows of oaks and spruce trees leading to Gross-Partsch, the headquarters hidden in the forest, East Prussia, all of Germany, the Third Reich determined to expand to the farthest reaches of the globe, and the eight meters of Adolf Hitler's irritated intestine converged in that solitary spot in the world occupied by Lieutenant Ziegler, the man who held the power of life and death over me.

"I am forbidding it now," he said to me. "Obersturmführer Ziegler: that is my name. Remember it well, because from now on you will do as I command—everyone will. Meanwhile, salute as you have been taught to."

As I mechanically held out my arm, Ziegler turned from me and swiped awkwardly at Beate's pouch, but it fell to the ground. A gust of wind carried some of the cards a meter or two away. He turned to the guards. "Get the women onto the bus."

"Yes, sir, Lieutenant. Move!"

Beate was the first to leave, Leni followed her, and slowly but surely the others joined them. The Obersturmführer stomped the pouch beneath his boot and turned to his subordinates. "Throw them away." With this, he walked off.

By the door he noticed Elfriede. "And what are you doing, hiding?" he said to her as he walked inside. "Get in line."

I moved toward her. When I reached her she touched the arm I had been slow to raise. There was apprehension in her gesture. I had run a risk, and for no reason. But then again, I didn't need a reason to die—if death had really been at stake—no more than I had a reason to live. That was why I wasn't afraid of Ziegler.

He had seen it, my inclination to die, and had had to look away.

14

Raising one's arm for the Nazi salute was no trivial matter. The Obersturmführer had doubtless taken part in many conferences at which they had explained it to him: in order for one's arm to be raised in a clear, incontrovertible manner, one has to contract every muscle in one's body, buttocks clenched, tummy in, chest out, legs joined, knees stiff, lungs full so as to exhale a mighty *Heil Hitler!* Every fiber, tendon, nerve has to perform the solemn task of stretching out one's arm.

There are those who hold their arm out weakly and stiffen their shoulder, which should instead remain low, distanced from the ear to avoid the least trace of asymmetry and to triumph in the athletic pose of one who cannot be defeated, or at least hopes not to be. There are those who, instead of holding it out at a forty-five-degree angle, hold it out almost straight up, but you're not raising your hand to express your opinion. Here, opinions are expressed by but one person, so fall in line and focus on doing your job well. Your fingers, for instance, mustn't be opened as though to apply nail polish to them. Join them together, hold them out straight! Raise your chin, smooth your brow, channel all your strength, all your intention along the trajectory of your arm, imagine using the palm of your hand to crush the heads of all those who lack the physique of victors. Men aren't all alike, race is one's soul seen from the outside, so put your entire soul into that arm and offer it to your Führer, that invincible man with the makings of a messiah. He won't return it to you, which means you can live relieved of that burden.

Obersturmführer Ziegler was undoubtedly an expert at the Nazi salute—he had been practicing it for years. Or perhaps he was simply talented. So was I, but I didn't make enough effort. My salute passed muster, but it was a performance without distinction. And yet as a little girl I had skated, had had a fair command of my body, so when at the beginning of the school year they would assemble us in the auditorium for a lecture on the Nazi salute, I would stand out for my aptitude, too proud to let myself be reproached. Over the course of the school year, though, I would gradually lapse into mediocrity, to the chagrin of my teachers, who would frown at me during the swastika-raising ceremony.

At the parade celebrating the arrival of the Olympic torch in Berlin—having begun in Greece, then passing through Sofia, Belgrade, Budapest, Vienna, and Prague—I saw the Jungvolk standing in line wearing their uniforms. After twenty minutes they couldn't stand still. They shifted from one foot to the other, supporting their outstretched right arm with their left hand, too weary to avoid the punishment in store for them.

The radio was broadcasting live recaps of the games. Due to the poor quality of the transmissions, the Führer's voice was raspy. Nevertheless, it crossed through the airwaves, stentorian and backed by the crowd who cheered and cried out to him as one, and traveled all the way to me. The nation that surrendered itself to him and unhesitatingly proclaimed it by shouting his name—a ritual, a magic formula, a word of limitless power—the nation gripped the heart, offering a sense of belonging that washed away the solitude to which every single person is relegated from birth. It was an illusion I couldn't believe in—I only wished I felt it inside me, not a rousing sentiment of victory but a comforting sense of connection.

My father angrily switched off the radio—my father, who believed National Socialism to be only a transitory phenomenon, deviant behavior among disorderly youths, a virus we had caught from Italy; my father, who at work had been passed over by colleagues who joined the Nazi Party. My father, who had always voted Zentrum, like good

Catholics did, and had then seen Zentrum backing the law that granted Hitler full powers, backing its own dissolution. My father was oblivious to that sudden, traitorous longing that had blossomed within me as I imagined the stream of people gulping down sausages and drinking lemonade together in the excitement of the holiday, persuaded that individual, irreducible human existences could merge together into a single thought, into a single destiny. I was eighteen at the time.

How old was Ziegler then? Twenty-three, twenty-five? My father died of a heart attack when Ziegler was certainly already in service, could perform an impeccable Nazi salute, knew the rules, and enforced them, was fully prepared to trample Beate's tarot cards beneath his boot and my insolence beneath his stony stare. He would have crushed any individual who stood between Germany and the achievement of its glorious designs.

That was what I was thinking of that afternoon, minutes after seeing him for the first time. He had just been transferred to Krausendorf and had already promised us that nothing there would be the same. What had happened to the officer who had commanded the barracks before him? We had crossed paths a few times in the hallway but he had never deigned to acknowledge our presence. Never would he have come out to the courtyard to scream at us. We were ten digestive tracts, and he certainly wouldn't have bothered speaking to digestive tracts.

As I sat on the bus, I thought of Gregor, thought that maybe he had trampled corpses rather than cards beneath his boots, and I wondered how many people he had killed before going missing. But Ziegler was a German man before a German woman; Gregor, a German before a foreigner. He would need much more self-hatred to give up on his own life. Or indifference. It wasn't Ziegler who angered me that day—it was my missing husband.

Actually, it was myself. In those who recognize it, weakness awakens guilt, and I realized that. As a child I had bitten Franz's hand.

15

"She's going to end up in lots of trouble." Augustine nodded at Ulla, who was standing off to the side of the lunchroom with the Beanpole and another guard as we waited for lunch to be served. Krümel was late that day, as he had been from time to time recently. I wondered whether there were problems with the supplies, if the impact of the war was reaching even our little corner of heaven on earth.

Ulla twirled a lock of her hair, fiddled with her necklace, its pendant dangling down to the curve of her bosom. No one could blame her—for too long we had been women without men. It wasn't the sex we were missing but the sensation of being seen.

"Women who drool over power are unbearable."

I stood corrected—Augustine could blame her. Laughing boisterously, Ulla tilted her head to the side and her dark brown curls slid onto a single shoulder, leaving part of her neck bare. The Beanpole stared at the white skin of that neck without taking any pains to hide it.

"It's the war that's unbearable."

Augustine wasn't surprised to hear me answer back to her, despite my now-customary apathy. After all, I had answered back to Ziegler when even she had said nothing.

"No, Rosa. You know what Hitler said? He said the masses are like women: they don't want someone to defend them, but someone to command them. *Like women*, he said. And that's because women like Ulla exist."

"Ulla is craving a little distraction, that's all. Sometimes frivolousness can be like medicine."

"A poisonous medicine."

"Speaking of poison, it's ready," Elfriede said, sitting down and spreading her napkin on her lap. "*Bon appétit*, ladies. As always, let's hope it's not our last."

"Give it a rest!" Augustine also sat down.

Ulla took the seat across from her but soon sensed she was being observed. "What?" she asked.

"Silence," ordered the Beanpole, who just a moment ago had been admiring her pendant. "Eat."

"HEIKE, DON'T YOU feel well?" Beate asked in a low voice.

Heike stared at her oatmeal. It was untouched.

"It's true. You're so pale," Leni said.

"You didn't put a curse on her, did you, little witchie?"

"Augustine," Beate said, "have you got it in for everybody today?"

"I feel nauseous," Heike admitted.

"Still? You don't have a fever, do you?" Leni reached over the table sideways, trying to feel her forehead, but rather than leaning in to let her, Heike remained sunk in her chair. "It wasn't your period, then. We don't have synchronized cycles," Leni mumbled, disappointed that her theory of sisterhood hadn't been confirmed. Heike didn't respond, and Leni nibbled on her fingernail, already closed up in herself, already the little girl who played hopscotch alone and continued to do so as an adult, even without a proper hopscotch court. "I was wrong," she repeated again after five minutes.

Augustine intentionally dropped her spoon, which clattered into her Aachen ceramic bowl.

"Order!" snapped the guard.

Potato pancakes were served along with a *Heil Hitler!* that I ignored. The SS guards were constantly coming in and out of the room, and the sight of the pancakes made my mouth water. Unable to control myself, I immediately grabbed one off my plate, burned my fingers, blew on them.

"You aren't eating?"

Recognizing the stern tone, I looked up.

"I don't feel well," Heike replied. "I must have the flu."

Leni seemed to return among us. Beneath the table she touched my leg with her foot.

"Taste the oatmeal. That's what you're here for."

Heike dipped her spoon into her dish, collected a scant milligram of oatmeal, and with unnerving slowness raised it to her lips, though her lips were sealed tight. She stared at the spoon but couldn't bring herself to put it into her mouth.

Ziegler's fingers squeezed both her cheeks like pliers until her mouth opened. "Eat."

Heike's eyes were watering as she swallowed. My heart raced.

"There, well done. A taster who doesn't eat is of no use to us. The doctor will determine if you have the flu. Tomorrow I'll have him give you a checkup."

"That's not necessary," she was quick to reply. "It's just a fever, that's all."

Elfriede looked at me, worried.

"Then eat what you've been served," Ziegler said, "and tomorrow we'll see." He glanced around, commanded the SS guards to keep an eye on Heike, and walked out.

The next day, Heike ate like the others, then asked to be escorted to the washroom. She did that for a while, relying on the alternation of the guards. She vomited quickly, trying not to be heard. In order to verify that it wasn't poisoned, the food had to remain in our stomachs for the established amount of time, and purposefully ridding ourselves of it wasn't allowed. We knew she was vomiting, though. Her eyes were deeply sunken into two dark hollows, her skin waxy. No one dared ask. How long would it be before they took our next blood sample?

"She has two children to feed," Beate said. "It's not like she can afford to lose her job."

"How long do you think her flu will last?" I asked with a sigh.

"She's pregnant," Elfriede whispered in my ear while we were in line. "Hadn't you realized that?"

I hadn't, no. Heike's husband was at the front. She hadn't seen him for almost a year.

WE WERE WOMEN without men. The men were fighting for our homeland—*First my people, then all the others! First my homeland, then the world!*—and sometimes they returned on leave, sometimes they died. Or they were declared missing.

We women, all of us, needed to be desired, because men's desire makes you exist more fully. Every woman learns that at a young age—at thirteen, fourteen. You notice that power when it's too early for you to handle it. It's not something you fought for and won, so it risks becoming a trap. It emanates from your body, still unknown to you—you've never looked at yourself naked in the mirror—and yet it's as if others have already seen you. Unless you exert this power it will consume you. Yielding power over oneself is easier than wielding power over others. It's not the masses who are like women, but the opposite.

Who was the father of the child Heike carried in her womb? I couldn't imagine him. She, however, I imagined with her head on the pillow, her other children sleeping at her side, and she, with her eyes still open, stroking her belly, her mistake. Maybe she had fallen in love.

At night I envied her. I pictured her in bed, frightened by her body's signals, exhausted from the nausea, and unable to sleep. But I also imagined her organs as they began to pulse. A life had been kindled, a heartbeat just beneath her navel.

16

THE INVITATION FROM MARIA FREIFRAU VON MILDERNHAGEN ARRIVED
in a card adorned with the family coat of arms. It had been delivered
by a messenger boy while I was at work. That's how I was saying it by
then: *I'm going to work*. Receiving the liveried boy at the door, Herta
was embarrassed not only by her stained apron but also by Zart, who
came over to greet him. The messenger boy freed his ankles from the
cat's endearments and tried to complete his task promptly but po-
litely. Herta had laid the sealed envelope on the credenza, curious to
know what it contained. However, since it was addressed to me she
would have to await my return.

The baroness, I read, was holding a soirée that weekend and would
be delighted if I attended.

"What does that woman want with Rosa?" my mother-in-law
grumbled. "She's never invited us. She doesn't even know her."

"She does know her," my father-in-law said, avoiding any mention
of the occasion on which I had met her, though Herta may have deduced it on her own. "I happen to think a little amusement would do
Rosa some good."

"I'm not so sure," I said.

Any form of amusement would have been an insult to Gregor. Nevertheless, the recollection of the baroness, that creamy complexion,
the way she had held Joseph's hands in her own—it gave me the same
sensation as a cloth draped on a chair beside the hearth which is then
raised to touch your cheek . . . that same warmth.

I could wear one of the few evening gowns I had brought with me from Berlin, I thought. *What are you going to do with all those?* Herta had asked, seeing me hang my things in the wardrobe in which she had made room for me. *Nothing. You're right,* I replied, picking up a hanger. *You've always been so vain,* she said.

It was true, but I had slipped those evening gowns into my suitcase because Gregor had given them to me, or because they brought to mind a moment I had spent with him—the year-end office party, for instance. He had stared at me the whole time, heedless of the rumors it would inspire at work the next day. It was then that I realized he liked me.

"Just what we needed," Herta grumbled, drying the dishes. She noisily stacked them in the credenza. It was May.

WHEN I CONFIDED to Leni that I had been invited to a soirée by the Baron and Baroness von Mildernhagen, she let out a squeal that drew the attention of all the others, so I was forced to tell them as well. "Anyway, I'm not going," I said.

The other women insisted. "Don't you want to visit the castle? It might be the only chance you'll ever get!"

Beate said she had rarely seen the baroness walking around town, children and governesses in tow, since the woman was always cooped up in her castle. It was because she was depressed, some said.

"Depressed? Her? Give me a break!" Augustine shot back. "She's always throwing parties, poor thing—only you're not invited."

"If you ask me, we never see her around town because she's often traveling the world," Leni said. "Who knows what wonderful journeys she's been on?"

Joseph had told me the baroness spent entire afternoons in the gardens, breathing in the scent of her plants, and not only in spring or summer—she also loved the smell of the rain-drenched earth and the colors of autumn. She had grown fond of Joseph, her gardener, because he grew and cared for her favorite flowers. When he spoke to me of her, I didn't picture her at all as being depressed, but rather a bit dreamy, a delicate woman protected within the walls of her own private Eden—no one would cast her out.

"She's a kind person," I told them, "especially with my father-in-law."

"Oh, please!" Augustine said. "She's just a snob. She's never seen around town because she thinks she's better than us."

"It doesn't matter what the baroness thinks," Ulla broke in. "All that matters is that you go to the party, Rosa. Do it for me, I beg you! That way you can tell me everything."

"About her?"

"Yes, but also about the castle and what a real soirée is like, how people dress for the occasion. . . . Speaking of which, what are you going to wear? As for your hair"—she tucked a lock of it behind my ear—"I can do it up for you."

Excited by this new diversion, Leni said she would help.

"Why did she send you an invitation? What do you have to do with her?" Augustine asked me. "Tsk! You're going to start putting on airs again."

"I've never put on airs."

But she had already stopped listening to me.

Joseph offered to be my chaperone, seeing as I didn't have one. According to Herta, neither of us should go. He repeated that I had the right to amuse myself. I didn't want to amuse myself, though, and I didn't care about my rights. For months I had been devoted to nursing a pain that distracted me from everything else, a pain so extensive that it had gone beyond the original object of that pain. It had become a personality trait.

On Saturday at around seven-thirty Ulla burst into the Sauer home. She wore the dress I had given her and was carrying a bag full of hair rollers. "You're wearing it at last" was the only thing I managed to utter.

"Well, today's a special day, isn't it?" she said, smiling at me.

Leni and Elfriede were with her too. We had said goodbye not long before on the bus. Leni must have nagged Ulla half to death to let her come, but Elfriede? What was she doing here in our kitchen, which Ulla had gotten it into her head to transform into a beauty salon? She hadn't said a word about my invitation to the castle, and now here she was, inside my house for the first time. I was too caught off guard to know how to receive her. Our intimacy had been confined to hidden, lowly places like the barracks washroom. This was a breach, a rupture, something we couldn't even acknowledge. Outside the framework of our time as food tasters, our friendship lost its urgency. It confused me.

I had the women make themselves comfortable, somewhat hesitantly, worried that Herta wouldn't enjoy having visitors. The somber spirit of our days had become a form of homage to Gregor, and she was devoted to her belief that her son would one day rise again. The least deviation from this was sacrilege. She already couldn't bear that I was going to the castle—who knew how much Ulla's festive spirit would upset her?

Instead my mother-in-law showed only a touch of uneasiness, and it was because she was being kind—she wanted to be hospitable but doubted she would manage to do it well.

I felt disoriented. The dress that Ulla was wearing was one I had worn myself in a now-remote era. The fabric, which was too warm for the season, now hung down the sides of another woman, yet the story it told was mine.

Herta boiled some water for tea and I took the good cups out of the credenza. "I don't have any cookies," she said apologetically. "If I had known, I would have made something."

"There's jam," Joseph said, coming to her rescue, "and bread. Herta's is delicious."

We ate bread and jam like children having an afternoon snack. We had never eaten together in a place outside the lunchroom. Did the other women think about poison whenever they brought food to their lips? My mother used to say that eating meant battling death, but only in Krausendorf had I believed it.

Having finished her first slice, Leni distractedly licked her finger and picked up another. "You like it, do you?" Elfriede asked, snickering. Leni blushed, and even Herta laughed. I hadn't heard her laugh for months.

Meanwhile, Ulla was anxious to do my hair. She stood up, her cup of tea still steaming, had Herta bring a basin with a little water in it, stood behind me, and dampened my hair with her hands.

"It's cold!" I protested.

"Oh, stop making such a fuss," she said.

Then, hairpins gripped between her lips, she began to wrap my locks, one by one, around the rollers, some larger, some smaller. From time to time I would tip back my head to catch a glimpse of her—she looked so serious—but she would push my head forward again. "Let me work."

Back when I was dating Gregor, I went to the hairdresser's once a week, wanting to look impeccable if he took me out to dinner. I would chat with the other women trapped in the mirror in front of me as the stylists teased and tamed our hair with brushes and hot irons. The sight of one's appearance spoiled by hair clips and barrettes, one's forehead pulled taut by combs, or half of one's face hidden behind a curtain of locks flipped forward, made it possible for us to talk about anything—about all the compromises marriage required, like the wives did, or about how amazing love was, like I did. Once, after listening to me, a woman slightly older in years had told me, *Dear, I don't like playing the part of Cassandra, but you should know it won't last forever.*

The recollection felt so far away, there in my in-laws' kitchen. Maybe it was because of that mismatched little group—Leni, Elfriede, Ulla, and Gregor's parents—gathered in the house where Gregor had spent his childhood. And along with them was me, who had once lived in the capital and spent my money at the hairdresser's every week, so young and naïve that the older women couldn't wait for their chance to begin to dampen my spirits in small doses—but only for my own good.

I tried to distract myself from the unfounded trace of concern that left my palms damp with perspiration. "Joseph," I said, "why don't you tell Ulla about the castle gardens?"

"Yes, yes, please!" she cried. "Oh, how I would love to see them! How big are they? Are there benches, fountains, gazebos?"

Before Joseph could even reply, Leni jumped in: "What about a maze? I love hedge mazes!"

My father-in-law smiled. "No, no garden maze."

"The kid thinks she's living in a fairy tale," Elfriede said, smirking.

"What's wrong with that?" Leni asked.

"Since she's lived this close to a castle her whole life," Ulla said, "it's to be expected, don't you think?"

"And where were you born, Elfriede?" Herta asked.

She hesitated before answering. "Gdańsk."

So she had been raised in a city too. How was it possible that after all those months I hadn't even known where she was from? Since every question seemed inopportune with her, I never asked any.

In '38 Gregor and I had passed through Gdańsk before setting off from Sopot. Who knew if Elfriede had been there as we walked down the streets of her city? Who knew if we had crossed paths without being able to imagine that years later we would share the same table, the same fate?

"Must've been hard," Joseph said.

Elfriede nodded.

"Who do you live with here?"

"I live alone. Leni, would you pour me some more tea?"

"For how long now?" Herta was trying to be kind, not indiscreet, but Elfriede made a noise with her nose—it sounded like she had a cold, but that was just her way of breathing. On certain winter afternoons, I still hear it.

"Done!" Ulla exclaimed, having placed a green hairnet over my head. "Now, please, don't touch it."

"But they're so tight. . . ." I wanted to scratch my scalp.

"Hands off!" Ulla slapped my wrist and everyone laughed, even Elfriede.

Luckily, Herta's question hadn't bothered her too much. There was something obstinate, even rude, about her secretiveness. I was allowed to get closer to her only when she decided I could, though at the same time I didn't feel rejected.

My discomfort faded and for a moment we were simply four young women focusing exclusively on beauty. Then, as if it were the right moment—as if the right moment for that question even existed—Leni asked, "Will you show me Gregor?"

Herta stiffened, drained of words.

Without a sound I stood up and went to my room.

"I'm sorry," Leni stammered. "I shouldn't have. . . ."

"What on earth were you thinking?" From her tone I could tell Elfriede was reproaching her.

The others remained silent.

Minutes later I returned to the kitchen, moved the teacups aside, and spread the photo album open on the table. Herta held her breath. Joseph put down his pipe, almost as though out of respect for Gregor, like taking off his hat.

I quickly flipped through the pages, some covered with a sheet of tissue paper, until I found him. In the first photograph he was sitting on a deck chair in the backyard, wearing a tie but no jacket. In another he was lying on the grass, wearing knickerbockers, the first buttons of his sweater undone. I was beside him, a striped kerchief on my head. They had taken the photo of us here, during our first trip together.

"That's him?" Ulla asked.

"Yes," Herta replied in a tiny voice. Then she tucked her upper lip into her mouth, pulling taut the skin beneath her nose. She looked like a turtle, she looked like my mother.

"You're a fine-looking couple," Ulla said.

"What about your wedding picture?" Leni was hungry for more.

I turned the page. "Here it is."

There they were, Gregor's eyes, those eyes that had studied me so closely on the day of my interview at the office, almost as if they wanted to search inside every atom, spot the nucleus, isolate it, pare away the rest, to directly access what mattered, what made me me.

I bashfully held a bouquet of flowers, the heads resting in the crook of my arm, the stems against my belly, as though to cradle them. One year later he would set off for the war. The following photograph was of him in uniform. After that he disappeared from the album entirely.

Joseph gently pushed Zart off his lap and went out back without saying a word. The cat followed him, but Joseph closed the door in his face.

ULLA TOOK THE rollers out of my hair and used her brush, which she then rested on the table. "Well, Frau Sauer, did I do a good job?"

Herta nodded unenthusiastically, then quickly said to me, "You need to get dressed."

A somber spirit had taken over once again. By now it was a familiar condition, for her a more-than-comfortable condition, since freeing herself from it would have been exhausting. I understood her. With my friends around, the photos of Gregor were no longer very different from the pictures Ulla would clip out of magazines—portraits of people you couldn't touch, with whom you couldn't talk, who might as well not have existed.

I dressed in silence, Herta sitting on my bed, lost in thought. She stared at the photo of Gregor at age five. He was her son, he had come out of her. How had she lost him?

"Herta, would you help me, please?"

Herta got up and did up my buttons one by one, slowly. "It's very low-cut," she said, touching my back. "You'll catch cold."

I walked out of the room, ready to go to the party yet feeling as though I had never decided to. Even Herta, perhaps, felt tricked into it. The other women were as bubbly as bridesmaids, but I was already married, no man awaited me at an altar. Why did I feel afraid, then, of what?

"The dark green of your gown looks good with your blond hair. And, not to compliment myself, but your hairdo flatters your round face," Ulla said. She looked so pleased it seemed like she was the one with the invitation.

"Have fun," Leni said from the doorway.

"Even if you don't have fun, remember everything," Ulla begged me. "I don't want to miss a single detail, got it?"

Elfriede was already outside.

"Aren't you going to say anything?"

"What do you want me to say, Berliner? It's risky to mix with people who aren't like you. Sometimes, though, you have no choice."

SAYING HELLO TO the baroness was the sole objective I managed to set myself for that evening, but I didn't know how to accomplish it. As soon as I walked into the reception hall, I accepted a glass of wine offered by a waiter—it seemed like a good way to familiarize myself with my surroundings. I took tiny sips of it as I wandered among the guests, who were all busy chatting. They were split up into such tight-knit groups that it was impossible for me to squeeze in anywhere, so I sat down on a divan beside a cluster of elderly ladies. Perhaps they were more tired or more bored than the others, because they found conversing with me to be an acceptable distraction. They complimented my satin gown, *The low-cut back looks good on you,* said one, *I love that embroidery on the shoulder,* said another, *I haven't seen many of that style before,* said a third. *A dressmaker in Berlin made it,* I replied. Just then other people arrived and when the ladies stood up to greet them they forgot about me. I walked away from the divan and leaned my bare back against the wallpaper, finishing my wine.

Studying the frescoes on the ceiling, I imagined I was tracing the figures' anatomies on a sheet of paper. I drew them with the nail of my first finger on the pad of my thumb. When I realized I was doing it, I stopped. I walked over to one of the picture windows, then checked yet again to see whether the baroness was finally free. She was still surrounded by people anxious to say hello to her. I should have gone over and included myself in the ongoing conversation but couldn't bring myself to do it. *You're always chatting away,* my mother would tell me. In East Prussia I had become laconic.

In the end, it was she who noticed me. I was standing there, partially hidden behind a long curtain. She walked over, looking happy to see me.

"Thank you for the invitation, Baroness von Mildernhagen. It's an honor to be here."

"You're quite welcome, Rosa. May I call you Rosa?"

"Of course, Baroness."

"Come, I'll introduce you to my husband."

CLEMENS FREIHERR VON Mildernhagen was smoking a cigar and entertaining two men. Seeing them from behind, if not for their uniforms I would never have recognized them as officers. Their relaxed posture—weight shifted onto one foot—wasn't proper military demeanor. One of the two was gesticulating adamantly, clearly trying to persuade the others of something.

"Gentlemen, may I present my friend from Berlin, Frau Sauer?"

The officers turned around.

I found myself facing Lieutenant Ziegler.

He furrowed his brow, staring at me as if trying to calculate the square root of a very long number. Perhaps he could see the surprise, the fear in me that appeared with a slight delay, like when you smash your knee against a sharp edge and for a moment it doesn't hurt, but then an intense pain shoots through it and grows stronger.

"My husband, Baron Clemens von Mildernhagen; Colonel Claus Schenk Graf von Stauffenberg; and Lieutenant Albert Ziegler," the baroness said, introducing us.

Albert, that was his first name.

"Good evening," I said, trying to keep my voice steady.

"It's a pleasure to have you here," the baron replied, kissing my hand. "I do hope the soirée is to your liking."

"Thank you, it's delightful."

Stauffenberg bowed. I didn't notice right away that he was missing a hand because my attention was drawn to the patch over his left eye. It gave him the air of a pirate that was far from threatening—quite the opposite, in fact. I was also distracted because I was expecting Ziegler to bow in turn, but he only acknowledged me with a little nod.

"I've noticed your conversation has been rather animated this evening. What are you talking about?" Maria asked with the impertinence that, as I would learn after we had spent time together, characterized her.

Ziegler narrowed his eyes and planted them on me. Someone else replied for him, perhaps the baron, or the colonel, but I didn't hear anything, I just saw a mist that clouded my vision and settled on my bare back. I shouldn't have worn this gown. I should never have come.

So the baroness doesn't know? Ziegler is going to pretend he doesn't know me? Am I supposed to tell the truth or play along? Is it a secret that I'm a food taster? Or is hiding the fact going to cause problems?

Ziegler's—no, Albert, that was his name—Albert's eyes were too closely set. He inhaled, dilating his feline nostrils, and pouted slightly, like a little boy who's upset because he just lost a football match—or, better, like a little boy who's eager to play football but has lost his ball and can't come to terms with it.

"You do nothing but discuss military strategies."

Was it possible that in the middle of a war that was claiming waves of victims every day, she was suggesting they speak of more frivolous topics, something more suitable for a social affair? Who was this woman? They said she was depressed. She didn't seem to be at all.

"Let's go, Rosa." Maria took my hand.

Ziegler noticed the gesture as though it were dangerous.

"Something the matter, Lieutenant? You've fallen silent. I must truly have been a disturbance."

"Don't even think it, Baroness," Ziegler replied. His voice was soft, calm, a voice I had never heard from him before. *I must tell Elfriede about it,* I thought.

I wouldn't.

"With your leave . . ." Maria pulled me from one guest to the next, introducing me as her friend from Berlin. She wasn't the kind of hostess who stops to chat with her guests only to move on a moment later, her sole purpose being to strike up conversations so that things run smoothly in every corner of the hall. Instead, she asked question after question, wanted to talk about anything at all, about the last time she had been to the opera and had seen *Cavalleria rusticana,* about our soldiers' still-high morale despite adversity, about the bias cut of my gown, which she praised in front of everyone, declaring that she would have an identical one made for her, but peach-colored, and not so low-cut, and in organza.

"It wouldn't be identical, then," I said, and she laughed.

All at once she sat down at the piano and, pressing her fingers onto the keys, sang "Vor der Kasern, vor dem großen Torstand eine Lanterne, und steht sie noch davor." From time to time she turned toward me, and with such insistence that I couldn't disappoint her: I began to sing softly, mechanically, but my throat was dry. Little by little the others joined us, and all together we longed for the time when Lili Marleen burned with love. But then again, the soldier knew—we, ourselves, knew—that soon she would forget him.

Where was Ziegler? Was he also singing? Who's going to be there now? we asked Lili Marleen in chorus, Who's going to be by the corner light with you? I thought of the woman who had distanced herself from the National Socialist Party, the woman who had left Germany, that white, sensual woman—did the lieutenant like Marlene Dietrich? Why should I possibly care?

Maria stopped, pulled on my arm, and made me sit down beside her on the bench. "Let's see if you know this one," she said, playing the unmistakable notes of "Veronika, der Lenz ist da." The first time I had gone to a Comedian Harmonists concert I was still a girl. I hadn't even met Gregor yet. The Großes Schauspielhaus was packed, and it seemed the audience's applause for the six young men in tuxedos would never end. That had been before the racial laws. Soon it would be discovered that the group had three Jews too many, and they would be prohibited from performing.

"Now it's your turn, Rosa," Maria said. "You have a lovely voice."

She didn't even give me the chance to reply. After the first two verses she stopped, forcing me to continue alone. I heard my voice echo off the tall ceilings, filling the hall, and it was as though that voice didn't belong to me.

This had been happening for months—I became detached from my actions; I couldn't perceive my own presence.

But Maria was satisfied, I could tell, and was also satisfied that she had chosen me as her friend. In the castle, in the large hall, with my eyes closed, I sang to the wavering accompaniment of a young baroness who had just met me and already she too was making me do as she wished.

You sing all day long, Rosa, it's becoming intolerable, Gregor said. *To me,* I replied, *singing is like diving underwater, Gregor. Imagine having a large rock weighing on your chest. Singing is when someone comes and pushes that rock off of you.* How long it had been since I had breathed so deeply?

All on my own I sang that love comes and love goes, until applause snapped me out of my daze. I opened my eyes, saw Albert Ziegler. He was at the far side of the hall, standing apart from the others, the end of a straight line leading directly to me. He still stared at me with that little pout of the boy left without a ball to play with. The boy had lost his power. He went home, having surrendered.

17

In may 1933, they lit the bonfire. I feared the streets of Berlin would melt and engulf us like lava. But Berlin was focused on celebrating and it didn't burn, it stomped its feet to the beat of the band, and even the rain stopped, making way for the oxcarts and the people rushing to the Opernplatz.

Once past the cordons, throats are parched by the smell of smoke, chests are scorched by the heat of the flames. Page after page curls up and falls to ash, and though Goebbels is a skinny man with a feeble voice he can bring that voice out to its fullest to exult, to look the ruthlessness of life straight in the eye, to repudiate the fear of death. Twenty-five thousand books taken from libraries and a league of celebrating students, youths who aspire to be men of character, not spineless men of letters. The age of Jewish intellectualism is over, Goebbels says, it's time to regain respect for death, and as hard as I try I can't figure out what he means.

A year later, during math class, I was looking out the window and staring at the tiny leaves of trees whose names I didn't know, watching the flapping wings of unknown birds, as Mr. Wortmann lectured. With his bald head, hunched shoulders, and thick mustache that compensated for his slightly protruding jaw, Wortmann certainly didn't have the looks of a movie star, yet all the girls in class adored him. He had piercing eyes and a matchless wit, which took all the strain out of learning.

When the door opened I was still lost in thought. Then, the click of handcuffs around wrists snapped me back to the classroom. The wrists in question were Wortmann's—SA officers were dragging him away. The formula on the blackboard remained incomplete. The chalk had fallen to the floor and shattered. It was May.

I leapt out of my chair and toward the door, but it was too late. Wortmann was already in the hallway, being escorted away by the SA officers. *Adam*, I cried out. That was his name. The professor tried to stop, to turn around, but the officers prevented him by speeding up. I shouted his name again and again, the other teachers trying every which way to hush me, with both threats and consolations.

Wortmann was made to do forced labor in a factory. He was a Jew or a dissident or simply a man of letters. We Germans, however, needed men of character, fearless men who respected death. Men, that is, who could let death be inflicted on them without uttering a word of complaint.

When the celebrations on May 10, 1933, came to an end, Goebbels announced he was satisfied. The crowd was tired, had run out of songs. The radio had concluded its transmission. The firemen had parked their trucks nearby and extinguished the blaze, but the fire had continued to creep beneath the ashes, had spread kilometers, had come all the way here. To Gross-Partsch, 1944. May was a merciless month.

18

I HAD NO IDEA HOW LONG HE HAD BEEN STANDING THERE.

The frogs seemed to have gone crazy that night. In my sleep, their incessant croaking had become the bustle of tenants racing down the stairs, clutching rosaries on which to count, the old women not knowing what saint to pray to, my mother not knowing how to persuade my father to seek shelter in the cellar. The siren was blaring and he rolled away from her, fluffed his pillow, and thrust his cheek into it. It was a false alarm. We climbed the stairs half asleep. My father said, *It's not worth it, if I have to die then I'll do so in my bed, I'm not going down to that cellar, I don't want to die like a mouse.* I dreamed of Berlin, the building where I was raised, the bomb shelter and the tenants squeezed together, and the clamor grew louder because of the frogs in Gross-Partsch, which had lamented all night before entering my dream. Who knew if he was there by then?

I dreamed of the old women's laments, one rosary bead after the other, while the children slept, one man snored, and upon the millionth *Pray for us* he pulled himself to his feet and spat out a curse, *Let me sleep!* the old women turning pale. I dreamed of a gramophone, the boys had brought it with them to the cellar and were inviting the girls to dance, playing "Das wird ein Frühling ohne Ende," and I sat off to the side, my mother saying, *Sing for me,* one hand encouraging me to get up, she whirled me around, and I sang at the top of my lungs, *A spring without end when you return,* I sang over the music, spinning around, and couldn't see my mother anymore. Then a wind lifted me up, pushing me fiercely, *The Abduction!* I thought. It had returned, and my mother wasn't there, my father was upstairs sleeping or pretending to, the gramophone had been silenced, as had my voice, I couldn't speak, couldn't wake up, and suddenly a massive boom as the bomb exploded.

My eyes shot open and I lay there in bed, sweating, until the numbness in my limbs subsided. Only afterward was I able to move. The darkness was stifling, so I lit the oil lamp and, as the frogs croaked away unperturbed, got up and went to the window.

And there he was, in the pale moonlight, had been there for who knew how long. He was a dark silhouette, a nightmare, a ghost. It could have been Gregor returning from the war but instead it was Ziegler standing on the road.

I was frightened. As soon as he saw me he took a step forward: immediate fear, without delay. He took another step: hundreds of sharp edges on which to smash my knee. I backed up and he stopped. I extinguished the lamp, hid behind the curtain.

It was an act of intimidation. *What did you say to the baroness, young lady, did you confess everything to her? No, Lieutenant, I swear, didn't you see for yourself? When she introduced us I pretended not to know you!*

Fists clenched, I expected to hear him knock on the door. I should run and warn Joseph and Herta. There was an Obersturmführer from the SS outside their house, in the middle of the night, and it was all my fault because I had gone to a party. Elfriede was right—for those like us, certain people only meant trouble.

Ziegler would enter, would drag us all into the kitchen, pillow-marks still on our cheeks, Herta's hair free of hairpins, a net covering her head. My mother-in-law would touch her temples with distress, my father-in-law would touch her hand, Ziegler would ram his elbow into the man's rib cage, Joseph would fall to the floor, and he would order him, *To your feet!* as he had done with Beate. He would force us to stay there lined up in front of the hearth, standing in silence. Then, stroking his holster, he would make me swear to keep quiet, to stay in my place. He would scream at Herta and Joseph even though they had nothing to do with it, because that was what the SS did.

THE MINUTES PASSED. Ziegler didn't knock.

He didn't burst into the house, didn't give us orders—he stood there, stock-still, waiting for who knew who, waiting for me. Inexplicably I too stood there and didn't call for help, because though my heart was pounding I had already realized it was something between him and me. No one else was involved. I was ashamed before Herta and Joseph, as if I had invited him. I knew at once that it would be a secret. Another one to add to my inventory.

I pushed the curtain aside and looked out the window.

He was still there. He wasn't an officer of the SS—he was a child demanding his ball back. Another step toward me. I didn't move. I watched him from the darkness. Ziegler came even closer. I darted back behind the curtain. Holding my breath, there was nothing but silence. They were all asleep. When I returned to the window, the road was empty.

IN THE MORNING, as I had breakfast Herta pressed me for details about the soirée. I was dazed, distracted. "Is something the matter?" Joseph asked.

"I didn't sleep well."

"It's springtime," he said. "Happens to me too. I was so tired last night I didn't even hear you come home."

"The baron had a servant accompany me."

"Well?" Herta asked, wiping her mouth with her napkin. "What was the baroness's gown like?"

IN THE LUNCHROOM I ate in a state of high alert. At each click of a boot against the floor I whipped my head around to look at the door to the lunchroom. It was never him. Should I ask to see him, show up at his office—the former principal's office—and warn him not to let me catch him like that again outside my window at night, or else . . . or else what? My father-in-law would grab his hunting rifle and persuade you to stop? My mother-in-law would inform the police? The police. Right. Ziegler wielded power over everyone in town, including me.

Besides, what would the other women think if I went to speak to him? I wasn't even able to tell them about the party at the castle, despite Leni's nagging—*What about the chandeliers, the floors, the fireplace, the drapes?*—and despite Ulla's insistence—*Was there anyone famous, what shoes did the baroness wear, did you at least put on lipstick?* I had forgotten to bring any lipstick. If I had gone to speak with Ziegler, Elfriede would have said, *You're always looking for trouble, Berliner,* and Augustine, *First you rub elbows with the rich and then you do the same with the enemy.* But Ziegler wasn't the enemy—he was German, like us.

The sound of heels on the tiled floor, the Nazi salute performed to perfection, and Augustine whispering, "Here's the bastard."

I turned around for the millionth time.

Ziegler was conferring with a few of his men. Nothing remained of the man who had been socializing with Baron von Mildernhagen the previous night at the soirée, nothing of the man who had appeared at my window.

Maybe it was a form of surveillance. Maybe he spent each night outside a different home, keeping an eye on the food tasters, *What an insane idea you've got into your head, maybe you dreamed it, an effect of the Abduction, Franz was right—you're just a sleepwalker.*

Ziegler turned toward us. From a distance he inspected the table to check whether we were all eating. I quickly lowered my head, feeling his gaze on the back of my neck. When I began to breathe again I searched for him with my eyes, but he was turned the other way. He wasn't even looking at me.

I WENT TO bed early. *You were right, Joseph, it's the springtime, it's wearing me out.* I drifted through a half sleep. The moment I closed my eyes, the skeins of voices in my eardrums came unraveled, my mother pounded her fist on the tablecloth, *Are you trying to get yourself fired?* my father pushed back his still-full plate and rose from the table, *Once and for all will you listen to me, I am not joining the party.* Outside, Gross-Partsch went still and inside my head a radio blared. The reception was terrible, it was all one long croak, or maybe it was the frogs again.

Finding myself awake, I sighed, the voices still echoing in my skull.

When I went to the window I saw only darkness, stared out until the moonlight carved the outlines of the trees. *What were you expecting, and why?*

I tossed and turned in my bed, pulled back the sheets, alert yet feeling numb, got up, returned to the window. Ziegler wasn't there. Why wasn't I relieved?

Lying on my back, I studied the wooden beams in the ceiling and with my finger traced the pattern on the sheet, then found myself drawing the oval of Ziegler's head, his nostrils shaped like the eyes of needles in the cartilage of his tiny nose, the narrow space between his eyes, and at that point I stopped, rolled over on my side, again got out of bed.

I poured myself some water from the carafe, drank a sip, lingered by the bedside table with the glass in my hand. A shadow darkened the pale moonlight—a pang of anguish. I looked over my shoulder and spotted him. He was closer than he had been the night before. I put down the glass, covered the carafe with a folded cloth, walked over to the window. I didn't hide. With clumsy fingers I turned the oil lamp brighter. Ziegler saw me standing in front of him, a white cotton nightgown beneath my robe, my hair tousled. He nodded. Then all he did was stare at me, as though it were an actual activity, one done simply for its own sake.

19

I KNOW A DOCTOR," ELFRIEDE SAID, HER EXPRESSION INDIGNANT, AS though we had made her name names through interrogation. The guards patrolled the courtyard, their hands clasped behind their backs, at times touching the circumference of our space like a tangent, at times crossing over it, and when they did, our words stayed trapped in our throats.

I looked at Augustine, who was sitting beside me on the bench, to ask her to confirm there was nothing else to be done. Leni wasn't far away behind her—I could hear her chatting with Ulla and Beate. Ulla wanted to convince Leni to change her hairstyle. She was eager to play the hairdresser again. Beate told them that two nights earlier she had calculated the Führer's astrology chart—she hadn't managed to find a new deck of tarot cards, so she had worked out a horoscope instead—and had discovered that the stars weren't in his favor. Things would very soon turn against him, perhaps as soon as summer. Leni shook her head in disbelief.

A guard's jaw dropped. He must have overheard everything, would push us inside and force us to speak. I gripped the bench's armrest. The guard's sneeze sounded more like a roar—it made him double over. Then he stood up straight again, pulled a handkerchief out of his pocket, and blew his nose.

"There's nothing else to be done," Heike said.

———

ELFRIEDE TOOK HER to a gynecologist and didn't allow anyone to go with them.

"I don't get it—why all the secrecy?" Augustine grumbled. "This is a delicate situation, Heike might need our help."

"Let's take care of Mathias and Ursula while she's gone," I said, to calm her.

We waited for Heike at her house with her children and Leni. We had tried to keep Leni out of it, but she wanted to know, kept asking questions. I was afraid it would shock her, but instead she had taken in the explanation without blinking an eye. Then again, others' pain doesn't sting as much as our own.

Beate wasn't there. Heike hadn't involved her. Beate was her oldest friend and she felt ashamed before her. Maybe Beate resented it, or, conversely, maybe she was grateful for not having to deal with the problem.

Mathias spent the evening arguing and making up with Pete, Augustine's son.

"Let's pretend you're France and Ursula is England," he said once he'd grown bored of every other game. "Let's pretend you two declare war on me."

"Where's England?" his little sister asked.

"No," Pete said, "I want to be Germany."

He was more or less Mathias's age—seven or eight. He had sharp shoulder blades and bony arms. If I had had a son, that was how I would have liked him to be, with prominent shoulder blades glistening with sweat like those of my brother when, as a boy, he would run about through the red spruce trees in Grunewald Forest and dive into the Schlachtensee. I would want my child to have blue eyes that squinted in the sunshine like Gregor's.

"Why Germany?" Augustine asked.

"I want to be strong," Pete replied, "like our Führer."

She tsked. "You know nothing about strength. Your father was strong, and he's gone now."

The boy blushed, hung his head: What did his father have to do with it, and why did she have to make him feel so sad all of a sudden?

"Augustine . . . ," I began, but didn't know what to say next. Her broad, boxy shoulders, and those slender ankles. For the first time I thought they might snap.

Pete ran into the next room. I followed him, Ursula right behind me. He had thrown himself onto the bed, belly-down.

"If you want to, you can be England," Ursula told him. "I don't want it anyway."

Pete didn't react.

"What do you want, then?" I asked, stroking her cheek.

She was four years old, the same age as Pauline now. Suddenly I missed Pauline, missed her breathing as she slept. I hadn't thought about her in so long. How was it possible to forget people, to forget children?

"I want my mother. Where is she?"

"She'll be back soon," I reassured her. "Listen, should we do something fun? All of us together?"

"Like what?"

"Let's sing a song."

She nodded unenthusiastically.

"Go call Mathias."

She obeyed, and I sat on the bed.

"Are you offended, Pete?"

He didn't reply.

"Angry?"

His head moved left and right, burrowing into the pillow.

"Not angry. . . . Are you sad, then?"

He turned to peek at me.

"My father died, too, you know," I told him. "I understand you."

He pulled himself up, sat cross-legged. "What about your husband?"

The last surge of light before the sun finally set lit up his face, turning it pale.

"Fuchs, du hast die Gans gestohlen," I sang in reply, tilting my head from one side to the other as I tapped my finger to the beat. "Gib sie wieder her." Where had I found that cheerfulness?

Ursula entered with Mathias and Augustine. They sat down on the bed with us and I sang the nursery rhyme all the way to the end. My father had taught it to me. Then the little girl begged me to sing it again, and had me repeat it over and over until she had learned it as well.

IT WAS DARK when we heard footsteps coming up the walk. The children were still awake, and they ran to the front door. Elfriede was supporting Heike, who walked without difficulty, though. Ursula and Mathias threw themselves onto her, clinging to her legs.

"Easy," she said, "take it easy."

"Are you tired, Mommy?" Ursula whispered.

"Why aren't you in bed?" Heike replied. "It's late."

"Make her rest." With this single instruction, Elfriede turned to leave.

"Don't you even want a cup of tea?"

"It's late, Rosa, and we're already past curfew."

"Why don't you sleep here, too?"

"No, I'm going."

She seemed cross, almost as though she had helped Heike against her will. She hadn't minded her own business, as she had warned me to do.

Heike wouldn't say where the doctor lived, nor would she call him by name. All she told us was that he'd had her drink a concoction whose ingredients he hadn't specified and had shown her the door, warning her that soon her contractions would begin. On the way home, they had had to stop in the woods. Sweating and moaning, Heike had expelled a clump of flesh, which Elfriede had buried at the foot of a birch tree while Heike tried to calm her breathing. "I'll never remember which tree," she said. "I'll never be able to go visit him."

THE PREGNANCY HAD been a mistake. There was nothing divine in creating life or taking it—it was simply something humans did. Gregor hadn't wanted to be the origin of any destiny and had reasoned that it was a question of meaning, as though giving life required some kind of meaning. But not even God had posed the same question to Himself.

It had been a mistake, a heartbeat just beneath the navel—Heike had stifled it. I was angry with her, and pitied her too. An emptiness was gouged within my belly, the summation of all the people I missed, including the child Gregor and I had never had.

WHEN I LIVED in Berlin, whenever I came across a pregnant woman I thought of intimacy. Spine curved back, legs parted slightly, palms resting on that big belly—all made me think of the intimacy between husband and wife. It wasn't the intimacy of love, of lovers. I thought of nipples growing larger, growing darker, ankles swelling. I wondered whether Gregor would be frightened of my body's metamorphosis, if he wouldn't like it anymore, if he would reject it.

An intruder takes up space inside your woman's body and deforms it, changes it for its own use and consumption, then comes out through the same hole you penetrated, barges through it with an aggressiveness you would never have dared. He has been where you will never be, it is he who will forever own her.

Yet that intruder is yours. Inside your woman, amid stomach, liver, kidneys, something that belongs to you has grown, and in such an intimate, internal part of her.

I wondered if my husband would tolerate my bouts of nausea, my urgent need to pee, my body reduced to its primordial functions; I wondered if nature was what he couldn't accept.

We hadn't experienced that intimacy, he and I. We had been parted too early. Maybe I would never put my body at the service of another, at the service of another life. Gregor had stolen that opportunity from me, had betrayed me like a dog that turns against its master. How long had it been since I had last felt his fingers on my tongue?

Heike had had an abortion and I continued to yearn for a child from a man who had gone missing in Russia.

HE NEVER ARRIVED before midnight, probably to be sure no one was awake except me, knowing I would wait up for him. What drove me to go to the window, what drove him to come, to struggle to make out my silhouette in the shadows? What was it that he couldn't do without?

The windowpane was a shield. It made the lieutenant less real, that lieutenant who said nothing, who did nothing but remain, persist, impose a presence I couldn't touch. I stared back at him because there was nothing else to do, since he had come, since it had happened. Even if I had put out the light, I would have known he was there. I wouldn't have been able to sleep. I stared at him, unable to imagine any consequences—the future finally severed from the present. The sweetness of inaction.

How had he known, the night of the soirée, that I would wake up? Did he think I hadn't yet gone to bed?

A few days after that evening, when I returned home, I found a decorated porcelain vase I had never seen. It was on the kitchen table and was full of dark purple flowers I didn't recognize. The room had never been filled with so much color.

"They're German irises," Joseph said, touching one of the petals with his callused fingers.

"A gift for you," Herta said. "I put them in water so they wouldn't wither, but take them to your room now." Her curt tone exposed my guilt. Had he—no, it couldn't be—had Ziegler sent me flowers? He certainly couldn't have included a card, couldn't have been so shameless. I didn't dare ask.

"They're from your friend," she said.

And Joseph: "I brought them with me from the castle. The baroness insisted."

"The baroness. She insisted," Herta said, mimicking him. "I thought you had an admirer," she added, and my throat went dry. I had to bite my tongue to feel saliva in my mouth again. It was salty, savory, tasted a bit like blood. "But an admirer would never have approached your father-in-law," she said, laughing.

Was she provoking me?

Joseph also laughed, and I realized it was a joke, nothing more.

Herta's peeved tone had been directed at the baroness, whom Joseph admired and who was interested in me. Herta was the only one who hadn't gained the woman's attention and she didn't like to feel excluded.

"Here," Joseph said, taking an envelope out of his pocket. I opened it.

Maria—that was how she had signed it—thanked me for attending her soirée and invited me to pay her a call. It would become a habit, spending a few hours at the castle in the early afternoons with the woman who had forced me to sing in front of Ziegler.

Who knew if it was the moment I had closed my eyes that he began to stare at me—he who in the courtyard, stomping on Beate's cards, had had to force himself to look away from me? Who knew if it was then, as the other guests were applauding while he kept his arms down at his sides, that he decided to come to my window with those same powerless arms? Or maybe he had never decided to, maybe he too had simply moved with the assurance of a sleepwalker.

In Krausendorf, his indifference toward me was absolute. If I happened to hear his voice, it left me paralyzed with terror. The other women noticed it but thought it was the same fear they also felt. Terror of the man who tyrannized guards and food tasters alike, and one morning had even exasperated Krümel—the chef had stormed out, slamming the door and shouting that everyone should know their place, that he knew what he was doing in his kitchen. Terror of the war, as things gradually grew worse and supplies began to arrive with more difficulty. If there were prospects of a food shortage even in the countryside, even at the Wolfsschanze, we were doomed. I would have asked Krümel what he knew, since we had been eating Williams pears and bananas less often, since he was always cooking the same dishes, and with less flair than before, but after our incident with the milk he hadn't spoken to me again.

When Ziegler went away at dawn—at first without a gesture, then raising his hand slightly in farewell, or shrugging his shoulders—I would feel lost. His absence settled in Gregor's bedroom, expanding until it pushed the furniture back against the walls, pressed me back against the window frame. At breakfast I returned to my real life—that is, to the surrogate of my real life. Only then, as Joseph drank his tea, slurping, and his wife reproached him with a light slap on the arm—jostling his cup and splashing a few drops onto the tablecloth—only then did I think of Gregor. I would nail the curtains to the window fixtures, tie myself down to the bed, and sooner or later he would give up. But at night Gregor disappeared because the world itself disappeared, life began and ended in the trajectory of the gaze connecting Ziegler and me.

IN THE WEEKS following the abortion I was cautious around Elfriede.

Often, sharing a secret doesn't bring people together—it separates them. Collective guilt is vague, shame an individual personal emotion.

I kept quiet about Ziegler's visits to my window to avoid sharing the burden of shame with my friends and instead bear it alone. Or perhaps I wanted to spare myself Elfriede's judgment, Leni's incomprehension, the chatter of the others. Or, more simply, what I had with Ziegler needed to remain untouched.

I hadn't even spoken of it to Heike, even though on the night of her abortion, while Augustine was putting the children to bed in the other room and Leni was snoozing in an old armchair, Heike had said to me, "It was a boy."

"You sensed it would be a boy?"

"No, not what I had inside me."

I swallowed, not understanding.

"The father," she said. "He's a boy, a child. The farmhand who helps us here. When my husband left, he took over for him. He's a fine boy, you know, very responsible, though he's barely seventeen years old. How could I have done such a thing . . . ?"

"What did he say about the pregnancy?"

"Nothing. He didn't know anything, and now there's nothing left to know—the pregnancy is over."

I had let her confess and hadn't confessed to her in turn.

Seventeen years old. Eleven fewer than her.

The birds twittered in the May sky, and the ease with which Heike's child had slid between her legs, the ease with which it had let itself be eliminated, crushed me.

It was a springtime ever ajar, ever vulnerable; it was a realm of desolation with neither a way to vent nor a means of catharsis.

Elfriede was leaning against the wall, smoking and staring at her shoes. I crossed the courtyard and walked up to her.

"What?" she said.

"How are you?"

"You?"

"Come to Moy Lake tomorrow afternoon?"

The ash on her cigarette grew longer until it sagged, then broke off, crumbled to dust.

"All right."

WE ALSO BROUGHT Leni, with her black swimsuit and pale complexion. Elfriede had a thin, elastic body as rough as linen. When Leni dove in we were astonished to see that in the ice-cold water—it was too early to go swimming, but we were in a rush to wash everything off ourselves, or at least I was—her gestures lost all their awkwardness. When wet, her skin was no longer that of a land creature. I had never seen her so self-confident before. "Are you coming in or not?" On her translucent cheeks, the dilated capillaries were butterfly wings—one flutter and they would fly up into the air.

"Where has this Leni been all this time?" I said to Elfriede, grinning.

"Hiding." Her gaze was fixed on a spot that was neither Leni nor the lake, a spot I couldn't see.

It sounded like an accusation, one directed at me.

"Things are almost never as they seem," she said. "That goes for people too."

With this, she dove in.

20

ONE NIGHT I UNDRESSED.

I opened the wardrobe and chose one of the evening gowns Herta had criticized, a different gown from the one I had worn to the soirée. I brushed my hair and put makeup on my face, though in the darkness Ziegler might not notice. It didn't matter. As I brushed my hair and powdered my cheeks, I rediscovered the anxious anticipation before a date. Those preparations were made for him, for he who lingered at my window as though before an altar, almost as if fearful to profane it. Or presenting himself before me was his way of facing the Sphinx. I had no riddles, nor answers, though if I had any I would have revealed them to him.

I sat at the window with the lamp lit, and when he arrived I stood up. I thought I saw him smile. He had never done that before.

If I heard someone stirring in the house, I would extinguish the lamp and he would hide. The moment I lit it again he would come back out into the open. It glowed softly, as I would cover the lamp with a cloth. There were blackout orders, anyone could have noticed us. If I suddenly feared Herta was about to walk in—why would she possibly have done that?—I would slip into bed. Once I had even dozed off, the tension having drained all my energy. Who knew how long he had waited before leaving? That tenacity, a form of weakness, was his power over me.

PRECISELY ONE MONTH after the soirée, I extinguished the lamp even though I hadn't heard a sound. On tiptoe, barefoot to soften my footsteps, I opened the door, made sure Herta and Joseph were asleep, went to the kitchen, and stepped out the back, made my way around the house toward my window, and found him crouching as he awaited some sign of me. To my eyes he looked tiny.

I stepped back and my right knee cracked. Ziegler shot to his feet. Standing in front of me, in his uniform, without the shield of the window separating us, I was as frightened as I was in the barracks. The spell came crashing down, reality revealing itself in all its candor. I was defenseless before the executioner, and it was I who had gone to him.

Ziegler moved, grabbed my arms. He buried his nose in my hair and breathed in. As he did, I too could smell his scent.

I entered the barn, he followed me. It was dark, not even a sliver of light. I couldn't see Ziegler but could hear him breathing. The mellow, familiar scent of the firewood calmed me. I sat down, so did he.

Blindly, awkwardly, guided by our sense of smell, we tumbled into each other's bodies as though each trying on our own body for the first time.

Afterward, we didn't say that no one should know but acted as though we had agreed on it. Both of us were married, even though I was alone now. He was a lieutenant in the SS. What would happen if it were known he had a relationship with a food taster? Maybe nothing, or maybe it was forbidden.

He didn't ask me why I had taken him into the barn, I didn't ask him why me. Our eyes had grown accustomed to the darkness when he begged me to sing to him. They were the first words he spoke to me. My mouth glued to his ear, below my breath, I sang. It was the nursery rhyme with which I had entertained Heike's daughter the night of the abortion, the one my father had taught me.

Naked in the barn, I thought of my father, the railroad worker, the man whose will had never been bent. Stubborn, my mother had called him, reckless. If he had known I was working for Hitler . . . *I couldn't refuse,* I would tell him if he returned from the land of the dead to ask me to explain my actions. Going against his own rules, he would slap me. *We have never been Nazis,* he would shout. I would cup my hand over my cheek in shock, would whimper that it wasn't a question of being Nazis, politics had nothing to do with it, I had never bothered with politics, besides, in '33 I was only fifteen, it wasn't like I had voted for him. *You're responsible for any regime you tolerate,* my father would scream at me. *Each person's existence is granted by the system of the state in which she lives, even that of a hermit, can't you understand that? You're not free from political guilt, Rosa.* My mother would intervene. *Leave her alone,* she would beg him. Yes, she would return as well, with her coat on over her nightgown, without even the good taste to change. *Let her stew in her own juice,* she would say to bring the conversation to an end. I would provoke her: *You're angry at me because I went to bed with another man, aren't you? You would never have done it, Mother.* And my father would repeat, *Rosa, you're not free from guilt.*

FOR TWELVE YEARS we had lived under a dictatorship yet almost hadn't noticed. What allowed human beings to live under a dictatorship?

We had no alternative—that was our alibi. I was responsible only for the food I ingested. A harmless gesture, eating. How could it be a sin? Were the other women ashamed of selling themselves for two hundred marks a month, an excellent salary, and unparalleled board? Ashamed of believing, as I believed, that immorality was sacrificing one's life if the sacrifice served no purpose? I was ashamed before my father, even though my father was dead, because in order to manifest itself shame requires a judge. We had no alternative, we said. But Ziegler must have had one, because it was I who walked out to him. I was a person who could accept that shame made of tendons and bones and saliva—I had held that shame in my arms, and it was at least a meter eighty tall, weighed seventy-eight kilos at most. Neither alibi nor justification, the relief of a certainty.

"Why did you stop singing?"

"I don't know."

"What's wrong?"

"That song makes me sad."

"You can sing a different one. Or not, if you don't feel like it. We can stay here and quietly stare at each other in the dark. We know how to do that."

Having returned to my room, in the silence of Herta and Joseph's slumber, I sank my head into my hands, unable to accept what had happened. Deep within me, euphoria sparked intermittently. Nothing had ever made me feel so alone, but in that solitude I discovered I was powerful. Sitting on the bed in which Gregor had slept as a child, I once again made a list of my sins and secrets, as I had done in Berlin before meeting him, and I was myself, and I was undeniable.

21

THE MIRROR REFLECTED AN EXHAUSTED FACE IN THE MORNING LIGHT. It wasn't from lack of sleep—the dark circles around my eyes, my subdued anguish, were a prophecy finally fulfilled. From the photo stuck in the mirror's frame, the unsmiling little boy was angry with me.

Herta and Joseph didn't notice a thing. How imperceptive human beings' trust is. Gregor had inherited it from his naïve parents—their daughter-in-law snuck out at night and they went on sleeping—and then he had heaped it onto me: a responsibility too great to bear once he left me alone.

A honk from the bus declared my freedom. I couldn't wait to leave. I was afraid of running into Ziegler, a splinter under my nail. I wanted to.

IN THE LUNCHROOM I was also served dessert. Topped with a spoonful of yogurt, the cake looked fluffy, but my stomach was in knots. I had barely gotten down the tomato soup.

"Don't you like it, Berliner?"

I shook myself out of it. "I haven't tried it yet."

Elfriede sliced with her fork what remained of her own piece of cake. "It's delicious. Eat it."

"As though she has any choice," Augustine said.

"What bad luck, not being able to choose whether or not to eat cake," Elfriede replied, "while everyone's starving to death."

"Let me try some," Ulla whispered.

No dessert for her that day, but she had been given eggs and mashed potatoes. Eggs were one of the Führer's favorite foods. He liked them sprinkled with cumin. The sweetish smell reached my nostrils.

"Careful. They'll rat on you," Augustine said, trying to dissuade her.

Ulla turned toward the Fanatics two, three times. Leaning over their plates, they were eating ricotta and cottage cheese. There was honey for them to dip it in. "Now!" Ulla said. I snuck her a bit of cake, which she hid in her hand. She popped it into her mouth only when she was sure none of the guards would see her. I ate as well.

IN THE COURTYARD, the high midday sun blurred the outlines of the houses near the barracks, silenced the birds, exhausted the stray dogs. *Let's go inside, it's too hot out here,* someone said. *Unusually hot for June,* someone else said. Seeing the other women walk sluggishly through the hazy air, I also moved, each step landing heavily, as though I were descending a staircase. I faltered, squinted my eyes to see more clearly. *It's hot out, unnaturally hot, it's only June, I'm dizzy.* I steadied myself on one of the swings, the chains were burning hot, nausea churned my stomach like a plunger, I felt it shoot up to my forehead, the courtyard was deserted, the other women already inside, standing in the doorway a backlit figure. The courtyard tilted, a bird swooped down, beat its wings hard. In the doorway was Ziegler, then I saw nothing else.

WHEN I CAME to, I was lying on the lunchroom floor. A guard's face eclipsed the ceiling. Vomit spurted to my throat, and just in time I rose onto my elbows and leaned to the side. As my sweat turned to ice, the sound of other regurgitations reached my ears, and another acidic gush burned my throat.

I heard the other women crying, couldn't distinguish them by the sounds. You can tell people's laughter apart—Augustine's chuckles, Leni's titters, Elfriede's snorts, Ulla's cascading laughs—but not crying. When crying we're all the same, the sound is the same for everyone.

My head was spinning. I glimpsed another body lying on the floor and a few women standing, their backs pressed against the wall. I recognized them by their footwear: Ulla's plateaus, the studs in Heike's clogs, the worn tips of Leni's shoes.

"Rosa." Leni broke away from the wall to come to my side.

A guard raised his arm. "Return to your place!"

"What do we do?" the Beanpole asked, wandering the room, at a loss.

"The lieutenant ordered that they all be kept here," the other guard replied. "None of them are to leave, not even those who haven't shown symptoms yet."

"Another one just lost consciousness," the Beanpole warned.

I turned to check the body I had seen sprawled out. It was Theodora.

"Find someone to clean the floor."

"They're going to die," the Beanpole said.

"My god, no," Leni gasped. "Call a doctor, please!"

"Would you be quiet?" the other guard told the Beanpole.

Ulla put her arm around Leni's shoulder. "Calm down."

"We're dying! Didn't you hear him?" Leni shrieked.

I looked around for Elfriede. She was across the room, sitting on the floor, her shoes submerged in a yellowish puddle.

The rest of the women weren't far from me. Their breathless voices and sobs amplified my feeling of malaise. I didn't know who had carried me inside from the courtyard and left me on that spot on the floor—Ziegler, maybe? Had he really been there in the doorway or had I only imagined it?—but it was to the same side of the lunchroom as the others. Out of instinct, my companions had huddled together; it's terrible to die alone. Elfriede, though, had withdrawn into a corner, her head between her knees. I called out to her. I didn't know if she could hear me over the noisy chaos of, *Let us out of here, bring a doctor, I want to die in my own bed, I don't want to die.*

I called out to her again. She didn't answer. "Please, make sure she's alive," I said, not knowing to whom. Maybe to the guards, who ignored me. "Augustine," I mumbled, "please, go check. Bring her over here to me."

Why was Elfriede like that? She wanted to die in hiding, like dogs did.

The French door to the courtyard was closed, a guard standing outside it. I overheard Ziegler's voice. It came from the hallway, or the kitchen. Amid the litany of sobs in the lunchroom and the bustle of footsteps racing back and forth through the rest of the barracks, I couldn't make out what he was saying, but it was his voice, and it didn't comfort me. The fear of death was a swarm of insects crawling beneath my skin. I collapsed.

Krümel's helpers came to wipe up the vomit with rags, and the dampness worsened the stench. They cleaned the floors, not our faces, our clothes. They left a bucket, scattered sheets of newspaper around, and walked out with the guards, who locked the door behind them.

Augustine shot over, grabbed the doorknob, and tried to wrench the door open, in vain. "Why are you locking us up in here? What are you going to do with us?"

Their faces already drained, their lips bluish, my companions inched toward the door. "Why are they shutting us up in here?"

I tried to get to my feet to join them, but didn't have the strength.

Augustine kicked the door violently, the others slammed their palms or fists against it. Heike banged her head against the wood slowly, repeatedly, an open display of desperation I would never have expected from her. Threats were snarled from the other side and all the women desisted, all of them except Augustine.

Leni came over and knelt beside me. I couldn't speak, but she was the one seeking comfort. "In the end, it happened," she said, "they poisoned us."

"They poisoned *them*," Sabine corrected her. She was slumped over Theodora's body. "You don't have any symptoms and neither do I."

"That's not true," Leni shouted. "I'm queasy."

"Why do you think they make us eat different foods, hmm? Why do you think they divide us into groups, you fool?" Sabine said.

For a moment Augustine detached herself from the door and turned to face her. "Yes, but your friend"—she gestured at Theodora with her chin—"ate fennel salad and cheese, while Rosa, for example, had tomato soup and dessert, but they both passed out."

I doubled over and retched. Leni held my forehead. I stared at my splattered dress, then looked up again.

Heike was sitting at the table, her face in her hands. "I want to go home to my children," she murmured, as though reciting psalms, "I want to see them."

"Then help me! Let's knock the door down!" Augustine shouted. "Help me!"

"They'll kill us," Beate said breathlessly. She too wanted to return to her children, to her twins.

Heike got up again, went to Augustine's side, but instead of ramming her shoulder into the door, she began to shout, "I'm fine! I haven't been poisoned. Do you hear me? I want to get out of here!"

I went ice-cold. She was saying out loud what had just crossed everyone's mind. We hadn't all eaten the same food. Identical fates weren't in store for us. Whatever dish it was that had been poisoned, some of us would die, others wouldn't.

"Maybe they're sending for the doctor," Leni said, not at all persuaded she was out of danger. "Maybe they can save us."

I wondered if a doctor actually could.

"They don't care one bit about saving us." Elfriede had pulled herself to her feet. Her stony face seemed to crumble as she added, "They don't care one bit. They're only interested in finding out what it was that poisoned us. All they need to do is perform an autopsy on one of us tomorrow and they'll find out."

"If one is enough," Leni said, "why do we all have to stay here?"

She didn't even realize she had uttered an abomination. *Let's sacrifice one of us*, she was proposing, *if it means sparing the others*.

If it were up to her, on what basis would she choose? The weakest among us? The one with the worst symptoms? One who didn't have children to care for? One who wasn't from the village? Or simply one who wasn't her friend? Would she count, chanting, *Backe, backe Kuchen, der Bäcker hat gerufen,* and let fate decide?

I didn't have children and I came from Berlin and I had gone to bed with Ziegler—Leni didn't know that last part. She didn't think I was the one who deserved to die.

I wished I could pray, but I no longer had the right to. It had been months since the last time, since my husband had been taken from me. Maybe one day, sitting by the hearth in his dacha, Gregor's eyes would open wide. *That's it,* he would tell his matryoshka, *now I remember. Far from here is a woman I love. I must return to her.*

I didn't want to die if he was alive.

THE SS DIDN'T reply to Heike's cries and she moved away from the door.

"What are their intentions? What are they going to do to us?" Beate asked her, as if Heike could know. Her friend didn't answer; she had tried to save her own skin, hers and hers alone, and since it hadn't worked she shut herself off in silence. Leni curled up under the table, repeated that she felt queasy, slid two fingers down her throat, gagged, only dry-heaved. Theodora continued to rock in a fetal position on the floor, helped by her friend Sabine, whose sister Gertrude gasped for air. Ulla had a headache and Augustine needed the bathroom. She tried to convince Elfriede to lie down beside me. "I'll help you," she said. Elfriede shoved her hand away. Isolated in her corner, she was gripped by more waves of nausea. She wiped her chin with the back of her hand, huddled up on her side. I was exhausted, my heartbeat slow.

I don't know how many hours went by. I know that at some point the door opened.

Ziegler appeared. Behind him, a man and a young woman in white coats. Serious expressions and dark medical bags. What did they contain? *Call a doctor,* Leni had pleaded, and voilà, one had come. Not even she could believe he was there to save us. The bags on the table, the click of latches. Elfriede was right: they didn't mean to administer a treatment—no one had bothered to hydrate us, take our temperature—they had simply isolated us there, waiting to see how things unfolded. They wanted to understand the cause of the affliction that was killing some of us. Perhaps they had already discovered it and we, those poisoned, no longer served a purpose.

We remained perfectly still, animals facing predators. *A taster who doesn't eat is of no use to us,* Ziegler had said. If we were destined to die, it would be best to speed things up. After that, they would clean the room, disinfect it, open the windows, let in some fresh air. *Putting creatures out of their misery is an act of mercy. It's done with animals, so why not with people?*

The doctor was in front of me. I flinched. "What do you want?"

Ziegler turned around.

"Don't touch me!" I shouted at the doctor.

Leaning over me, Ziegler grabbed my arm. He was centimeters from my face, like the night before—he could smell my stink, would never kiss me again. "Be quiet and do as they say." Then, standing up: "All of you, be quiet."

Under the table, Leni hugged her knees to her chest, as if by doubling up over and over she might make herself smaller than a handkerchief, might hide in someone's pocket. The doctor felt my pulse, raised my eyelids, listened to my breathing with a stethoscope pressed to my back, and went off to check on Theodora. The nurse wiped my brow with a damp cloth, gave me a glass of water.

"As I was saying, I'll need a list of who ate what," the doctor explained as he turned to go. The young woman and Ziegler followed him out and the door was locked again.

The swarm of insects beneath my skin became an insurrection. Elfriede and I had eaten the soup and that sweet, sweet cake. The two of us definitely shared the same fate. I had been punished for what I had done with Ziegler, but what was Elfriede guilty of?

Either God is perverse, or He doesn't exist, Gregor had said.

Another wave of nausea shook me to the core. I spewed out the food for Hitler that Hitler would never eat. They were mine, those groans—guttural, indecent, inhuman-sounding. What of me remained human?

Suddenly I remembered, and it was like crashing down to earth. The Russian superstition Gregor had mentioned to me in his letter—did the same thing go for German soldiers? *As long as your woman is faithful, you'll never be killed,* it went. *So I suppose,* Gregor had written, *I have no choice but to count on you.* But I wasn't a woman to count on. He hadn't realized that, he had trusted me, and he had died.

Gregor had died and it was my fault. My heartbeat slowed further still. Breathlessness, plugged ears, silence. Then my heart stopped.

22

I WAS AWAKENED BY A FURY OF BANGS.

"We have to use the washroom! Open up!" Augustine was hammering her fists on the door. No one had helped her break it down. The French door to the courtyard was locked, the sun had set. Who knew if Joseph had come looking for me, if Herta was waiting at the window?

Augustine picked up the bucket beside me.

"Where are you taking it?"

"You're awake?" she asked with surprise. "How do you feel, Rosa?"

"What time is it?"

"Dinnertime was a while ago but they didn't bring us anything to taste. We don't even have anything to drink anymore. They've all gone. Leni has been a torment. She's been crying so hard she's dehydrated now too, and she didn't even throw up. She's healthy as a horse, and so am I," she added, sounding almost apologetic.

"Where's Elfriede?"

"Sleeping, over there."

I saw her. She was still lying on her side. From the pallor of her dark complexion she looked like she was made of flint.

"Rosa," Leni said, "are you better?"

Augustine crouched over the bucket wearily. After her, other women resorted to doing the same. There was no way it would be large enough for all of us to use—someone would end up wetting themselves or urinating on the floor, which was already filthy and foul-smelling.

Why wouldn't they open up? Had they abandoned us in the barracks, evacuated it? My temples throbbed. I dreamed of breaking down the door and escaping, never to return. No doubt guards were out there, though—they had been given specific orders. They would never open the door, they didn't know how to handle the problem of the women in their death throes, had set it aside until further orders.

With Augustine's help I pulled myself up, teetering on my unsteady ankles, and used the bucket as well. She and Beate had to hold me up by my underarms. It wasn't humiliating, it was just my body surrendering. I remembered the bomb shelter in Budengasse, remembered my mother.

My urine was boiling hot, my skin so sensitive that it ached to the touch. My mother would have said, *Cover up, Rosa, don't catch cold.* But it was summer, the wrong season in which to die.

Peeing was as sweet as a dying wish being granted. I thought of my father. He had been a righteous man, he would be able to plead on my behalf. And so I prayed, despite no longer having the right to. I prayed I would die first, not wanting to witness Elfriede's death. I didn't want to lose anyone else. My father, though, wouldn't forgive me, and God was already distracted.

THE FIRST THING I felt was a chill throughout my body, then light-headedness.

I opened my eyes to the ceiling. It was dawn.

They had swung the door open and my body had awoken. Maybe the SS imagined they would find a couple of bodies, maybe more, which they would need to carry out. Instead they found ten women whom the sound of the key turning in the lock had just torn from broken sleep. Ten women who had crusty eyelashes and parched throats but were alive, all of them.

The Beanpole gaped at us in silence from the doorway, as frightened as if he were staring at ghosts, while another guard pinched his nose and stepped backward, his heels echoing off the tiles in the hallway. Were we ghosts? Without speaking, we warily made sure our limbs worked, checked our breathing. Mine flowed between my lips, through my nostrils. I was alive.

Only when Ziegler arrived and ordered us to stand up did Leni crawl out from under the table, did Heike move her chair in a daze, did Elfriede slowly roll onto her back and seek the strength to sit up, did Ulla let out a yawn, and did I unsteadily rise to my feet.

"Line up," Ziegler said.

Placated by the aftereffects of the illness, or simply tamed by fear, we formed a row of prostrate bodies.

Where had he been all that time, the Obersturmführer, my lover? He hadn't carried me to the washroom, hadn't laid a dampened towel on my temples, rinsed my face. He wasn't my husband, had no need to see to my happiness. As I was dying, he was busy safeguarding the life of Adolf Hitler, his and his alone, tracking down the culprits, interrogating Krümel, the assistant chefs, the kitchen helpers, the guards, the entire SS unit housed in the headquarters, as well as the local suppliers and those farther away—he would have interrogated even the train conductors, journeyed to the very ends of the earth to track down the guilty party.

"Can we go home?"

I wanted him to hear my voice, to remember me.

He looked at me with those tiny eyes, two stale hazelnuts, and ran a hand over them to massage them. Or maybe he simply didn't want to see me. "The chef will be here soon," he said. "You need to resume your work."

My stomach knotted. I saw hands clapped over mouths, fingers clutching bellies, queasy expressions. None of us, however, said a word.

Ziegler left and the guards accompanied us to the washroom, two at a time, so we could freshen up. The lunchroom was cleaned, the French door to the courtyard left open for a while, and breakfast was ready earlier than usual. The Führer must have been hungry, he couldn't be kept waiting a minute longer. He had spent the night nibbling his fingernails just to sink his teeth into something, or perhaps the un-foreseen incident had ruined his appetite, his stomach had grumbled but it was gastritis, flatulence, a nervous reaction. He had fasted for hours, or maybe he had a supply of manna that had fallen from heaven one night just for him and had been stockpiled in the bunker in case of emergency. Or he had simply endured his hunger, since he could endure anything, had stroked his German shepherd Blondi's soft fur, having kept her too on a strict diet.

We sat down at the table in our soiled clothes, an unbearable stench. We held our breath and waited to be served. Then, with our customary submissiveness, once again we began to taste the food, as we had the day before. The sun illuminated our plates and our haggard faces.

I chewed mechanically, forcing myself to swallow.

THEY EXPLAINED NOTHING to us, but at last they drove us home.

Herta came outside to greet me with a hug. Then, sitting on my bed, she told me, "The SS visited one farm after the other. They grilled the suppliers. The shepherd thought they were about to kill him right there in the barn, they were so furious. Recently there have been other cases of poisoning in town, and no one knows what from. We were fine, though—that is, we suffered, but for you."

"Fortunately no one died," Joseph remarked.

"He went looking for you," Herta said.

"Joseph, you were out there?"

"Leni's mother was there too," my father-in-law replied, almost as if to play down his concern, "and the farmhand who works for Heike, and sisters and sisters-in-law, and other old folk like me. We stood there outside the barracks asking for news but no one would tell us anything. They threatened us every which way until we were finally forced to leave."

Herta and Joseph hadn't slept. I don't know how many people in town had slept that night. Not even the children had drifted off, until terribly late, exhausted from sobbing, before the watchful eyes of grandmothers and aunts. Heike's children asked for their mother, *I miss her, where is she?* Little Ursula calmed herself by singing my nursery rhyme, though she couldn't remember the words anymore. The goose was stolen, the fox was dead, the hunter had shot him, tinged him red. Why had my father sung me such sad stories?

Even Zart, Joseph told me as he stood beside Herta, had watched the front door all night as though expecting me to return from one moment to the next, or as though there were an enemy lying in ambush. And there was. There had been for eleven years.

23

HE WOULDN'T COME BACK. HE WOULDN'T DARE APPEAR AT THE WINDOW after what he had done. Or he *would* come, just to measure his power. But I had been the one to lead him into the barn. Did I really expect special treatment? The favorite lady. The lieutenant's whore.

Though the night was hot I closed the windows, fearing Ziegler would sneak into the room, fearing I would find him beside my bed, or on top of me. My throat tickled at the thought.

I banished it, rolled the sheet down to the foot of the mattress, sought cool patches on which to rest my calves. If he dared come I would hurl my rejection right in his face.

Lighting the lamp with the customary cloth over it, I sat down at the window. The thought that he might be the one to reject me—after seeing me indecent, covered with vomit—made me angry. He could do without me. I, instead, waited for him, scrutinizing the dark countryside, barely making out in the darkness the dirt road, the bend, and, farther up, the turn leading to the castle, where it had all begun. At one o'clock I extinguished the lamp—a matter of pride, an admission of defeat. Ziegler had won. After all, he was stronger. I lay down again, my muscles so tense my back hurt. The alarm clock ticked, making me nervous. All at once a faint, high-pitched noise terrified me.

Fingernails against the windowpane. A wave of fear brought back my nausea of the day before. In the silence, only the fingernails scratching and my heart pounding.

When the sound stopped I leapt out of bed. The windowpane silent, the road empty.

"How are things today, ladies? I'm pleased you've recovered."

With effort, I swallowed. The other women also stopped eating and they all looked at Ziegler—stealing glances, almost as though it were forbidden but they couldn't help it—then we all stared at one another, our faces pinched.

After the poisoning, after the lunchroom had shown itself for what it was—a trap—whenever the SS guards spoke to us we felt panic rising. If it was Ziegler, we sensed imminent danger.

Ziegler walked around the table, stepped over to Heike, said, "You must be pleased it's all over." For a fraction of a second I thought he was talking about the abortion. Heike might have thought the same thing; she nodded with little jerks of her head, too rapid to hide her nervousness. Leaning over her shoulder, he reached out and picked up an apple from her plate. With the air of someone at a luncheon on the grass, he bit into it. The sound of his bite was crisp, sinister. He chewed as he walked, chest out, arms behind him, as though every step were in preparation for a dive. It was so strange, his walk. Why, then, did I miss him?

"I wanted to thank you all for your cooperation during the emergency."

Augustine stared at the apple in the lieutenant's hand, one of her nostrils quivering. Elfriede's nose was stopped up, as always, and she was breathing with difficulty. A lattice of stagnant blood had turned Leni's cheeks purple. I felt exposed. Ziegler strolled and chewed with such coolness I thought he might change his tone from one second to the next; we were expecting a dramatic twist, were prepared for the worst, impatient for it to arrive.

But Ziegler completed his walk around the table, stopped behind me. "We couldn't have done things any differently, though in the end, as you've seen for yourselves, the crisis is over. Everything is under control," he said, "so enjoy your meal." He placed the apple core on my plate and left.

Beate reached across the table and with two fingers picked it up by its stem. I was so shaken I didn't even wonder why. Glistening with his saliva, the pulp around the seeds was already darkening.

HE WANTED TO blackmail me. *Everyone will know who you are.* Wanted to torture me. Or just see me—a pang of nostalgia. We had made love. It could never happen again. If no one found out about it, that night would never have existed. It was in the past, couldn't be touched, it was as though it hadn't happened. Maybe with time I would even come to wonder whether it actually had happened, I wouldn't be able to say, and would be being honest.

I started eating again, drank my milk, set the cup on the table far harder than I meant to. It wobbled, tipped over. "I'm sorry." The cup rolled over to Elfriede, who set it upright. "I'm sorry," I said again.

"It's nothing, Berliner." She handed it to me and laid a napkin over the puddle of spilled milk.

I went to bed early, searching in vain for redemptive sleep. My eyes open wide, I imagined Ziegler had come. I feared he would walk up, scratch the windowpane with his fingernails as he had the night before, that he would smash the window with a rock, grab me by the neck. Herta and Joseph would come running, wouldn't understand, I would confess, would deny it to my dying day. The light out, I trembled.

THE NEXT DAY the Obersturmführer came out into the courtyard after dinner. I was talking to Elfriede, who was smoking. He headed straight for me. I instantly fell silent. "What is it, Rosa?" Elfriede asked.

"Throw away that cigarette."

She turned around.

"Throw it away at once," Ziegler repeated.

She let go of it hesitantly, almost as if wanting to take one last puff to avoid wasting it all.

"I didn't know smoking was forbidden," she said in her defense.

"From now on it *is* forbidden. No one smokes in my barracks. Adolf Hitler detests smoking."

Ziegler was mad at me. He was taking it out on Elfriede, but it was me he was angry with.

"A German woman mustn't smoke." He tilted his head, breathed in my scent, as he had done four nights earlier outside my window. I flinched. "Or at least she mustn't smell like it."

"I never have," I said.

With her eyes Elfriede begged me to be quiet.

"Are you sure?" Ziegler said.

THE APPLE CORE had turned brown. Beate rested it on the table beside a black candlestick and a tiny box. She lit the candle with a match. It was early evening, before curfew, and it was still light out, but her twins were already in the bedroom, sleeping. Ulla, Leni, Elfriede, and I were sitting around her.

Heike wasn't there. Ever since her abortion, she and her childhood friend had grown somewhat apart, without having decided to. Heike had simply kept her out of one of the most significant events of her life, and this had caused a distance. Actually, she had become more introverted around all of us, almost as though having shared such a secret with us we were a burden to her. She couldn't forgive us for knowing something she would rather forget.

Augustine, on the other hand, had wielded her usual skepticism toward all that gibberish about Beate being a witch and had stayed home, using her children as an excuse.

We're going to punish Ziegler, Beate had said. *If it works, fine. If it doesn't, at least we'll have some fun.*

She opened the box. It contained pins.

"What do you mean to do?" Leni asked, slightly worried. Inflicting pain on Ziegler didn't bother her—it was that the bad things you wish on others might come back to you one day. She was worried about herself.

"I take something the lieutenant touched," Beate explained, "and I stick pins into it. If we all focus on imagining that the apple core is him, pretty soon the lieutenant won't be feeling so good."

"What nonsense," Elfriede said. "I came all the way here for a bunch of nonsense."

"Oh, don't be a killjoy like Augustine!" Beate told her. "Can't you just play along? Look at it as a way to pass the time. Did you have anything better to do tonight?"

"After that, do you burn the apple core over the candle?" Leni was the most interested among us.

"No, that's just to create atmosphere." The little witch was really having fun.

"Sticking pins into a chewed-up apple? Never heard of anything like it," Elfriede said.

"We don't have anything else that's been in contact with Ziegler," Beate pointed out. "We need to make do."

"Hurry up," Elfriede said, "before it gets dark out. I have no idea why I listen to you."

Beate took a pin from the box. She pointed it at the upper part of the apple core and pierced the deteriorated pulp. "A pin in his mouth," she said. I had kissed it, that mouth. "That way we won't hear him screaming at us anymore."

"Right," Leni said, giggling.

"No, girls, let's stay serious, otherwise it won't work."

"Beate, hurry up," Elfriede insisted.

By the light of the candle, her fingers cast a long, flickering shadow. When it neared the apple core it darkened it, made it an eerie object, more or less the shape of a human body, Ziegler's body, which I had known.

Beate stuck more pins into it, saying aloud anatomical parts. Shoulders, which I had clung to. Belly, which I had rubbed against. Legs, which I had encircled with my own.

I had been in contact with Ziegler. They might as well have stuck pins into my flesh—it would have been more effective.

Beate focused on what was left of the red peel attached to the stem. "Head."

My neck stung.

"Is he dead now?" Leni asked in a low voice.

"No, we're missing his heart."

Her fingers moved closer with deliberate slowness. My breath began to grow short. The pin was just about to pierce the seed when I thrust my hand in the way.

"What are you doing?"

"Ow!" A drop of blood pooled on my finger, glimmered in the candlelight.

"Are you hurt?" Beate asked.

Elfriede blew out the candle, getting up.

"Hey, why'd you do that?" our hostess asked.

"Come on, that's enough," she replied.

I was hypnotized by the blood on my fingertip.

"Rosa, what's gotten into you?" Leni was already anxious.

Elfriede came over to me, and the others watched in silence as she pushed me into the bedroom.

"Still scared of your own blood, Berliner? Can't you see it's just a tiny speck?"

The twins were sleeping on their sides, cheeks squashed against arms, mouths open as if in a compressed, deformed O.

"It's not because of that," I mumbled.

"Look." She grabbed my wrist, slid my fingertip between her lips, sucked. Then she checked to see if it was still bleeding, sucked on it again.

A mouth that doesn't bite, or the chance to unexpectedly attack the other.

"There," she said, letting go of my finger. "Now you know you won't bleed to death."

"I wasn't afraid I would die. Don't make fun of me."

"Then what was it? Did you get spooked? You're a city girl—you disappoint me."

"Sorry."

"Are you apologizing for disappointing me?"

"I'm worse than you think."

"How should you know what I think?" She raised her chin in a comical air of defiance. "How presumptuous."

It made me want to laugh.

Then, to justify myself, I said, "The other night, in the barracks. It was terrible."

"It was terrible, yes, and it might happen again. There's no avoiding it," she said. "We can hide as long as we want, but sooner or later death will track us down all the same." Her expression turned sharp. It was just like the one she wore during the blood draw on our second day. But then her features gave in to resignation and her eyes comforted me. "I'm afraid too. More than you are."

I looked at the minuscule prick on my fingertip, which had dried, and my words slipped out: "I love you."

Her surprise left her speechless. One of the twins let out a rodent-like sound, wrinkled his nose as though from a sudden itch, turned beneath the sheets, and rolled over, belly-up, arms raised, spread out. He looked like Baby Jesus already surrendering for crucifixion.

"You're right," I said. "It's nonsense."

"What, that you love me?"

"No, this charade with the pins."

"Oh. Thank goodness." She took my hand, squeezed it. "Let's go back to the others."

Only right before stepping into the kitchen, only then, did I let go.

I DIDN'T GO to the window that night, nor any of the following nights. I thought I had finished it, that it was over. He didn't come back—or, if he did come back he didn't scratch his nails against the windowpane. Perhaps he had never come and the screech had been the sound of my bones.

I missed him. It wasn't like missing Gregor, fate taking a sharp turn, the annulment of all promises. It wasn't that serious. It was restlessness. I clutched the pillow, the cotton rough, combustible. It wasn't Albert Ziegler—it was me. The inertia he had disturbed. I bit the pillowcase. The roughness between my teeth made me shudder. Instead of Ziegler it could have been anyone, that's what I thought. I had made love to him because I hadn't made love for too long a time. I tore off a strip of cloth, chewed it, a thread got caught between my canines. I sucked on it, wrapped it around my tongue, swallowed it, like I had when I was a little girl. It didn't kill me this time either. *What I'm missing isn't Albert Ziegler*, I told myself, *it's my body.*

WHO KNEW HOW many days later, the Beanpole appeared in the lunchroom and ordered me to my feet. "You've been stealing again."

What was he talking about? "I haven't stolen anything."

Krümel had claimed responsibility for the bottles of milk in my bag. I had never been found guilty.

"Move."

I looked over at Theodora, Gertrude, Sabine. They were as stunned as I was. It hadn't been the Fanatics who accused me.

"What is it I supposedly stole?" I asked breathlessly.

"You know perfectly well," the Beanpole said.

"Berliner." Elfriede shook her head, a mother who'd run out of patience.

"I swear it!" I shouted as I stood up. I hadn't gotten myself into trouble again, she had to believe me.

"Come along." The Beanpole pulled me by the arm.

Leni pinched her nose shut, squeezed her eyes closed.

"Go on, out in front of me." He guided me out of the lunchroom, escorted by another guard.

In the hallway I turned around, tried once again to ask what theft I had been accused of. "Did Krümel tell you something? He's just mad at me."

"He's mad at you because you steal from the kitchen, Sauer. But now you're going to regret it."

"Where are we going?"

"Be quiet and walk."

I pressed my palms against his chest. "I beg you, you've known me for months. You know I would never—"

"Get your hands off me! How dare you?" He shoved me away by the shoulder.

I made my way forward, my breathing ragged, until we were outside Ziegler's office.

The Beanpole knocked, was told to enter, made me go in, was dismissed, though it was plain to see he was consumed with curiosity. I wondered whether he would stay outside and eavesdrop.

Ziegler clearly didn't. He came over to me, gripped my arm so hard it hurt, my joints coming apart, my bones clattering to the floor. Then he pressed me against him and I was intact, I hadn't shattered to pieces.

"Did Krümel tell you something?"

"If you don't come outside tonight I'll break the window."

"Did he tell you about the milk? Was it him who made you think of the excuse of theft?"

"Are you listening to me?"

"How do we explain it away, this story you've come up with? What am I going to tell the other women?"

"Unless you want to confess to stealing, despite having already been pardoned once, you'll tell the others it was all a misunderstanding, that everything is fine now."

"They'll never believe it."

He scrutinized me. I had to close my eyes for a moment. I breathed in the scent of his uniform—it lingered on him even when he was naked.

"You meant to kill us," I said.

He didn't reply.

"You would have killed me."

He continued to scrutinize me, seriously, as always.

"Say something, for heaven's sake!"

"I've already told you: if you don't come outside I'll break the window."

A pain shot through my forehead. I raised a hand to my temple.

"What is it, Rosa?"

It was the first time he had called me by my first name.

"You're threatening me," I said, and the pain vanished all at once. Through my body spread sweet relief.

24

WITHIN HOURS WE WERE LYING ONE BESIDE THE OTHER LIKE TWO people in a field staring up at the sky, even though there was no sky above us. The heat with which Ziegler had embraced me that afternoon in his office had disappeared—knowing I was still available was enough to calm him. As soon as we entered the barn he had lain down and hadn't touched me. His uniform still on, he was silent. Maybe he was sleeping—I didn't know what his breathing sounded like in his sleep—maybe he was thinking, but not of me. I lay there beside him in my nightgown. Our shoulders were touching, and the fact that this contact left him unresponsive demoralized me. I was already addicted to his desire. He had needed to do so little—decide to come to my window one night—for it to happen. I had responded to that desire as though to a summons. And now his indifference was humiliating. Why had he brought me here, if he wouldn't even say a word to me?

His shoulder pulled away from mine. As though pushed by a gust of wind, Ziegler moved, sitting up. I thought he was about to leave, and without explanation—after all, it was without explanation that he appeared outside the first time. After all, I had never asked him anything, never asked for a reason.

"It was the honey," he said.

I didn't understand.

"It was a shipment of bad honey. That's what poisoned you."

The delicious cake Elfriede had liked so much. "They sold you tainted honey?" I sat up as well.

"Not deliberately."

I touched his arm. "Explain."

Ziegler turned, and his voice reverberated against my face. "It happens. Bees feed off a noxious plant somewhere around the hive and taint the honey, that's all."

"What plant? And who said so? And what did you do to the producer?"

"People don't die from honey. Or at least, very rarely." The sudden warmth on my cheek was his hand.

"But you didn't know it wasn't lethal. While I was vomiting and shivering and fainting, you didn't know that. You would've let me die." I put my palm on his hand to push it away. He squeezed it.

Ziegler shoved me back and my head fell to the ground with a soft, buttery thump. He covered my face with all five fingers, his palm sealing my mouth shut, his fingertips squeezing my forehead. He pressed down on my nose, my eyelids, as though wanting to crush them, reduce them to a pulp. "You aren't dead."

Releasing his grip on my face, he stretched out on top of me, slipped his fingers under my rib cage, clasped the twelfth rib almost as if to detach it, to reclaim it at long last on behalf of the entire male gender.

"I thought I was going to die," I said. "You thought so too, and you didn't do anything."

He raised my nightgown and bit the rib he hadn't managed to pull free. I thought it would break between his teeth, or that his teeth would break. But the rib seemed to roll beneath his incisors, soft, chewy.

"You aren't dead," Ziegler said against my chest. He kissed me on the mouth, said, "You're alive," and his voice caught in his throat, a sort of cough. I caressed him as one might caress a child, as one might say, *Everything's fine, nothing's happened.* Then I began to undress him.

25

I WENT OUT EVERY NIGHT TO MAKE LOVE TO HIM, WALKING BRISKLY TOWARD the barn with the determination of someone going to face the inevitable. It was a soldier's march. Questions crowded my mind. I silenced them. The next day they would return to torment me, but when I went into the barn they were rags snarled in wire fencing, unable to get through the barrier of my will.

There was, in that act of going outside, a rebellion. In the solitude of my secret I felt complete freedom; relieved of all control over my own life, I succumbed to the arbitrariness of events.

We were lovers. It would be naïve to look for a reason for which two people become lovers. Ziegler had looked at me—no, actually, he had seen me. In that place, at that time, it had been enough.

Maybe one night Joseph would open the door and find us there, lying together, a Nazi uniform draped over us. Why hadn't it happened yet? In the mornings I thought it would be just—I wanted to be dragged onto the scaffold to face the collective scorn. *So that explains the whole story about the theft, a misunderstanding my foot, now it's all clear,* the other women would say. *A Berliner secretary,* Herta would say, *I knew she couldn't be trusted.*

In the darkness I clung to my lover's body so I wouldn't fall, and suddenly I felt life accelerating, consuming my body, my hair falling out, my nails breaking.

———

"Where did you learn to sing? I've been meaning to ask you that since the night of the party."

Albert had never asked me a personal question before. Was he really curious about me?

"In Berlin, at school. We had a chorus, met two afternoons a week. At the end of the year we would perform for our parents. What torture, for them."

"But you're an excellent singer."

He said it with such a familiar tone, as though we had been chatting for years. Instead, it was the first time.

"I had a very good teacher who knew how to motivate us. I liked singing and she would give me solos. I always had fun at school."

"I didn't, not at all. Just think: my elementary school teacher used to take us to the cemetery."

"The cemetery?"

"To teach us to read. From gravestones. The writing was large and all uppercase, there were letters and numbers . . . she found it a convenient method."

"A practical woman!"

Was laughing with him possible?

"In the morning she would line us up in pairs and walk us down to the graveyard. We had to keep quiet out of respect for the 'poor souls' and read one gravestone each. Sometimes I was so shaken by the idea that there was a dead person under the ground that I couldn't utter a word."

"A likely excuse," I said, laughing.

It was possible; he laughed too.

He said, "At night all those dead people would come to mind and I would imagine my mother or father under the ground, and I wouldn't be able to sleep."

What was happening to us? We were two strangers sharing our life stories. Did physical intimacy spawn compassion? I felt an incomprehensible protectiveness toward his body.

I needed his thumbs squeezing my nipples, pinning me to the wall. Once acted upon, though, our impetuosity dissolved. It became tenderness, the untrustworthy tenderness of lovers. I was thinking of Ziegler as a little boy—that was what was happening to me.

"The teacher would make us count our heartbeats too. 'There is no such thing as boredom,' she would tell us. 'If you become bored, you can take your pulse'"—Ziegler grasped his wrist with his other hand—"'and count. One. Two. Three. Each heartbeat is one second, sixty seconds are one minute. You can know how much time has passed even without a watch.'"

"She thought *that* was a good way to kill boredom?"

"I would do it at night when I couldn't sleep because I was thinking about the dead. It seemed disrespectful to go there and trespass on their space. I thought sooner or later they would seek revenge."

In an evil monster's voice, I said, "And they would take you to the netherworld?" I grabbed his wrist. "Come on, let's count your heartbeats like your teacher taught you." He let me do it. "You're quite alive, Lieutenant Ziegler."

It takes a great deal of curiosity to imagine people when they were little. Ziegler as a child was the same person as now, but most of all he was another—he was the starting point of a destiny that would include me. With that child I was forming an alliance. He wouldn't hurt me. That was why I could play with Albert, that was why I was laughing—my hand over my mouth to avoid making noise—in the banal way lovers laugh, laugh over nothing.

"The dead seek revenge," he said.

I wanted to hold him in my arms, that child afraid of death, make him fall asleep with a world of caresses.

We fell silent for sixty consecutive beats of his heart, then I tried to go back to our conversation. "I had excellent teachers. I was in love with my high school math teacher. His name was Adam Wortmann. I often wonder what happened to him."

"Well, my teacher died. And not long afterward, her sister, who lived with her, died too. Her sister always wore funny hats."

"They arrested Mr. Wortmann. They came into the classroom to take him away. He was a Jew."

Albert said nothing, nor did I.

Then he slipped his wrist out of my grasp and picked up his jacket, which lay on the firewood.

"Leaving so soon?"

"I must." He stood up.

His chest was furrowed in the center. I loved to run my finger down that gully, but he didn't give me time. He buttoned his uniform, pulled on his boots, mechanically checked the gun in his holster. "'Bye," he said, straightening his hat without waiting for me to leave too.

26

SINCE THE ARRIVAL OF SUMMER, THE BARONESS HAD OFTEN INVITED ME to the castle. I would go there in the afternoon after work, before the bus returned to pick me up again. We would stay out in the garden, just she and I, like two adolescent girls who need exclusivity in order to consider it friendship. In the shade of the oak trees, amid the carnations, peonies, and cornflowers, which Joseph had planted in clusters instead of rows—*After all, nature isn't orderly,* Maria said—we would talk about music, theater, film, and books. She would lend me novels to read, and I would bring them back after having formed an opinion of them, knowing that she would want to discuss them for hours. She asked me about my life in Berlin, and I wondered what she found interesting in my former everyday petit bourgeois existence, but she seemed passionate about everything, and everything piqued her curiosity.

The servants now greeted me as a regular guest, would open the gates to me with a *Welcome, Frau Sauer,* would accompany me to the gazebo and go to call her if need be, if Maria wasn't there already, sipping a drink while reading a book and fluttering her fan. She said that inside the house there was too much furniture, it stifled her. I found her excessive, ostentatiously over-the-top, but her delight in nature was sincere. "When I grow up," she joked one day, "I want to be a gardener so I can plant whatever I like!" She laughed. "Don't get me wrong: Joseph is an excellent gardener and I'm lucky to have him here, but I've asked him to try to grow an olive tree and he says the weather isn't the best. I'm not giving up, though! Ever since I visited Italy I've dreamed of having an olive grove behind the house. Olive groves are delightful, don't you think, Rosa?"

I wasn't thinking. I was just letting her enthusiasm wash over me.

ONE EVENING, AS she opened the gate, a maid told me the baroness was in the stables with her children—they had just returned from a ride on their horses—and wanted me to join her there.

From the dirt path leading to the stable I saw all three of them, each standing beside a horse. Maria stroked the mane of hers, the tight vest around her trim torso flattering her figure. She was a petite woman but the jodhpurs made her hips rounder. Still, from the looks of her it seemed impossible that she had given birth to two children.

"Rosa!" cried Michael and Jörg, running over to me.

I knelt down to hug them. "How adorable you look in these hats."

"I have a riding crop too," Michael said. He showed it to me.

"I have one as well, but I don't use mine," the elder brother said, "because just the sight of it will make the horse be good." Jörg was nine. The rules of submission were learned at a young age.

Maria's shadow stretched out over us.

"Here's your mother," I said, standing up. "Hello."

"Hello, dear. How are you?" A smile spread out like the mark of a finger over her creamy complexion. "Forgive us, we're late." She was always kind. "I thought it would be worse, going riding on such a sunny day, but the children insisted and I indulged them. It turns out they were right. We had a lovely ride, didn't we?"

Her children nodded, bouncing up and down around her.

"I must look a fright, though," she went on, running a hand over her head. She wore her hair up, copper-colored locks escaping the combs. "Would you care to go for a ride, Rosa?" The idea suddenly seemed irresistible to her—I could see it in her eyes.

"Oh, yes! Do!" the children said, lighting up.

"Thank you," I replied, "but I've never even been on a horse before."

"Try it, Rosa! It's fun!" Michael and Jörg came over to bounce up and down around me.

"I have no doubt it's fun, but I don't know how."

In their world it was probably absurd, someone not knowing how to ride a horse.

"Please, Rosa. It would mean so much to the children. Our groom will help you."

That was what happened with her: the possibility of disappointing her became out of the question.

And so I went into the stable just as I had begun to sing at the party—only because the baroness wanted me to. The smell of dung, hooves, and sweat was soothing. That the smell of animals was soothing was something I had discovered at Gross-Partsch.

When I drew near, the horse snorted, jerking its head back. Maria rested her arm on its neck. "Easy," she said.

The groom pointed to the stirrup and told me, "Slip your foot in there, Frau Sauer. No, the left one. That's it. Now, gently pull yourself up. Lean on me." I tried but fell back. He held me up. Michael and Jörg burst out laughing.

Maria frowned at them. "Does that seem kind to our friend?"

Regretful, Michael said, "Would you like to ride my pony? He's shorter."

Jörg immediately joined in. "We'll help you get on!" With this he came over and pushed on my calves. "Up you go!" His brother stepped to his side and also began to push.

Now it was Maria who was laughing, a childish laugh, her tiny teeth showing. I was already perspiring, though I didn't back out of their moment of amusement. The horse continued to snort.

The groom lifted me up by the waist and finally I was in the saddle. He told me to sit up straight and not to pull on the reins—he would guide the animal for me. We made our way out of the stable, the horse trotting along, me bouncing slightly, clinging on with my legs to avoid losing my balance.

It was a short ride just outside the stable, the horse being led by the halter, and I atop it, also being dragged along.

"Do you like it, Rosa?" the baroness asked.

I felt ridiculous. An excessive sentiment I couldn't help feeling. Inviting me to ride their horse had been a gesture of hospitality, but it made the difference between those people and me plain to see. "Thank you," I replied. "The children were right. It's lots of fun."

"Wait!" Michael cried out to the groom.

The boy shot over to me and handed me his riding crop. What was I supposed to do with it? The horse was docile, just like me. I took it from him all the same, then asked the groom to help me down.

In the gazebo we sipped cool lemonade. The children had been entrusted to the governess, had changed clothes, and had come back to greet their mother, who was still in her riding outfit. Her slightly disheveled hair didn't tarnish her elegance. Maria was aware of it. "Go off and play, now," she told them.

I was taciturn, and the baroness didn't understand why. She took my hands in hers, as she had done with Joseph. "He's missing," she told me, "he isn't dead. Don't be discouraged."

She had taken it for granted that it was Gregor I was brooding over. Whenever she or anyone else reminded me of what condition they all expected me to be in—that of a worried wife—I scared myself.

I hadn't pushed Gregor out of my mind—it wasn't that. He was as much a part of me as were my legs or my arms. Quite simply, you don't walk while thinking constantly about the movement of your legs, you don't do the laundry while concentrating on your arms. My life went on and he was oblivious to it, like my mother when she would leave me at school and go home without me, like my mother when I lost the new fountain pen she had given me. Someone might have stolen it, someone might have put it in their pencil case by accident—I couldn't search my classmates' book bags. A new fountain pen, a brass one, which my mother had bought for me, and I had lost it, but she had no idea, she made my bed and folded my sweaters in a state of complete innocence. My pain at the wrong I had done to her was so great that the only way to bear it was to love my mother less, to say nothing, to keep it a secret. The only way to survive my love for my mother was to betray that love.

"Everything's going to work out, you know. Even if one loses hope,"

Maria said. "Just think of poor Stauffenberg. We thought he would end up blind last year, when his car drove through that mine field in Tunisia. Instead, thank heavens, he lost an eye but he's fine."

"Not only an eye. . . ."

"Yes, he lost his right hand as well. And the pinkie and ring finger on his left hand. But he didn't lose his charm. I've always told his wife, Nina, 'You married the handsomest one.'"

I was struck by her liberty in speaking like that about a man who wasn't her husband. It wasn't brazenness, though—there was no malice in Maria—just enthusiasm.

"With Claus I can talk about music and literature, like I can with you," she said. "As a child he wanted to be either a musician or an architect, but then at age nineteen he joined the army. Such a shame, he had talent. I've heard him many times objecting that this war has gone on for too long. He believes we're going to lose it. Nevertheless he's always fought, and with a great sense of duty. Perhaps it's also because he's quite devout. One day he quoted to me Stefan George, his favorite poet: 'A silent artist who surpassed himself, and waits bemused for God to do his own.' They're the final lines of *The Knight of Bamberg*. But Claus doesn't wait for help from anyone. He takes the initiative, believe me, and he's not afraid of anything."

She let go of my hands and drank until her glass was empty. All that rattling on must have made her thirsty. The maid arrived with a cake topped with cream and fruit, and Maria thumped her chest. "Poor me, I'm such a glutton! I eat sweets every single day. To compensate, I never eat meat. That will work in my favor, don't you think?"

It was an unusual custom in those days. I didn't know anyone who voluntarily went without meat, except the Führer. Actually, I didn't *know* the Führer. I worked for him but had never met him.

Once again, Maria misinterpreted my silence. "Rosa, you really are feeling down today." There was no point denying it. "We must do something to cheer you up."

She invited me upstairs to her room, where I had never been before. Soft light came in through a giant, open picture window, which took up almost the entire wall. In the middle of the room was a round table in dark wood, cluttered with books. Everywhere, vases filled with flowers. Nestled in one corner was the piano, and pages of sheet music had fallen onto the bench and rug. Maria picked them up and sat down. "Come, now."

I stood behind her. Over the piano hung a picture of Hitler.

It was a three-quarters portrait, with him looking straight ahead. His eyes indignant, weighed down by the bags beneath them, cheeks flaccid. He wore a long gray overcoat opened just enough to reveal the Iron Crosses he had earned in the Great War. His arm was bent, his fist planted on his hip, making him look far from a fighting man, more like a mother scolding her child, a housewife resting for a moment after scrubbing the floors with lye. There was something feminine about him, so feminine that his mustache looked fake, as though it were glued on for an imminent cabaret act. I had never noticed that before.

Maria turned and saw I was staring at the photo. "That man is going to save Germany."

If my father had heard her.

"Whenever I see him it feels like I'm talking to a prophet. He has magnetic, almost violet eyes, and when he speaks it's as if the air moves. I've never met a more charismatic person."

What did I have in common with this woman? Why was I there in her bedroom? Why, for some time now, had I found myself in places I didn't want to be in and acquiesced and didn't rebel and continued to survive whenever someone was taken from me? The ability to adapt is human beings' greatest resource, but the more I adapted, the less human I felt.

"It isn't hard to believe he receives piles of letters from his female admirers every day! Over dinner with him I was so excited that I didn't touch my food. And later on, when we were saying goodbye, he kissed my hand and said"—she tried to imitate his voice—"'Dear child, do try to eat more. Can't you see you're too thin?'"

"You aren't too thin," I objected, as though that were the point.

"I don't think so either. No thinner than Eva Braun, at least. And I'm even taller than she is."

Ziegler had also mentioned her, the Führer's secret girlfriend. It was strange to think about him with the baroness right there in front of me. Who knew if she had noticed something, if at the thought of Ziegler my expression had changed?

"But Hitler also made me laugh a lot, you know. At one point he notices me taking a hand mirror out of my purse and tells me that as a boy he'd had one just like it. Silence falls. 'Mein Führer, what were you doing with a lady's hand mirror?' Clemens asks. Such cheek! And Hitler says, 'I used it to reflect sunlight into my teacher's eyes to blind her.' Everyone bursts out laughing." Maria was laughing herself just then, thinking it would make me laugh too. "One day, though, the teacher makes a note in her register when he does it, so between lessons he and his classmates go to peek at what she's written. As soon as the bell rings again, they return to their desks and begin to chant, all together, 'Hitler likes to bully me, he plays with light so I can't see.' That's what was written in the register. . . . It sounded like a children's rhyme! The teacher was right: Hitler was a bully, and in some ways he still is."

"Is that why he's going to save Germany?"

Maria frowned. "Don't treat me like a fool, Rosa. I won't abide it from anyone."

"I didn't mean to be disrespectful," I said sincerely.

"We need him, you know that. It's a question of choosing between Hitler and Stalin, and anyone would choose Hitler. Wouldn't you?"

I knew nothing about Stalin or the Soviet Union except for what Gregor had told me: the Bolshevik paradise was a pile of hovels inhabited by beggars. My anger toward Hitler was personal. He had taken my husband from me, and because of him day after day I risked dying. My very existence was in his hands—that was what I detested. Hitler nourished me, and that nourishment could kill me. But then again, as Gregor would say, giving life to someone always means condemning them to die. Before creation, God contemplates annihilation.

"Wouldn't you, Rosa?" Maria repeated.

I had the urge to tell her about the Krausendorf barracks, about how the SS had treated us when they believed we had been poisoned. Instead, I nodded mechanically. Why should my experience as a food taster move her? Maybe she already knew. The baroness dined with the Führer and invited Ziegler to her parties. Were they friends, she and the lieutenant? Suddenly I wanted to talk about him instead of Hitler, wanted to see him through her eyes. My experience as a food taster had lost interest even to me.

"Change always comes at a cost, unfortunately. The new Germany, though, will be a place where we'll all live a better life. Even you."

She raised the piano lid, the German cause momentarily set aside. She had other things to focus her attention on. Because Maria was passionate about everything with equal intensity. We could go on about the Führer or the cake with cream and fruit, she could recite a poem by Stefan George or sing a tune by the Comedian Harmonists, whom her beloved Führer had forced to split up. Everything had equal importance to her.

I didn't blame her. I couldn't blame anyone anymore. In fact, I had grown to love the way she swayed her head to the music, her eyebrows raised as she coaxed me to sing.

27

I asked Albert if he had ever met Adolf Hitler in person. Yes, of course he had met him, what a silly question. I begged him to describe what it felt like to be next to him. He, too, mentioned Hitler's magnetic eyes.

"Why do you all talk about his eyes? Is the rest of him so unbearable?"

He gave me a little slap on the thigh. "Such insolence!"

"Ooh, so defensive! Well? What's he like?"

"I don't feel like talking about the Führer's physical appearance."

"Then show him to me! Take me to the Wolfsschanze."

"Right. Sure."

"Hide me in your jeep, in the trunk."

"Have you really never seen him? Not even at a parade?"

"Will you take me?"

"Where do you think you'd be going, to a party? In case you haven't heard, there are barbed-wire barriers with electric currents running through them. And land mines. You can't imagine how many rabbits they've blown up."

"How horrible."

"Now do you understand?"

"But I'll be going in with you."

"No, you don't understand. To get into the last ring, which is where Hitler lives, you need a pass, but he needs to invite you first, and besides that you'd be searched. Not everyone is welcome into the Führer's home."

"An inhospitable man."

"Cut it out." My joking was bothering him, as though I were be-littling his position. "He didn't have headquarters built in the forest just so he could let in anyone."

"You told me two thousand people live there, and four thousand people work there! It's practically a city. Who's going to notice if I go in too?"

"I can't understand why it's so important to you. There's nothing to see there, in that place where the sun never shines."

"Why does the sun never shine there?"

An irritated sigh. "Because there are nets strung between the trees, with piles of leaves covering them. And trees and bushes are growing on the roofs of the bunkers. Whoever looks down from overhead sees only forest. They can't find us."

"How brilliant," I joked yet again. Why was I doing it? Maybe I was unsettled by the fact that so much energy had been expended to barricade them, to entomb them.

"You're getting on my nerves."

"I just want to know where you spend your time. Are there women in there too?"

He faked a scowl.

"Well?"

"Unfortunately," he said, grinning, "not enough of them."

I pinched him on the arm. He grabbed hold of my breast, squeezed it.

"At least bring me a strand of the Führer's hair. I'll frame it."

"You'll what?" He rolled over and straddled me.

It was almost morning. The first light was filtering in between the slats in the walls. I stroked the faint tattoo on his left underarm. *AB Rh NEGATIVE*, it read, beside his identification number. He flinched because it tickled. I persisted until he defended himself by trapping my wrists.

"Why do you want one?"

"I'll hang it over my bed. . . . But if you can't pull out a strand of his hair for me, I'll settle for a hair from Blondi." I laughed as Albert nipped at my collarbones, my funny bones.

"Would you really want a relic of a man who's always doing this?" He curled the corner of his lips upward repeatedly.

His imitation of the Führer's tic made me burst out laughing. I cupped my hands over my mouth to muffle the sound. Albert laughed reflexively—a low, rolling chuckle.

"First you defend him and then you disparage him?"

"He really does that. It's not my fault."

"I think you're making it all up. You've believed the stories put out by his detractors. You're playing right into his enemies' hands!"

He twisted my wrists until they cracked. "Say that again!" he dared me.

It was almost dawn. We should have parted, but I couldn't stop staring at him now that I could see his face. There was something in the lines in his forehead, in the curve of his chin, something that frightened me. I stared at him and couldn't grasp the synthesis of his face, only the rigidity of his protruding jaw, the deep groove in his brow—surviving beams in scaffolding that had collapsed. Hardness is vulgar precisely because it lacks cohesion. Like a number of vulgar things, however, it can be exciting.

"You should have become an actor, not an SS officer."

"That's enough. You've gone too far!" He squeezed my throat with one hand while keeping my wrists trapped with the other. He squeezed for a few seconds, I don't know how many, and the pain spread to my temples. I opened my eyes wide and only then did he relax his grip.

He stroked my breastbone and then began to torture me with tickles using his fingers, his nose, his hair. Laughing, I continued to be frightened.

ALBERT TOLD ME a few stories about the Führer. It seems he was the one who really enjoyed doing impressions. Over meals, Hitler would often tell an anecdote involving one of his men. He must have had an excellent memory, because he never left out a single detail. The man in question would willingly allow himself to become the subject of derision—would be honored by it.

Hitler was wild about Blondi, his German shepherd. He would

take her for a walk and to run every morning, though Eva Braun couldn't stand her. Maybe the woman was jealous, given that the dog had access to her lover's bedroom, while she had never even been invited to the Rastenburg headquarters. Then again, she wasn't an official girlfriend. She told him Blondi was a calf, not a dog, while Hitler detested smaller breeds, which he deemed unsuitable for a great statesman, and referred to Eva's Scottish terriers, Negus and Stasi, as dusting brushes.

"She sings better than you, you know," Albert told me.

"Braun?"

"No, Blondi. I swear it. He asks her to sing and she starts barking, louder and louder. The more he encourages and praises her, the more she barks, almost howling. Then he tells her: 'Not like that, Blondi! You should sing with a lower voice, like Zarah Leander.' And the dog, I swear to you, the dog obeys."

"Did you see this for yourself or did you only hear about it?"

"Sometimes I end up at the nighttime tea. He doesn't always invite me. But then again, I prefer not to go. They always last forever and no one ever gets to bed before five in the morning."

"As though you slept more than that anyway. . . ."

He touched the tip of my nose.

"So you can go back to the Wolfsschanze whenever you like, with curfew and lights-out?"

"I don't go back," he said. "I sleep in Krausendorf, in the barracks, on the sofa."

"You're mad."

"You think my mattress is any more comfortable? Besides, my room is little more than a cubbyhole. It's hot out now but I can't turn on the ceiling fan, the sound drives me insane."

"Poor Lieutenant Ziegler, the light sleeper."

"And when do you make up for the sleep you lose with me?"

"Since I moved to this place I've had insomnia."

"We all have insomnia. Even him."

Once, he told me, the Führer's men used gasoline to exterminate the insects infesting the area and in the process inadvertently killed off all the frogs too. Hitler couldn't fall asleep without their strident lullaby, so he sent a party of men out to search the entire forest for frogs.

I imagined the SS men in the dark of night, their feet sinking into muddy swamps where mosquitoes and gnats—which hadn't been exterminated and were breeding peacefully—would be amazed at having so much young blood on which to feast, so many robust German men on which to leave their marks. The German men were terrified at the thought of returning without a prize. I imagined one of them pointing his flashlight around, chasing after the leaping frogs but being unable to catch them. He calls to them sweetly, like he would call to my Zart, a soft smacking of his lips, as though wanting to kiss them, to liberate Prince Charming to wed. At last, beaming, he manages to scoop up a frog in his hands, but a second later it slips away and in his attempts to catch it again he falls, his face ending up smeared with slime.

Everything considered, it turns out to be their lucky night. Hitler has granted them the opportunity to go back to being children, something that will never happen again. The frogs are put back in their place around his lodgings. I imagined the SS men encouraging them: *Croak, oh, please croak, little frog.* The Führer once again shows clemency. Then he goes to bed.

Albert had also fallen asleep, his cheek flattened against my belly. I lay awake, listening carefully for the slightest noise. The barn was our lair. Every criminal has one.

28

Tonight the Wolf can't sleep. He can talk nonstop until dawn. One after the other, the SS men nod off, their heads drooping and then sinking into their palms, their elbows propped on the table, wobbling though still supporting the weight. The important thing is that someone, even just one of them, stays awake. Tonight the Wolf doesn't want to fall asleep, not at all, doesn't want to let himself go, sleep can be deceptive. How many people have closed their eyes convinced they would open them again in a moment, but instead were swallowed up by sleep? It's too similar to death for it to be trusted. *Sleep,* his mother would tell him, and she would wink at him with her good eye. She had earned herself a beating that evening, her husband preferring her with purple cheekbones—even more when he was drinking. *Shhh,* his mother would say, *sleep now, my little Wolfie.* But the Wolf already knew you needed to be constantly alert, that you couldn't let down your guard; traitors were everywhere, everywhere an enemy ready to annihilate you. *Hold my hand,* his mother would hold it, *stay here with me,* the SS officer nods. He waits for the powder to take effect, for the Führer to drift off to sleep, waits until he succumbs, watches over his breathing—mouth open, sleeping like an infant. Now the SS officer can leave, can let him rest.

The Führer has been left alone and death lies in wait, a phenomenon beyond all control, an enemy that can never be defeated. *I'm afraid. Of what, little Wolfie? Of the fat Dutchwoman who tried to kiss me in front of everyone at the Berlin Olympics. How silly you are. I'm afraid of traitors, of the Gestapo, of stomach cancer. Come here, sweetheart,*

I'll rub your belly, the tummy ache will pass, you'll see, you ate too much chocolate. Poison, I'm afraid of poison. But I'm here, you can't be afraid. I taste your food like Mother drips milk from the bottle onto her wrist, like Mother tests the baby food in her own mouth, it's too hot, she blows on it, feels it on her palate again before spoon-feeding it to you. I'm here, little Wolfie. It's my devotion that makes you feel immortal.

29

We had spread our blankets out on the grass. The lake was slightly rippled but the temperature was perfect for swimming. Ursula and Mathias didn't want to get out of the water. Heike was lying on her side, asleep. Ulla was sitting in a rowboat on the shore, legs crossed, and from time to time would adjust the straps on her swimsuit. Leni, on the other hand, had immediately dived into the water and had been swimming ever since, as though to cross a finish line. I was reading a novel Maria had lent me and between one page and the next kept an eye on Heike's children.

Not far from our blankets, something caught my attention. Two large branches, one driven into the earth, the other nailed to the first one, forming a cross. On one side of the cross hung a military helmet.

When had the soldier fallen, in what war? And more important, had he died right there? Or had a parent, a wife, a sister decided to commemorate him with a cross beside the lake because it was a sweet, restful place? Because it was a place where the son, the husband, the brother had held diving contests with his friends as a child?

Sooner or later Gregor would also deserve a cross in a place he had loved, but I had no right to commemorate him.

Ursula's voice made me turn around.

"Mother!" Heike awoke with a start. "Mother, Mathias swam far from shore and now he's drowning!" Ursula screamed.

I ran to the water's edge. Heike followed me. "I can't swim," she said. "Go get him, please."

I dove in. I tried calling out to Leni, but she was a tiny speck in the distance and didn't hear. She was the best swimmer of us all. I wasn't trained myself, I moved slowly and grew tired quickly. Where was Ulla?

I advanced one arm stroke after the other. "Don't worry," Heike shouted to her son, and Ursula did the same. I swam as quickly as I could. I saw Mathias's head sinking and reemerging. He was thrashing and swallowing water. I didn't want to assume such a huge responsibility all on my own. Why wouldn't that fool Leni come back? And Ulla, who had she gone off to flirt with, for her not to have noticed? I was already out of breath and Mathias's head was still far away. I rested for a moment, *Just for a moment, now I'll start swimming again,* but Mathias sank once more and didn't come back up. With all my strength I shot forward and as I did I saw a man swim over swiftly, dive underwater, and a moment later reappear with the boy on his back. Within minutes he had pulled him back to shore.

When I had caught my breath, I swam over to them.

Mathias, lying on the water's edge, had already regained his color.

"Why did you go so far out?" Heike was shouting. "I told you not to!"

"I wanted to reach Leni."

"You're so thoughtless!"

"Come on, calm down. He's fine," Ulla said.

Two young men stood beside them, arms crossed, watching the scene. One of them must have been the man who had pulled Mathias out of the water.

"Thank you for beating me to it," I said. "I was already exhausted."

The taller of the two replied, "Don't mention it." Then he turned to the boy. "If you like, I'll teach you to swim properly. But only on condition that you won't go so far out into the water until you've learned how."

Mathias nodded and stood up, suddenly reinvigorated.

"I'm Heiner," the young man said, holding out his hand to him.

The boy introduced himself in turn.

"And I'm Ernst," the other one said. Then he punched Heiner on the shoulder. "Well done, Sergeant."

They were two young soldiers from the Heer. Heiner was a film enthusiast, and at the front he had spent most of his time behind a movie camera, but he had also been made projectionist. "These days, true cinematographic art is the documentary," he explained to us a while later, sitting on Heike's towel. We had all huddled together, even Leni, who had returned from her long swim, during which she hadn't realized what was going on behind her. "When the war is over," Heiner said, "I'm going to become a movie director."

Ernst, on the other hand, had always dreamed of fighting in the Luftwaffe—he had been designing and building model airplanes since elementary school—but he had a congenital eye defect, so he had had to settle for joining the ground forces.

They had set up a movie hall not far from the Wolfsschanze. A tent where they showed whatever was allowed—which wasn't much. Among the films, though, were some real jewels, Ernst explained, and, staring at the pale, glowing skin revealed by Leni's black swimsuit, he said, "It would be nice if you could all come watch a movie with us now and then."

Ulla rattled off a series of films Zarah Leander had starred in. "And *To New Shores?* Do you have that? Or *Heimat?* It's my favorite!"

We became friends, most of all because of Leni, who had welcomed Ernst's interest unquestioningly, without wondering if she wanted him. She had subscribed to his desire almost as if responding to an assignment she couldn't refuse. She was an exemplary victim, Leni. If she hadn't been so afraid, out of all of us she would have been the perfect food taster.

WITH ZIEGLER, I hadn't behaved any differently than Leni.

In the morning, Herta's eyes seemed to follow me and Joseph's silence to conceal disappointment. In Krausendorf, the SS guard searched me too eagerly, as though he could sense that my body was profane. In the lunchroom, Elfriede studied me like the day I had worn my checkered dress—I hadn't taken it out of the wardrobe in ages—until she guessed what I had kept so well hidden. Or maybe I simply couldn't believe I was getting away with it.

In the afternoons I would often search for some trace of Albert in the barn. I had no reason to go in there and hoped I wouldn't be noticed by Herta, busy baking bread despite the heat. Joseph was at the castle, tending the garden where Maria played with Michael and Jörg if the governess wasn't looking after them.

I opened the old door and the dry smell inside the barn tickled my nostrils. In the future I would forever associate that smell with Ziegler, and every time I would feel my hips crumble. Hips that yield, that shatter. I no longer know how to describe it, to describe love, any other way.

No trace of Albert, of us. The tools, the discarded furniture, nothing was out of place. Everything was just as it always had been, our encounters left behind no mark in the world. They happened in suspended time, a scandalous blessing.

30

"ALBERT, DID YOU HEAR THAT?" HE HAD FALLEN ASLEEP. I SHOOK HIM.

His mouth pasty, he swallowed before whispering, "No, what is it?"

"Noises. Like someone's pushing on the door."

"Maybe it's the wind."

"What wind? Not even a leaf is stirring."

It's Joseph, I thought. *He knows, he's known for weeks, he's tired of pretending. It was Herta, she incited him, I dared to offend her in her own home: In my own home, Joseph, can you believe it?*

I pulled on my nightgown, stood up.

"What are you doing?" Albert asked.

"Get dressed!" I nudged him with my bare foot. I couldn't stand the thought of my in-laws opening the door and bursting in on such an indecent sight.

When Albert stood up, on instinct I sought a way to hide him, to hide us. But where? The door continued to creak. Why weren't they opening it?

They had gone to the door, driven by anger, but then just outside the barn they had frozen. They didn't want to witness the scene. Maybe they would go back to bed. I was the person most like a child to them, they could forgive me, or harbor toward me constant resentment without making a fuss, without openly confronting the situation—the silent resentment in every family.

The noises continued. "Do you hear it now?"

Albert said, "Yes," and his voice sounded tinged with anxiety.

I wanted to get it over with, so I rushed to the door, opened it.

When he saw me, Zart let out a muffled meow. He had caught a mouse, was gripping it between his sharp teeth. Its head was falling off. I backed up in disgust. Herta and Joseph weren't there.

"An unexpected gift?" Albert whispered. Realizing I was out of my wits, he was trying to calm me.

"The cat knew I was here."

Finally someone had noticed. No, we couldn't get away with it. Zart knew our secret. He had killed a mouse and brought it to us here. More than a gift, it seemed like a warning.

Albert pulled me back inside, shut the door, held me in his arms gently, then tightly. He had been scared. Not for himself—what did he have to be afraid of?—but for me. He didn't want me to suffer because of our relationship, didn't want me to suffer at all. I held him close, wanted to take care of him, prove it to him. In that moment, I thought that ours was a worthy love, one worth no less than any other, no less than any other emotion that had refuge on earth, that there was nothing wrong, reprehensible, if when I embraced him I began to breathe again—slowly, like Pauline in the bed with me in Berlin.

31

LISTENING TO IT WITH MY EYES CLOSED, THE SOUND OF THE LUNCHROOM would have been a nice sound. The clink of forks against plates, the splosh of water being poured, the thunk of glass on wood, the clack of footsteps against the floor, mouths chewing, voices overlapping, birds singing and dogs barking, the distant rumble of a tractor drifting through the open windows. It would have been nothing other than a moment of conviviality. It's endearing, the human need to eat so as not to die.

But if I opened my eyes I saw them—the uniformed guards, the loaded weapons, the confines of our cage—and the dishes would once again clink, the compressed sound of something on the verge of exploding. I thought of the night before, of the terror that they had discovered me, of the dead mouse. I could no longer bear the lie, it was as if I carried it on my back, and was amazed no one else could see it. Still, I wasn't relieved. Sooner or later they would see it. I lived in a state of high alert.

That morning, as I was leaving the house to wait for the bus, the cat rubbed against my ankles and I brusquely sidestepped him. *I know your secret, you're not safe,* he threatened. *Why are you angry at the cat?* Herta asked, and I felt like I could die.

THE OTHER WOMEN went outside. I stayed in my seat. The sound of the lunchroom had been interrupted, but Zart's claws scratching the barn door continued to torment me.

"Berliner?" Elfriede came to sit down beside me, her elbow upright on the table, her hand cupping her chin. "Can't digest?"

I tried to smile. "Well, you know, poison gives me a touch of heartburn."

"Milk can help with that. But please, don't go stealing it this time."

We laughed. Elfriede turned her chair to the side to have a view of the courtyard.

Heike was on the swings and Beate was pushing her—two schoolgirls at recess. Maybe when they were little they had played like that.

"They're really close friends," I said, noticing that Elfriede was watching them too.

"And yet," she replied, "Beate wasn't there when Heike had that problem."

It was the first time she had mentioned the abortion, though she avoided calling it by its name.

"But it was Heike who didn't involve her," I objected. "Who knows why?"

"Because she didn't want to tell her about the seventeen-year-old."

So Elfriede knew about him too. During their walk through the woods Heike must have confided in her.

"They're still together," she added. "People use love to justify all kinds of things."

The comment stabbed my heart. In my mind once again I saw the barn door, Albert growing nervous, then the dead mouse in Zart's jaws. I had to summon my courage to say, "And you think it's wrong?"

"The point, Berliner, is that anyone can justify anything. They always find an excuse." She turned to look at me. "If she really thought she was doing nothing wrong, Heike would talk openly about it with her closest friend. You know why she isn't ashamed around us? Because we aren't so dear to her heart."

She looked up and to the left, as though still reflecting on it. "Or," she said, "Heike imagines Beate isn't ready to know. That she doesn't want to know. Sometimes knowing is a burden. And she'd rather not give her that burden. In any case she's lucky she didn't have to keep it all to herself."

She had caught me—it was me she was talking about, she was asking me to confess. I didn't need to keep everything to myself, I could share that burden with her. She wasn't Beate, she would understand.

Or would she tell me I was behaving worse than Heike?

It didn't matter to me anymore. At least with Elfriede I wanted to be honest, delude myself that I was better than I had become. She would tell me the dead mouse wasn't a bad omen, and I would believe her.

She stood up, went over to one of the guards, asked to be escorted to the washroom. It was a signal, she wanted me to follow her, it had happened before. Or had she been trying to suggest just the opposite? *Never confess it to me, don't make me your accomplice.*

Her fitted skirt went halfway down her calves, her muscles flexed and relaxed as she walked toe to heel. Her poised, lofty gait enchanted me. From the start Elfriede had had that effect on me—if my eyes caught sight of her they remained transfixed. That must have been why I found myself quickly following in the wake of her footsteps, reaching the guard and saying, "I need to go too."

In the washroom, Elfriede was closing a stall door when I stopped her.

"Don't you have to go?" she asked.

"No, I can wait. I need to talk to you."

"But I can't wait."

"Elfriede—"

"Listen, Berliner, we don't have much time. Can you keep a secret?"

My organs banged together.

Elfriede slid a hand into her pocket, very gingerly, and pulled out a cigarette and a box of matches. "I come here to sneak a smoke. Secret revealed."

She crouched in one corner of the stall, lit the cigarette, inhaled. Smiling, she blew the smoke into my face. I was leaning against the doorframe, and that breeziness which Elfriede occasionally displayed, rather than dissuading me made me even more anxious to speak to her. She would understand me, she would calm me.

From outside came a woman's voice. Elfriede pulled me against her, quickly shut the door. She took one last puff, put the cigarette out against the tiles, and, holding a finger to her lips, said, *"Shhh,"* as a woman entered and went into one of the free stalls.

We were as close together as the first time, but now Elfriede wasn't trying to intimidate me. She stared at me with two sly eyes I had never seen on her before, the cigarette between her fingers and her left hand fanning the air to dispel the smell of smoke. This rule-breaking spirit amused her, a grunt escaped her nose, and she pinched it shut, tucking her head into her shoulders. We were so close, face-to-face, and all at once I felt like laughing too. For a moment I forgot where I had met her, what had led me to her. For a moment the fullness I felt from inhabiting the same space as her made me as giggly as a schoolgirl. We were two high schoolers, Elfriede and I, hidden away in the washroom, sharing a harmless secret, one that wouldn't have been worth adding to my inventory.

As soon as the woman left the washroom, Elfriede pulled her face close to mine, her forehead touching my forehead. "Should I relight it," she said softly, "or do you think it's dangerous?"

"The guard is probably wondering what happened to us," I replied. "Pretty soon he'll come get us. . . ."

"Right." Her sly eyes sparkled.

She pulled out the matchbox.

"But if you want to light it, I'll wait here with you until you finish it."

"Really?"

"At least two puffs."

The match sputtered, the tiny flame burned the paper.

"Then you take one of them," she said, slipping the cigarette into my mouth.

I drew in the smoke awkwardly. More than inhaling it, I swallowed it. It made me feel slightly nauseous.

"Not even coughing. Well done." Elfriede smiled, taking back the cigarette. She took a deep drag, closing her eyes slightly. She was calm, or at least seemed to be. "And if they happen to catch us, Berliner? What will you do then?"

"I'll stay by your side," I said, resting my hand on my chest theatrically.

"Anyway, if they catch us," she said, "they'll punish *me*. What do you have to do with it?"

Just then the guard decided to knock. "Coming out?"

Elfriede tossed the cigarette into the toilet, flushed it, opened the door to the stall we were hiding in, then the washroom door, and walked out.

We went back in silence, Elfriede suddenly focused on something I couldn't even imagine. Her eyes weren't sparkling anymore, she wasn't laughing, the intimacy of a moment before had vanished. I felt something like shame.

We weren't two high school girls playing around, and I didn't understand her.

In the lunchroom she remembered. "Oh, Berliner, what was it you wanted to talk to me about?"

If I didn't understand her, why would she have understood me?

"Nothing important."

"Oh, no, please. I didn't mean to interrupt you. I'm sorry."

It was too dangerous to tell her, to tell anyone, about Ziegler. How ridiculous, believing I could do it.

"It was nothing, really."

"As you wish."

She seemed disappointed. She headed toward the courtyard and, almost to delay her, to keep her with me a moment longer, I said, "When I was little, while my brother was sleeping I leaned into his crib and bit his hand, hard."

Elfriede didn't reply, waited for me to finish.

"Sometimes I think that's why he doesn't write to me anymore."

32

THOUGH I KNEW ALBERT HAD A WIFE AND CHILDREN, WHEN HE TOLD me he was going home to Bavaria the second week in July it was as if I had never known. During the months when we had been seeing each other, he had never gone away on leave. His family was an abstract concept, wasn't any more real than a husband who was missing or dead or simply resolved never to return to me.

I curled up on my side, isolating myself in the darkness. Albert touched my back, I tried to shake him off, he didn't give up. What did I expect, that he would cancel his leave so I wouldn't be left alone to picture him tucking in his children and climbing into bed with her?

At first it had been easy to think of distancing myself from him—in fact, it had been a need. I imagined him with other women. I saw Ulla riding him, Albert clutching her hips until his nails left marks down her skin as he craned his neck to suck her pointy breasts. I saw Leni shocked at the touch of his fingers between her legs, capillaries bursting on her face as he deflowered her. I fantasized it was Albert who had impregnated Heike. It didn't cause me pain, but relief, a sort of exuberance: I could lose that man.

Nevertheless, the night he told me about his leave it was like having a door slammed in my face. Albert slammed it right before my nose and shut himself up in his bedroom with his wife, with his life separated from mine, and didn't care that I was out there waiting for him.

"What should I do?" he asked, his palm still resting on my back.

"Whatever you want," I replied without turning around. "I'm returning to Berlin after the war, so if you prefer you can forget about me right now."

"But I can't."

It made me laugh. It was no longer the foolish laughter of lovers. The decline had begun and I laughed with spite.

"Why are you being like this?"

"Because you're ridiculous. We're trapped down here and can't wait to get out. On top of that you're an SS officer and you bed a woman who has no choice."

He pulled his palm away from my back. The loss of that contact made me feel in danger. He didn't reply or even get dressed, didn't fall asleep. He lay there, exhausted. I hoped he would touch me again, that he would embrace me. I wanted neither to sleep nor to see the dawn.

I went back to thinking we didn't have any right to speak of love. We were living in a severed era, one that upset all certainty and broke up families, crippled every survival instinct.

AFTER WHAT I told him, he might have been convinced I let him into the barn out of fear and not because of the intimacy between us, which felt age-old.

Between our bodies there was a sort of kinship, as though we had played together as children. As though at eight years old we had bitten each other's wrists to leave behind a "watch," the mark of our dental arches that glistened with saliva. As though we had slept in the same crib long enough to believe each other's warm breath was the very smell of the world.

And yet that intimacy never became habit. I would run a finger down the furrow in the middle of his chest and my personal history would be razed to the ground, time would be suspended, an endless loop. I would rest my hand on his belly and Albert would open his eyes wide, curve his spine.

NEVER HAD I believed I could trust what he told me, because he told me so little. When he spoke, there was a hint of exclusion in his words. He hadn't ended up at the front—a heart murmur had exempted him—but the rigor and devotion with which he had served Germany had made him scale many ranks of the Waffen-SS. Then one day he asked to be assigned to different functions. *Different from what?* I asked him once. He didn't reply.

That night, though, after I rejected him, while I had my back turned to him, in the silence he said, "They committed suicide. We were in Crimea."

I turned toward him. "Who committed suicide?"

"The SS officers, the Wehrmacht officers, all of them. Some became depressed, others alcoholics, others impotent." A grimace turned his face unrecognizable. "And some killed themselves."

"What were you doing there?"

"Some of the women were beautiful. They would stand there, all naked. They had to undress. Their clothes were washed and packed in suitcases to be reused. They would photograph them."

"Who would? What women?"

He lay still, facing the beams overhead almost as though he weren't talking to me.

"People would come out of curiosity, even bring children along, and they would take photographs. Some of them were beautiful—it was impossible to take your eyes off them. One of my men couldn't handle it. One morning I saw him fall to the ground, on his rifle. He'd fainted. Another confessed to me that he couldn't sleep. . . . One must carry out one's duty with joy," he said, raising his voice.

I covered his mouth.

"That's what is expected of us," he went on, his mouth against my hand. He didn't remove it—it was I who pulled away. "What else could I tell him? I knew it, knew the men were fucking them. They fucked them all, even if it was forbidden, but in any case those women would never be able to tell anyone. Double rations of food: getting rid of fifty people a day is hard work even for us." Albert's face furrowed.

Fifty people a day. I was frightened.

"Then, one morning, one of them snapped. Instead of aiming at them, he turned his rifle on us and fired. We returned fire."

I could have known then about the mass graves, about the Jews who lay prone, huddled together, waiting for the shot to the back of the head, could have known about the earth shoveled onto their backs, and the wood ash and calcium hypochlorite so they wouldn't stink, about the new layer of Jews who would lie down on the corpses and offer the backs of their heads in turn. I could have known about the children picked up by the hair and shot, about the kilometer-long lines of Jews or Russians—*They're Asian, they're not like us*—ready to fall into the graves or climb onto trucks to be gassed with carbon monoxide. I could have learned about it before the end of the war. I could have asked. But I was afraid and couldn't speak and didn't want to know.

WHAT DID WE know back then?

In March of '33 the newspaper announced the opening of the camp in Dachau, with its capacity for five thousand. A labor camp, people said. Not that they talked about it willingly. A man who had been there, the doorwoman mumbled, said the detainees had to sing "Horst Wessel Lied" as they were being whipped. *Ah, so that's why they call it a "concert camp,"* joked the street cleaner, continuing to sweep. The street cleaner could have played the enemy propaganda card—everyone played that, to drop the subject—but he hadn't thought fast enough. And those who returned from down there said only, *Please, don't ask me, I can't tell you,* and at that point people certainly did start to worry. *A place for criminals,* the grocer said with assurance, especially if there were clients listening. *A place for dissidents, for Communists, for those who can't keep their mouth shut.* "Dear Lord, make me say nothing they would not allow, I don't want to be sent away to Dachau": it had become a prayer. *They make them put on new boots destined for the Wehrmacht,* people said, *and they walk around in them for a while, to soften them. That way the soldiers who wear them later on don't run the risk of getting blisters on their feet.* At least that risk they avoided. *A reform institute,* the locksmith explained, *you go there and they brainwash you, when you get out you're completely over your desire to grumble.* How did the song go? "Ten Little Grumblers." Even little children knew it. *If you misbehave, I'll send you to Dachau,* parents threatened. Dachau in place of the boogeyman; Dachau, *the* place of the boogeyman.

I had lived in terror at the thought that they might take away my father, who just couldn't keep quiet. *The Gestapo's keeping an eye on you,* one of his coworkers had warned, and my mother had shouted, *Do the words "defamation against the National Socialist State" mean anything to you?* My father didn't answer, slammed the door. What was he aware of, the rail worker? Had he seen them, the trains packed with people? Men, women, and children crammed into cattle cars. Did he too believe the project was only to resettle the Jews out East, like they claimed? And Ziegler, did he know everything? About the extermination camps. About the Final Solution.

NAKED AND FEELING threatened, I felt around for my nightgown. I was afraid he would notice and get angry. He turned toward me.

"They said it wasn't a problem, that we could be reassigned to other functions. And I was one of those who left. There was an abundance of volunteers—that's how I got the transfer. Nothing changed, there were others to fill my place."

I slid away stealthily, slowly, almost as if I weren't authorized to move. "It's dawn," I said, getting up.

He nodded with his chin, his customary gesture. "All right," he said. "Go to bed."

"Have a nice trip."

"See you in twenty days."

I didn't reply. His was a cry for help, but I didn't understand that. No—I denied it to him.

I could make love to Ziegler while ignoring who he was. In the barn there were only our bodies, our joking, and that little boy I had formed an alliance with—nothing else. No one else. I could make love to Ziegler even if I had lost a husband at the front, a husband who had also killed, killed soldiers and civilians, and perhaps he too had become sleepless or impotent or had fucked Russian women—*They're Asian, they're not like us*—because he had learned how to make war, and he knew that was how war was made.

———

YEARS LATER I imagined Ziegler sitting on his cot in Crimea, elbows on his knees, forehead weighing on his interlaced fingers. He doesn't know what to do. He wants to leave, to ask for a transfer. He's afraid it might jeopardize his career. If he leaves the Einsatzgruppen, he'll probably never be given any more promotions. It isn't a question of morals. Russians, Jews, Gypsies . . . he's never cared anything about them. He doesn't hate them, but he doesn't love the human race either, and he certainly doesn't believe in the value of life.

How could anyone see value in something that can end at any moment, something so fragile? One sees value in things that have strength, which life doesn't, in things that are indestructible, and life isn't—to the point that someone might come along and ask you to sacrifice your life for something that has more strength. The homeland, for example. Gregor had decided to do that, by enlisting.

It isn't a matter of faith. Ziegler has seen it with his own eyes, the miracle that is Germany. He's often heard his men say, *If Hitler were to die, I would want to die as well.* Everything considered, life matters so little, and devoting it to someone fills it with meaning. Even after Stalingrad the men continue to have faith in the Führer, and the women to send him birthday gifts of cushions they've embroidered with eagles and swastikas. Hitler has said his life won't end with death: that is when it will begin. Ziegler knows he's right.

He's proud to be on the right side. No one loves losers. And no one loves the entire human race. One can't cry over the interrupted existences of billions of individuals starting from six million years ago. Wasn't that perhaps the original agreement, that every existence on earth had to be broken off sooner or later? Hearing with one's own ears the distressed neighs of a horse being tortured causes more torment than the thought of some unknown man who's dead, dead because history is made of dead men.

There's no such thing as universal compassion—only being moved to compassion before the fate of a single human being. The elderly rabbi who prays with his hands on his chest because he knows he's about to die. The Jewish lady, so beautiful, about to be disfigured. The Russian woman who's locked her legs around your hips and for a moment makes you feel so protected.

Or Adam Wortmann, the mathematics teacher, whom they arrested before my eyes. The victim who back then incarnated for me all the others, all the victims of the Reich, of the planet, of God's sin.

ZIEGLER IS AFRAID he won't get used to the horror and will spend every night sitting on his cot without closing an eye. He's afraid he *will* get used to the horror and will stop feeling pity for anyone, even his own children. He's afraid he'll go insane. He needs to ask for the transfer.

His Hauptsturmführer will be disappointed—of all people, Ziegler, who had never backed down, who had persevered despite his health problems. Who's going to inform Himmler? He had made an excellent impression, he won't accept having made a mistake.

Ziegler has blood that hisses instead of flowing silently without bothering anyone. It seems to be roaring as he's on his cot and isn't getting sleepy. And so he asks to be transferred and gives up everything, but his heart doesn't stop hissing. It's defective, it can't be fixed, there's no remedy for things that are born flawed. Life, for example. There's no remedy for it. Death is its destination. Why shouldn't men take advantage of that?

When he arrives in Krausendorf, Obersturmführer Albert Ziegler realizes he's going to remain Obersturmführer forever. No more ranks to scale. He has a loser's longing for vengeance and imposes the same strictness that took him to the top, and yet he feels like he's falling apart. Then one night he comes to my window and begins to stare at me.

FOR YEARS I thought that his secrets—the secrets he couldn't confess, the secrets I didn't want to hear—were what kept me from truly loving him. That was foolishness. I knew little more about my husband. We had lived under the same roof for barely a year and then he set off for the war. No, I didn't know him. Besides, it's between strangers that love happens, between people who don't know each other and are eager to break down the barriers. It happens between people who frighten each other. It wasn't the secrets but the fall of the Third Reich that our love couldn't survive.

33

In summertime the smell of the swamps grew so powerful that it was as though everything around me were decomposing. I wondered if I too would soon begin to rot. It wasn't Gross-Partsch that was ruining me—I had been tainted from the start.

July '44 heaped muggy days upon us, the humidity making our clothes stick to our skin, along with platoons of crane flies: they besieged us, hounded us relentlessly.

There had been no news from Albert since his departure. Everyone disappeared without writing to me anymore.

One Thursday, right after work, Ulla, Leni, and I went to see a film with Heiner and Ernst. The heat was unbearable. Shut up inside the tent, without even a window to let in some air, we would suffocate. But Ulla insisted. The idea of a movie after lunch had her all excited, and Leni wanted to spend time with Ernst. *Come on, please, come on*, she kept saying.

The film was almost ten years old and had met with incredible success. It had been shot by a woman, one who always did as she pleased—at least that was what Ulla said, and Ulla knew everything about the people in show business. Maybe she had read it in the magazines she thumbed through back at the barracks, or maybe it was her own notion, but she was convinced there were feelings between the director and the Führer. After all, the woman was rather pretty.

"She has the same name as you," Ernst told Leni, opening the tent to let her in. "Leni Riefenstahl." Leni smiled and shyly looked around inside for a place to sit. She had never seen the movie, unlike me.

The wooden benches were almost all full. The soldiers had rested their muddy boots on the spots in front of them. When they saw us come in, some of them composed themselves and wiped off the wood with the back of their hands while others stayed there, leaning back casually, arms crossed, with no intention of disturbing their torpor. Sabine and Gertrude were there too. I recognized them by the braids coiled on the sides of their heads. They turned around and though noticing us didn't stoop to acknowledge our presence.

We sat down in the spots our chaperones found for us—Ernst and Leni in a row on the right, Heiner, Ulla, and me on the left.

Wild about all kinds of technological innovation, Heiner said *Triumph of the Will* was an avant-garde film. He was thrilled by its aerial shots, the plane slicing through the clouds, penetrating the sooty white mass without fear of getting stuck in it.

I read the words superimposed on the images—"20 years after the outbreak of the World War," "16 years after the beginning of German suffering," "19 months after the beginning of the German rebirth"— and the clouds seemed to come rushing at me, blinding me. From up there, with the tall bell towers, Nuremberg was beautiful. The shadow that the plane cast over it was an anointing, not a threat.

Glancing at Leni, I saw her lips parted, her tongue between her teeth, struggling to understand everything there was to understand. Maybe before the movie was over Ernst would put his arm around her waist. Maybe Leni's jutted-out chin was the sign of expectation, an offer being made.

I fanned myself with my hands, and when Heiner announced, "Here, it's going to land now," to get Ulla and me to pay attention, I grumbled. On the screen, the Führer's nape was too bare, as pitiful as any bare nape, and the Wagnerian exaltation in the background did nothing to remedy it. The Führer returned the simultaneous salute of the thousands of raised arms but kept his elbow bent, and his hand wobbled on his wrist—almost as if he were excusing himself, *I have nothing to do with it.*

I couldn't have known, only later would I learn, that just then, not far from the tent that the soldiers had set up as a movie theater, another hand was fumbling around a briefcase. Though lacking two fingers, the hand clutched a pair of pliers and broke a glass capsule to release the acid that would corrode the wire, a thin metal wire. Ten minutes and it would dissolve.

The colonel gritted his teeth, and his nostrils flared. He had to wrap everything in a shirt and shove it back into the briefcase, well hidden among the documents, and to do so he had only one hand—actually, only three fingers. His forehead was beaded with sweat, but not from the muggy air.

Time was up. The meeting had been moved back to twelve-thirty because of Mussolini's imminent visit, and Field Marshal Keitel, who was waiting outside his quarters in the Wolfsschanze, quarters which the colonel had made up an excuse to return to, called out to him to hurry up. He was running out of patience. Even earlier Keitel had taken the liberty of pressing him, though with the respect due to a wounded officer such as Claus Schenk Graf von Stauffenberg, the charming colonel of whom Maria was so fond.

Stauffenberg came out carrying the briefcase. Keitel scrutinized it. Nothing more normal than going to a meeting with a briefcase full of documents, but perhaps Stauffenberg was gripping it too tightly, and that was the odd detail that stuck out to Keitel. "They're all here," the colonel said. "The documents about the new Volksgrenadier divisions I'll be presenting to the Führer." The field marshal nodded and walked alongside him. Any odd detail became of secondary importance, given their urgent need to arrive at the meeting in the Lagebaracke.

I was sweating inside that unbearable tent where I had gone only to please Leni, who was talking intently with Ernst and giggling, her cheeks sprayed red, along with her ears and neck, as if the blotches had invaded every centimeter of her skin.

Ulla was spying on them instead of watching the movie, and Heiner had started drumming his fingers on the bench. He was bored by the speeches of the party officials—not because of what they were saying but because of the repetition of the shots. He tapped his pointer finger on the wood almost as if to tell the orators to hurry up, but at the National Socialist Party Congress of September 5, 1934, everyone wanted to speak their mind. Rudolf Hess, who that day hadn't yet been declared insane by Hitler, shouted from the screen, "You were our guarantor of victory. You'll be our guarantor of peace."

Who knew if General Heusinger would agree with that prediction? I couldn't have known, only later would I learn, that when Stauffenberg walked into the conference room, Deputy Chief of the General Staff Heusinger, to Hitler's right, was reading a discouraging report. It said that after the latest breach of the central Russian front, the position of the German troops had become very dangerous. Keitel glared at Stauffenberg: the meeting had already begun. *Twelve thirty-six,* the colonel thought, *six minutes and the acid will eat through the wire.*

His back to the door, sitting at a heavy oak table, Hitler was fiddling with the magnifying glass he needed to study the maps spread out in front of him. Keitel sat down to his left while Stauffenberg took a place beside Heinz Brandt. While in our tent Dietrich's recorded voice demanded that the foreign press tell the truth about Germany, Colonel Stauffenberg's nostrils flared again as he breathed deeply. Anyone who looked him in the eye would have understood, but he wore a patch over the left one and his head was bowed. Trembling slightly, he pushed the briefcase under the table with his foot, slid it across the floor so it was as close as possible to the Führer's legs. He licked off a drop of sweat that had trickled to his lips and slowly, one step after the other, left the room. No one took any notice. They were focused on the map Heusinger was gesturing at grimly. Four minutes, Stauffenberg counted, and the wire would be completely consumed.

In the makeshift movie theater set up by the Wehrmacht soldiers, Ernst took Leni's hand and she didn't pull back. In fact, she rested her head on his shoulder. Ulla looked away, bit her fingernail, and Heiner nudged me, though not to comment on their idyllic scene. "The second part is amazing. Remember when the eagle fills the entire shot, without sound?" he asked me, almost as though the quality of the movie were a question of honor—his own. From the screen came Streicher's admonishment: "A people that does not protect its racial purity will perish!"

Inside Stauffenberg's briefcase, the metal wire was corroding. Expressionless, the colonel walked away from the building somewhat stiffly. He certainly couldn't run, but his heart was thumping as though he were running.

In the Lagebaracke, Heinz Brandt leaned over the map for a better look—the writing was tiny and it wasn't like he had a magnifying glass—and knocked his boot into the abandoned briefcase. He pushed it away from them with an automatic gesture, absorbed as he was in Heusinger's report.

Twelve-forty. Stauffenberg didn't stop. Stiffly, he carried on walking. Two minutes left.

"Make the German worker an upright, upstanding, proud, and decent citizen, enjoying equal rights!" Ley's voice thundered inside the tent, and by then Ernst was already holding Leni tightly against him. He seemed to be planning to kiss her. Even Heiner noticed. Ulla was just about to stand up and leave when he stopped her by whispering in her ear, "Have you seen the lovebirds?" I thought of my father, of when he said Nazism had done away with class conflict through conflict among the races.

Standing straight-backed on the screen, Adolf Hitler personally saluted the army of fifty-two thousand labor service men in attendance, all lined up in rows.

"Shoulder spades!" he shouted.

The spades snapped back like rifles and a deafening blast thundered through the tent, hurling us off the bench. I felt my head slam against the ground, then nothing, no pain.

As I died, I had a final thought: Hitler was dying too.

34

For several hours after the explosion, I couldn't hear out of one ear.

A shrill whistle pierced my eardrum, monotonous, relentless, like the sirens in Berlin. Whatever note it was, it rang in my skull, muffling the outside world, cocooning me from the havoc that had been wrought.

A bomb had exploded inside the Wolfsschanze.

"Hitler is dead," said the soldiers, scrambling back and forth. The projector, left atilt by the blast, played only darkness, a constant hum, and Leni trembled with the same desperation as she had the first day in the lunchroom. She was no longer concerned with Ernst, who in a state of panic was asking Heiner, "What do we do now?" Heiner didn't reply.

"He's dead," said Ulla, and she was surprised, because no one would ever have believed in Hitler's death. She had gotten back to her feet before the rest of us, had looked around as though drowsy, and said, "It's over." It was barely a murmur.

Facedown, I saw my mother's eyes, the nightgown under her coat. She had died dressed in a ridiculous outfit. I had hugged her, her scent lingered on her, I had seen my mother dead beneath the bombs as a tone I couldn't identify rang in my eardrums. It was a punishment devised just for me, I thought.

But the Führer was enduring the same pain as me, and not only that. To make his way out of the wreckage of the Lagebaracke, he leaned on a miraculously unscathed Keitel, though most of the people at the far end of the table had been wounded and four officers, including Brandt, had died on the spot. With his chimney-sweep face, his smoking head, marionette arm, and striped trousers like a hula skirt, Hitler looked far more ridiculous than my mother.

It's just that he was alive. And determined to get revenge.

HE ANNOUNCED IT over the radio at about one in the morning. Herta, Joseph, and I listened to him as we sat around the kitchen table, exhausted yet awake. We had done nothing but sit glued to the radio, even forgetting to eat dinner. That day the afternoon shift in Krausendorf had been canceled, the bus hadn't come to get me, and in any case they wouldn't have found me. I managed to return only several hours later, on foot and speechless, leaving behind Leni and Ulla, who couldn't stop speculating: What would happen now that Hitler was dead?

But Hitler was alive, and through the Deutschlandsender microphones he delivered a message to the nation and all of Europe: the fact that he had escaped death was a sign that he would accomplish the task entrusted to him by Providence.

Mussolini had said so too. Having arrived at four in the afternoon due to a delay with his train—though the meeting had been held early to accommodate him—he wandered the ruins with his battered friend, who the year before had sent a Nazi commando to Gran Sasso to free him from the prison where he had been confined.

Hitler's calves were burned and one of his arms was paralyzed. Nevertheless he had taken Mussolini around the ruins because if he had gone to bed, as his doctor advised, who knew what nonsense the world would start saying about him?

Faced with the danger his friend had undergone, the Duce wielded his expected optimism: it was impossible for the two of them to lose, after that miracle. And he was the one who had granted that miracle, though Hitler didn't realize it. The change of schedule had caused problems for his assailants, who'd had time to arm only one of the two bombs they had planned to set off, and one hadn't been enough. Mussolini had saved his life.

Over the radio the Führer screamed that it had been the work of a band of criminals, people who had nothing in common with the spirit of the Wehrmacht, nor with that of the German people. They would be mercilessly annihilated.

Joseph chomped down on his pipe, his jaw creaking. He had risked losing me too, not only a son he had never buried, and the rigid posture with which he sat, his fist clenched on the tablecloth, kept away even Zart, who was crouching beneath the table.

The whistling in my head continued to torture me. Then Hitler uttered Stauffenberg's name: it was like being stabbed in the ear, which I covered with my hand. The contrast between the hot cartilage and my cool palm momentarily soothed me.

Stauffenberg was responsible, the Führer said, and I thought of Maria. I had no way of knowing that the colonel had already been shot, nor what fate was in store for my friend.

The window was open on that July night. No one was on the road, the barn was closed. The frogs croaked unperturbed, oblivious to the risk that their master had run just hours ago, oblivious to the fact that they even had a master.

"We will settle accounts in the way we National Socialists are accustomed," Hitler shouted, and Joseph's pipe snapped between his teeth.

35

Maria was arrested the next day along with her husband, taken to Berlin, and locked up in prison. The news spread around town immediately, spreading down the milk line and around the well, through the fields at dawn, and even at Moy Lake, where children were playing in the water, including Heike's, who had learned to swim. Everyone imagined the big castle empty now that the baron and baroness were gone and the servants had had to bar the shutters. I imagined the townspeople breaking down a door, the servants' entrance perhaps, and being surrounded by a luxury, a magnificence that they had never witnessed before, then leaving through the front door as though after a soirée, perhaps hiding booty under their shirts or in their trousers. But the castle was guarded day and night, and no one could go inside.

Joseph was out of a job too. "It's better off this way," Herta said. "You're old. Haven't you noticed?" She seemed angry at him for having had anything to do with the baroness, but actually she was only worried that they would come to interrogate him, to capture him.

She was concerned about me too, and grilled me: What had I spoken about with that woman, did I know who she really was, had I met any strange people at her home? Suddenly Maria had become dangerous, someone it would be better to keep a distance from. My kind, spoiled friend. They had locked her in a cell without sheet music, had taken from her the gown with the bias cut she had had made, the one almost identical to mine.

Hitler had decided to act swiftly, the people's court instead of a military court, summary trials and immediate executions by hanging, a noose around the neck, one made of a piano string hung from a butcher's hook. Not only those suspected of having had even the slightest part in the assassination attempt, but even their relatives and friends were all rounded up and deported, and anyone who offered refuge to those being sought was executed. Clemens von Mildernhagen and his wife Maria had been Colonel Stauffenberg's longtime friends, they had had him over to the castle on many occasions. According to the prosecution, Stauffenberg had plotted with other conspirators there; the baron and baroness of Gross-Partsch were devious.

But what did the prosecution know about Maria's universal enthusiasm, about her smoothly polished thoughts? She knew about flowers, songs, and little else, only what she needed. Maybe the colonel had schemed behind their backs, secretly using the castle as a base for his meetings, maybe the baron had been in on it and had kept his wife in the dark. I had no idea. After all, I didn't have a relationship with him. I knew, though, that Maria had loved both Stauffenberg and Hitler, and they had both betrayed her.

On my bedside table, next to the oil lamp, was the last book she had given me, which I hadn't returned to her: poems by Stefan George. Her dear Claus had given it to her, according to the dedication written on the frontispiece. It must have been very precious to her, and yet she had lent it to me. Suddenly I realized that Maria cared about me, more than I cared about her, that more than anything else I was amused by the levity with which she interacted with the world.

I tore the pages out of the book one by one, crumpled them up, and lit a small fire in the backyard. Seeing the flickering flames rise and twist, Zart scurried into the house. I was burning a book all on my own, with neither a band nor oxcarts, nor even the clucking of the hens to celebrate. I was terrified by the possibility that if the Nazis came looking for me they might find Stauffenberg's dedication on the book of George poems and arrest me. I was burning a book to renounce Maria. But the fire, which destroyed all I had left of her, was also the clumsy rite by which I was saying goodbye.

Joseph was interrogated. They soon released him, and no one came for me. I don't know what became of Maria's sons. They were only children and, as everyone knows, Germans love children.

THE NEW DIRECTIVES to defend the Führer also involved us food tasters. Forced to pack suitcases, we were taken from our homes. Herta watched me disappear around the Gross-Partsch bend, my nose glued to the bus window, and anxiety stung her like it had on my first day.

In the courtyard, in addition to searching us, the guards checked our suitcases. Only after that could we go inside. Krausendorf became lunch, dinner, and dormitory. It became our prison. We were allowed to sleep at home only on Fridays and Saturdays. The rest of our time was dedicated to the Führer, who had bought our whole lives, and for the same price—no negotiations allowed. Segregated in the barracks, we were soldiers without weapons, high-ranking slaves.

ZIEGLER RETURNED THE day after the assassination attempt, entered the lunchroom, and announced that as of that moment we would be under constant surveillance. Recent events had demonstrated that no one could be trusted, much less us, lowly country women accustomed to lying with beasts, what did we know about honor, or loyalty, we had probably heard it over the microphones of the German radio—*Always practice loyalty and honesty*—but that went in one ear and came out the other with us potential traitors, who would sell our children for a piece of bread and spread our legs for anyone, given the opportunity. He, however, would isolate us like caged animals. Things would be different now that he was back.

The SS guards hung their heads. To me they looked embarrassed by his rambling tirade that had nothing to do with the bombing. It seemed more like a personal outburst. Maybe the Obersturmführer had caught his wife in bed with another man, they thought. Maybe he had been browbeaten at home—some women bossed their men around—so now he had to make up for it by pounding his chest and raising his voice: ten females kept in check were what he needed to feel like a man, control over an unusual barracks made him feel that he had power, that he was authorized to abuse it.

I was the one who thought that.

Air whistled through Elfriede's nostrils and Augustine cursed beneath her breath, with the risk that Ziegler might hear. I stared at him, waiting for his eyes to meet mine, but he avoided them. That was what had me convinced he was talking to me. Or he had simply drawn from a list of clichés to piece together an effective speech, one with just the right dose of insults, like any monologue to which no reply is expected. Maybe he had something to hide, he, who had been chatting with Stauffenberg and the baron that May night at the castle. I wondered if his colleagues had grilled him, if someone had suspected him. Or if he had become so unimportant that no one had noticed him together with the man behind the conspiracy and his presumed accomplices. Ziegler was frustrated, furious: just when something tremendous happened, he hadn't been there.

Then I told myself it was plausible that he had gone back to Bavaria at that very moment on purpose, that I had understood nothing, neither about him nor about Maria, they had all lied to me. I never learned the truth, never asked.

COTS WERE LAID out for us in the classrooms on the second floor, an area of the barracks we had never been to before. Three tasters per room, except for the larger one, in which they put four cots. They let us choose our beds and our roommates. I took the one against the wall beside Elfriede, and then there was Leni. Looking out the window, I saw two guards. They paced the school perimeter, the patrol lasting all night. One of them noticed me and ordered me to get to bed. The Wolf was on guard, keeping close watch, wounded and burned, a trapped and vicious creature. And Ziegler slept in the outermost ring of the Wolfsschanze; the heart of the headquarters was off-limits to him.

"I miss you," he said a few mornings later, crossing paths with me in the hallway. I had fallen behind. My ankle had buckled and I had lost a shoe. The SS guard watched me from a distance as he walked the line of women to the lunchroom. "I miss you." I looked up, my foot still bare, my ankle throbbing. The guard came over in a show of concern and I slipped my shoe on, sliding a finger into the heel as I teetered on only one leg. My instinct was to lean on Albert, and his instinct was to support me. He held out a hand. I had known his body and couldn't touch it. I couldn't believe it had been his, now that I wasn't touching it anymore.

A love like that, which has no past, no promises, no obligations, dies out from indolence. The body grows lazy, it prefers inertia to the effort of desire. Just being able to touch him again—his chest, his belly, simply my hand on the fabric of his uniform—would have been enough to feel time fall to dust, enough to open wide the depth of our intimacy. But Albert froze and I composed myself. Standing up straight, I began walking again without replying. The guard who had just reached me clicked his heels and saluted him by extending his arm just as Obersturmführer Ziegler let his own arm fall.

36

On Saturdays and Sundays, during my hours off work, I spent my time with Herta and Joseph. We picked vegetables in the garden, wandered the forest, sat out back chatting or saying nothing, grateful all three of us could be there in the same place, I having lost my parents, they their child. It was on that shared loss, on the very experience of loss, that we based our bond.

I still wondered whether they suspected my nights with Ziegler. Having deceived them made me feel unworthy of their affection, though it didn't make mine any less sincere. That it was possible to omit parts of one's existence, that it was so easy, had always shocked me; but it's only by being oblivious to others' lives as they pass by, it's thanks only to this physiological lack of information, that we avoid going insane.

My sense of guilt had extended to Herta and Joseph because Herta and Joseph were right there in flesh and blood, while Gregor was a name, a thought upon waking, a picture in the mirror frame or the photo album, a handful of memories, a sudden outburst of tears at night, a feeling of anger and defeat and shame. He was an idea, Gregor. He was no longer my husband.

If I wasn't with my in-laws, I dedicated my free time to Leni, who wanted to meet up with Ernst when he went off duty but was afraid to go alone. And so she would bring along me and Ulla, or Beate and Heike with their respective children. Some days even Elfriede would come, despite the fact she couldn't stand the two Wehrmacht soldiers and did nothing to hide it.

"So am I a great soothsayer or aren't I?" Beate said early one Sunday afternoon, sitting at a little table in a café on Moy Lake.

"You mean about Hitler?" Elfriede said, provoking her. "You predicted things would go badly for him, and as you can see you got it wrong."

"What did you predict?" Ernst asked.

"She's a witch," Ulla said. "She did his horoscope."

"Well, actually he did risk dying," Heiner said. "You weren't far off, Beate. No one can bring down our Führer, though."

Elfriede stared at him hard. Heiner didn't notice. He drank deep from his beer stein and wiped his mouth with the back of his hand.

"We risked dying ourselves," she pointed out. "They almost managed to poison us, and we don't even know what with."

"It wasn't poison," I said. "It was honey, tainted honey."

"How do you know that?" she asked me.

All at once my legs went rubbery.

"I don't know," I stammered. "I . . . I deduced it. The ones who got sick had eaten honey."

"Where was the honey?"

"In the dessert, Elfriede."

"Actually, it's true," Heike said. "Beate and I didn't throw up . . . you two were the only ones who ate dessert that day."

"Sure, but there was yogurt on the cake too. Besides, Theodora and Gertrude were sick, and it's not like they ate dessert. They were eating dairy." Elfriede was irritated. "How can you say it was the honey, Rosa?"

"I've already told you, I don't know. I just guessed."

"No, you stated it as a fact. Did you find it out from Krümel?"

"Krümel doesn't even talk to her anymore!" Ulla said. Then she turned to the two soldiers and, to include them in the conversation, explained, "She got in lots of trouble, our Rosa." The two said nothing, not understanding.

"I can blame that on Augustine. On Augustine and the rest of you," I said, turning to Heike and Beate.

"Don't change the subject," Elfriede said stubbornly. "How do you know it's true? Tell me."

"She's a soothsayer too!" Beate joked.

"What's a soothsayer?" little Ursula asked.

My legs without a drop of strength. "Why are you getting so worked up, Elfriede? I told you I don't know. I was talking about it with my father-in-law. We must've figured it out together."

"If you think about it, they didn't serve us honey again for a while after that," Ulla said, thinking aloud. "What a shame. The cake you let me sneak a taste of was delicious, Rosa."

"Exactly, you see?" I said, seizing the opportunity. "Maybe I figured it out from the fact that they stopped giving us honey. In any case, what difference does it make now?"

"What's a soothsayer?" Ursula repeated.

"It's a witch who can tell what's going to happen," Beate told her.

"Mother knows how," one of her twins bragged.

"It still makes a difference, Rosa." Elfriede wouldn't stop staring at me. I couldn't hold her gaze.

"If you'll let me continue!" Beate said, raising her voice. "I wasn't talking about the Führer. I'm not as good with horoscopes as I am with cards, and Ziegler stole those from me." The tremor I always felt whenever he was mentioned. "I was talking about Leni."

Leni shook herself from the enchantment she fell into whenever Ernst was near.

He pulled her closer and kissed her forehead. "You predicted Leni's future?"

"She saw a man." I spoke in a low voice as though not to be heard by Elfriede, so she would forget I was there.

"And some people think he showed up," she said. Only I heard the sarcasm in her voice, or maybe the guilt I felt over lying to her distorted my perception.

Ernst drew his mouth to Leni's already ruby-red ear. "Is it me?" He laughed. Heiner did too, as did Leni. I followed suit, forcing a laugh.

We were all laughing. We hadn't learned anything. We thought it was still all right to laugh, thought we could trust—trust life, trust the future.

Elfriede didn't. She stared at the bottom of her cup, the idea of reading the coffee grounds not even occurring to her. She had waged a battle to the death with the future, and none of us had noticed.

THE SAME NIGHT that Leni's enchantment was shattered, the Abduction returned. As Leni silently pushed back her sheets and left the room barefoot, Elfriede was breathing hard—not snoring, it was a sort of squeak. I was covered with sweat, but no one was holding me close.

I was sleeping deeply, dreaming, and at first I wasn't there in the dream. There was a pilot, and he was hot. He drank a sip of water, slid his finger under his collar, then prepared to fly the plane in a perfect curve. In the bull's-eye he saw a red patch in the darkness, a fiery moon, or the star of Bethlehem—this time, however, the Magi wouldn't follow it, there was no newborn king to pay tribute to. And yet in Berlin a young woman with a creamy complexion and red hair, a woman exactly like Maria, had just gone into labor, and in the dark of a cellar that resembled the one in Budengasse a mother whose son was at the front said, *Push, I'll help you,* and an instant later the blast of a bomb sent her hurtling backward. The children who were sleeping woke up wailing, the ones awake began to scream, the cellar became a mass grave in which their bodies would be piled up once the lack of oxygen had snuffed them out. Pauline wasn't there.

When Maria's heartbeat stopped, her unborn child lost its only chance to come into the world. It remained floating in the placenta, oblivious that its destiny had been to come out—how strange, one death that contains another.

Outside, instead, there was oxygen. It fed the flames, which rose dozens of meters and illuminated the now-roofless buildings. In the explosion the rooftops had flown off like Dorothy's house in *The Wonderful Wizard of Oz,* trees and billboards whirled through the air, and the gaping holes in the houses would have revealed—if someone had peeked inside them—the vices and virtues of their inhabitants: an ashtray still dirty with cigarette butts or a vase full of flowers that remained standing though the walls around it collapsed. Neither men nor animals, however, were in any condition to peek—they were curled up on the floor or had already been burned to cinders, black statues captured in the act of drinking, of praying, of caressing their wife to make up after a foolish argument. Night-shift workers had melted in the boiling water of the burst furnaces, prison inmates had been buried alive under the rubble before having finished serving their time, and at the zoo the lions and tigers lay still, looking like they had been stuffed.

Ten thousand feet overhead, the bombardier could still see that incandescent light in the bull's-eye and drink another sip of water and undo a button, could tell himself that the light was nothing but a cluster of stars—that was why, although dead, they continued to shine.

Then, suddenly, the bombardier was me. I was the one moving the controls, and the very instant I realized it I remembered I didn't know how to maneuver those controls. I was going to crash. The fighter plane began to plummet, air pockets spun around in my chest, and the city came closer and closer. It was Berlin, or maybe Nuremberg, and the plane's pointy nose was aimed straight at it, about to smash into the first wall it encountered, plunge into the ground. My vocal cords were anesthetized, I couldn't call out for Franz to tear me out of the grip of the Abduction.

"Help me!"

I awoke, my limbs covered with a film of ice-cold sweat.

"Help me, Rosa."

It was Leni, and she was crying. Elfriede also woke up. She switched on the flashlight she kept under her pillow. The SS guards hadn't thought of furnishing the classrooms with bedside tables and lamps, but she had thought ahead. She saw that little slip of a girl kneeling beside my bed and asked, "What happened?"

I pulled myself up to put my arms around Leni but she wouldn't let me. She touched herself between the legs.

"Tell me what happened!" Elfriede insisted.

Leni opened her hand: the palm was pale, its lines jagged and deep. They formed a grid of barbed wire; who knew what Beate would have read in it? Her fingertips were bloody. "He hurt me," she said, crumpling onto the floor. She curled up into a ball, becoming so tiny I thought she might disappear.

Elfriede ran barefoot into the hall—her heels thudding fiercely, with rage—and stopped by the only open window. Leaning out, she saw the rails of a ladder propped against the wall and, in the vanishing point where the two lines converged, Ernst's silhouette. He had just rested his feet on the ground.

"You'll pay for this," she promised him, her fingers gripping the windowsill. The guards might hear her. She didn't care. Where had they been while a soldier from the army had snuck into the barracks? Had they been distracted? Had they turned a blind eye? Had they been hitting the bottle? *Go ahead and run, my friend, but tomorrow it's my move.*

Ernst looked up, didn't reply, ran off.

WHEN HE ASKED her to meet him at midnight at the third window in the hallway on the left, Leni agreed. *You're an adult,* she told herself, *you can't back out of it.* Besides, Ernst liked Leni that way, never knowing what to say, frugal with her words, an eternal beginner. He seemed amused by precisely that—the constant need to coax her out into the open from where she'd hidden herself away, the light touch of a finger on her shoulder to bring her back without making her jump out of her skin.

Leni couldn't disappoint him, couldn't risk losing him, that was why she had said, *Yes, I'll be there,* and at the stroke of midnight, despite the darkness, despite the guards, she had appeared at the window, which she had left open a crack before dinner so it could be opened without making noise when Ernst scrambled up the ladder. The moment he crawled in through the window they joyfully embraced, united by their secret, conspiring romantically, excited by the need to elude the security, and looked for a classroom where they could hide away and be together. Unfortunately the classrooms were all occupied because in the only one without cots SS guards were playing cards to kill the boredom of their nighttime shift.

"Let's go to the kitchen," Ernst suggested. "The guards certainly won't include it in their rounds."

Leni shook her head. "We'd need to go downstairs, they would discover us!"

Ernst held her tight. "Do you trust me?" And without realizing it Leni was already going down the steps, and no one heard them, no one stopped them. Holding the sergeant by the hand, Leni guided him to the kitchen. What a disappointment to learn that Krümel had bolted it shut. It came as no surprise, though; the Führer's food supplies were stored there. *Give Krümel the respect he's due, or there will be no cake for you,* the chef would say. Leni didn't want to disrespect him and felt ashamed. Perhaps noticing how sorry she was, Ernst stroked her cheeks, ears, neck, nape, back, sides, thighs, in a moment had pulled her against him, closer than ever before, the protrusions of her body pressing against his, his lips on hers in a long kiss, and, walking backward, slowly, maintaining contact the whole time, he led her through the first unlocked door he found.

It was the lunchroom, though only when he bumped into a chair in the dim light coming through the windows did Leni realize it. But then, how could she ask for anything better? The room was familiar to her, the crude table made of heavy wood, the unadorned chairs, the bare walls—for almost a year now she had spent several hours a day in this room, it was a second home, there was no need for her to be afraid, she wasn't anymore, she could do it, *Slow your breathing, Leni, or better yet, take a deep breath, you're grown up now, you can't back out of it. As a child Ernst would throw paper airplanes out the window of his classroom in Lübeck and dream of flying while you were learning to read, held your finger beneath each printed letter, moved it mechanically across the page, saying aloud one syllable at a time until pronouncing the entire word, and you dreamed of becoming very good at it one day, better than the classmates who didn't need to use their finger, could already read so quickly that they got fed up waiting for you. And you didn't know you two would meet years and years later, you and that boy who wanted to become a pilot—this is the astonishing thing about love, all the years when neither of you knew the other even existed, and you lived far away, hundreds of kilometers apart, and you grew up and grew tall, him more than you, and you filled out and he was shaving already and you both came down with fevers and got better and school ended and it was Christmas and you learned to cook and one day he was conscripted and it all happened without you having met each other, you might never have met each other, what a risk you both ran, the very thought tugs at your heart—it would have taken nothing, the slightest deviation, a slower footstep, a poorly wound watch, a more attractive woman met a moment before seeing you, just one moment before, Leni, or simply Hitler not invading Poland.*

Ernst slowly moves the chairs aside, takes Leni in his arms, and rests her on the table, the same one at which we food tasters eat, the same one Leni moved away from to vomit on her first day, and because of that patent weakness of hers I chose her as a friend, or she chose me. When she finds herself lying on the wood—her nightgown too thin not to feel her backbone pressing against the hard surface—Leni doesn't resist, this time doesn't ask to leave.

Ernst stretches out on top of her. At first it's his shadow that engulfs her, then the muscles of a young soldier rejected by the Luftwaffe that weigh heavier and heavier on her hips, on the knees that Leni doesn't know to spread.

She'll have to learn—all girls do, and she will too. You can get used to anything, to eating on command, gulping it all down, holding back waves of nausea, braving poison, death, oatmeal, *Heike, you have to taste it, otherwise Ziegler will be angry, we don't need women who don't obey, here people do what I want, which is what the Führer wants, which is what God wants.*

"Ernst!" His name escapes her all at once, as a sob.

"Darling," he moans.

"Ernst, I need to go. I can't do it in here, I can't be here, I don't want to be."

It was then, as I slept and the Abduction returned, as Elfriede slept and breathed hard through her nose, in our shared bedroom upstairs, three beds, one empty, as the other women tried to fall asleep despite their concern for their children, whom they had been forced to entrust to their grandparents, to a sister, a friend, they certainly couldn't bring them along to the barracks, couldn't escape by jumping out the window—if only they knew there was a ladder—it was then that Ernst tried the kind way to persuade Leni, and since that didn't work, since she was struggling and making noise, he covered her mouth with his hand and did as he pleased. After all, she had shown up for the rendezvous. She knew it was going to happen. That was the only reason he was there that night.

37

Elfriede stood up from the table and walked toward the Beanpole. Leni saw the feisty bounce in her step and understood—she, who was so unintuitive. "Wait!" she cried. Elfriede didn't wait. "It's none of your business," Leni said, also getting up. "It's none of your concern."

"You think you don't have any rights?"

The question disoriented Leni, who was already blue in the face.

"A right is a responsibility," Elfriede added.

"And so?"

"If you can't assume it, someone will have to do it for you."

"Why are you doing this to me?" Leni's voice was breaking.

"I'm doing something to you? Me?" Elfriede sniffed, drew a breath. "Do you enjoy victimhood?"

"It's not your problem."

"It's everyone's problem, don't you see?" Elfriede shouted.

The Beanpole shouted even louder. He pulled away from the corner, ordering them both to be quiet and sit down.

"I need to talk to you," Elfriede told him.

"What do you want?" he asked.

Leni made one last attempt. "Please . . . ," but Elfriede pushed her out of the way and I went to her aid. I wasn't trying to take Leni's side, it was just that she was the weaker one, she always had been.

"I need to inform Lieutenant Ziegler of an event that occurred in the barracks," Elfriede explained, "an event that is an offense to the barracks itself."

The grimace on the Beanpole's face might have been astonishment. No one had ever demanded an audience with Ziegler, not even the Fanatics. He probably didn't know if such a request was legitimate, but what Elfriede said confused him. Besides, that argument between two food tasters, it must have had some significance.

"Out in the courtyard, all of you," he ordered with a certain satisfaction over his own prompt response.

I dragged Leni with me.

"It's my business," she murmured, "why does she have to make it public? Why does she have to humiliate me?"

The others walked out a few at a time.

"You stay here," the Beanpole told Elfriede, and she pressed her back against the wall.

"Are you sure about this?" I asked her softly, so as not to be overheard by the guard as he left the room.

Elfriede replied with an assertive nod of her chin, then closed her eyes.

LENI SLUMPED TO the ground. Though I don't think it was intentional, she had sat down in the exact center of the faded hopscotch court, the magic perimeter that hadn't protected her from anything. I plopped down at her side. The others swarmed around her, bombarding her with questions, especially Augustine. "Enough," I said. "Can't you see she's beside herself?"

Out of the corner of my eye I peeked at the lunchroom but couldn't see Elfriede. As soon as the crowd around Leni had dispersed, I walked over to the door. The sound of footsteps on the floor made me back up. "Let's go." It was the Beanpole's voice. The footsteps doubled. Only when the asynchronous, differently paced noises had faded into the distance did I peer inside. Elfriede was walking down the hall with the guard.

Against all expectations the lieutenant had agreed to receive her. It must have been because of the boredom of the weeks following the assassination attempt, which he had missed. He was looking for a distraction. Or maybe it was his bitterness about the new arrangements.

Nothing was to happen without his knowing about it. I felt in danger, almost as if by entering his room Elfriede might see in Albert what I saw in him, might see me deep in his eyes and discover everything.

Elfriede appeared before Ziegler to report Ernst Koch, a noncommissioned officer of the Heer. She said the night before, though entry was forbidden, the sergeant had sneaked into the barracks, where the food tasters slept, German women employed by the Führer, and despite his being a representative of the Reich, an army man with the duty to defend us from the enemy, he had raped one of the women, a German, just like him.

ZIEGLER FOUND OUT the names of the guards on duty that night and summoned each of them, along with Ernst and Leni. He couldn't wait to inflict punishment—that must have been it.

In response to the Obersturmführer's questions in the dimly lit principal's office, at first Leni—she told me later—reacted by clamming up, then mumbled that it was her fault, Sergeant Koch had misunderstood, she hadn't been clear, had agreed to meet him in the barracks but had instantly regretted it. Had there been intercourse or hadn't there? Leni didn't deny Elfriede's account. Ziegler asked her if she had consented. Leni quickly shook her head, stammering that no, she hadn't.

Despite her incoherent statements, Ziegler didn't let the question drop. He reported Ernst Koch to the Wehrmacht authorities, which after a series of questions and verifications would determine whether to send the young man before a military court.

When Leni went to see Heiner and asked for news about Ernst, he was courteous yet cold, almost as if he was afraid that meeting with the victim—that is, the accuser—was unwise. He didn't justify his friend, but he didn't open up to her either. *I've ruined his life*, Leni said.

I didn't talk about it with Elfriede because I was afraid I would give myself away, like I had with the honey. *I'm sorry*, she had told me that Sunday afternoon as we returned to the barracks, *it's just that I get nervous when I remember the day they poisoned us—that is, when we were sickened by the honey, from what you said.* I shook my head. *Don't worry, who knows if it really was the honey after all?*

I was a coward. That was why I couldn't understand why she would involve herself in a situation that had nothing to do with her, against the wishes of the person directly affected. That chivalrous attitude was ridiculous. For years every heroic act had seemed ridiculous to me. I was embarrassed by any form of initiative, any trust, especially in justice—a remnant of romantic idealism, a naïve, false sentiment detached from reality.

The news spread among the tasters. The Fanatics didn't spare us their comments: *First you sneak him into the barracks and then you say it was his fault? No, no, dear, that's no excuse.*

Augustine tried to comfort Leni, to tell her how admirable Elfriede's gesture had been, she should be grateful. Leni wasn't persuaded. Would they summon her to testify in court? She had never even managed to utter a word at the blackboard. Why had her friend inflicted this torture on her?

I gathered my courage and went to Elfriede, who was surly even with me.

Annoyed, I told her, "Protecting someone who doesn't want to be protected is an act of aggression."

"Oh, really?" She pulled the unlit cigarette out of her lips. "Would you think that about a child?"

"Leni isn't a child."

"She can't defend herself," she shot back, "just like a child."

"Who among us can defend ourselves here? Be objective! We've had to put up with all kinds of oppression here. It's not always a question of choice."

"You're right." As though it needed to be extinguished, she smashed the cigarette against the wall until the tobacco burst out of the torn paper. Then she walked away. The conversation was over.

"Where are you going?"

"There's no escaping destiny," she said without turning around. "That's the point."

I could have followed her but didn't. She wasn't listening to anyone anyway. *Suit yourself,* I thought.

Whether Elfriede had been right to report Ernst against Leni's wishes I couldn't say, but there was something about the whole thing that made me uncomfortable, something that left me with a dark feeling of foreboding.

38

I spotted Ziegler in the hallway and twisted my ankle on purpose. My foot slipped out of my shoe, my knee buckled, I fell to the
floor. He walked over and held out his hand. I took it. He helped me
up. The guard had also come over. "Everything all right, Lieutenant?"

"She's hurt her ankle," Ziegler replied. I didn't say a word. "I'll take
you to the washroom. You can run cold water over it."

"Don't bother, Lieutenant. I can take her mysel—"

"It's no problem." Ziegler walked off. I followed him, pretending
to hobble.

When we were in the principal's office he locked the door, grabbed
my face in his hands furiously, squeezing my cheeks, and kissed me.
All I had to do was touch his chest with my finger to relapse.

"Thank you for what you did."

He had decided to protect one of us rather than cover for a noncommissioned officer. He seemed to be on our side, on mine.

"I've missed you," he said, pulling up my skirt and baring my thighs.

I had never touched him in broad daylight before, had never seen
so clearly his brow furrowed with desire, the gaze of someone who
fears everything might dissolve from one moment to the next, an
adolescent impulse. We had never made love in a place that wasn't
mine—no, a place that wasn't Gregor's family's. I had desecrated the
barn and now we were desecrating the barracks. That place was Hitler's. It was ours.

Someone knocked. Ziegler quickly did up his trousers, I slid off the desk, trying to smooth my skirt with my palms, neaten my hair. I stood there as he spoke with the SS man, who glanced in my direction. I lowered my head, then turned three-quarters away, slicked down my hair again, and looked at the paperwork on the desk to escape his interest. It was then that I saw the dossier.

On the first page was written: *ELFRIEDE KUHN / EDNA KOPFSTEIN.*

My blood ran cold.

"Where were we?" Ziegler whispered, embracing me from behind. I hadn't noticed he had dismissed the guard. He spun me around, pulled me close, kissed my lips, teeth, gums, the corners of my mouth. "What's wrong?" he said.

"Who's Edna Kopfstein?"

He pulled away and, after lazily circling around his desk, sat down and picked up the dossier. "Don't ask." He slid it into a drawer.

"Please, tell me what's going on. What does that woman have to do with Elfriede? Why do you have a file on Elfriede? Do you have one on me as well?"

"That isn't information I can share."

No, he wasn't on our side. He had reported a noncommissioned officer only because it was within his power, and he wanted to wield that power.

"Well, what can you share with me? Until a minute ago you were embracing me."

"Please, return to the lunchroom."

"So now you're treating me like a subordinate. I don't follow your orders, Albert."

"But you must."

"Because we're in your stupid barracks?"

"Don't make a fuss, Rosa. Pretend you never saw it. It'll be better for everyone."

Cursing, I leaned over the desk and grabbed him by the collar of his uniform. "I'm not going to pretend anything. Elfriede Kuhn is my friend!"

Ziegler stroked the backs of my hands, my knuckles. "Are you sure? Because there *is* no Elfriede Kuhn. At least, if there is one, she isn't the woman you know." He yanked my hands off his collar. I staggered backward and he grabbed me by the forearms. "Edna Kopfstein is a U-boat."

"What do you mean?"

"Your friend Elfriede is an imposter, Rosa. A Jew."

I couldn't believe it. Among Hitler's food tasters was a Jew.

"Show me the dossier, Albert."

He stood up, came over to me. "Don't you dare breathe a word of this to anyone."

There was a Jew among us, and it was Elfriede, of all people.

"What's going to happen to her?"

"Rosa, are you listening to me?"

"I have to tell her. She has to escape."

"You're so funny." A grimace flashed over his face, the same grimace I had glimpsed in the barn once. "You plan to have her escape and you actually tell me?"

"Are you going to send her away? To where?"

"This is my job. No one can stand in my way, not even you."

"Albert. Help her, if you can."

"Why should I help a clandestine Jew who's been making fools of us? She hid all this time, changed her identity, ate our food, slept in our beds, thinking she could trick us! But she can't. She's wrong about that."

"Please. Make the dossier disappear. Who gave it to you?"

"I can't make a dossier disappear."

"You can't? Are you admitting you're of no importance around here?"

"That's enough!" He clamped his hand over my mouth. I bit his fingers. He slammed me against the wall and I hit my head. Squeezing my eyes shut, I waited for the pain to spread and reach its peak and then lessen. The moment it vanished I spat in his face.

I found myself with the barrel of his gun pressed against my forehead. Ziegler wasn't shaking. "You will do as I command."

That was what he had told me the first time, in the courtyard, when his little eyes, so closely set they made him look cross-eyed, hadn't managed to frighten me. The same hazel-colored irises stared at me, now that the metal was stamping a cold ring onto my skin. I felt a tic below my cheek, couldn't swallow, my throat sealed in a knot, two tears welled up by my tear ducts—I wasn't crying, it was the inability to breathe.

"Very well," I murmured.

And all at once Ziegler lowered the gun, shoved it awkwardly into its holster, his eyes locked on to me. Then he held me tight, his tiny nose on my neck, asked me to forgive him, touched me, my collar-bones, femurs, ribs, as though making sure I was still intact. He was pathetic.

"Forgive me, please," he said. "You gave me no choice." He repeated, "Forgive me."

I couldn't speak. I was pathetic. We were pathetic.

"If she runs away it'll be worse," he said, his face buried in my hair.

I said nothing, and he added, "You mustn't tell her anything. I'll do what I can, I promise you."

"Please."

"I promise you."

When I returned to the lunchroom, the ladies asked me where I had been.

"You should see your face," said Ulla.

"She's right," Leni said. "You're pale."

"I was in the washroom."

"This whole time?" Beate asked.

"Oh, god, don't tell me we've got another one," Augustine said, glancing at Heike.

Heike hung her head. So did Beate, who had to pretend she hadn't heard.

"You're as tactless as always, Augustine," I said, trying to deflect their attention.

Heike looked at me, then looked at Elfriede, then hung her head again.

I also looked at Elfriede, all through lunch. Every time she caught me doing it I felt my heart squeezing like a bellows.

As I was getting on the bus someone grabbed my arm. I turned around.

"Berliner, what's wrong? Still afraid of the sight of your own blood?" Elfriede smiled, our inside joke.

I had to tell her. Even if I trusted Ziegler, I couldn't trust a lieutenant in the SS. Elfriede had to know what was going on. But what would she do? Would she run away? How could I help her? Only Ziegler could—there was no alternative. He had promised me. *If she runs away it'll be worse*, he said. I had to believe him. We were pawns in his hands. I needed to stay quiet—it was the only way to save Elfriede.

"I've never gotten used to it," I told her, "to blood."

With this, I sat down beside Leni.

The next day the ladies continued to tell me I was acting strangely. Had I heard from Gregor, by chance? Received another letter from the headquarters of military families? I hadn't. *That's good. You know, we were all worried. What's wrong, then?*

I wanted to confide in Herta and Joseph, but they would ask me how I knew what I knew, and I couldn't confess that. The afternoon when Ulla had put my hair into rollers and Elfriede and Leni had drunk tea, after they all left, Herta said she hadn't been able to figure out Elfriede. *Yes, there's something about her,* Joseph agreed, pressing down the tobacco in his pipe with a tamper, *something sorrowful.*

I spent the week in terror that they would come and take Elfriede away as inexorably as they had arrested Mr. Wortmann. I never looked out the window, not at the birds or trees or flowers. Nothing could distract me, I had to stay on guard, watch over Elfriede. There she was, sitting across the table from me, eating roasted potatoes with linseed oil.

Friday arrived.

No one came for her.

39

ZIEGLER WALKED IN AS WE WERE ALMOST FINISHED TASTING BREAKFAST. He and I hadn't locked ourselves away in the office again, there had been no further contact between us.

We were eating cake with honey, walnuts, cocoa, and raisins, which Krümel called "Führer Cake." I don't know if it was the Führer who came up with the recipe or if the cook had been the one to combine in a single pastry everything his boss liked, as a tribute to him.

After that day I never ate raisins again.

Standing stiffly in the doorway, legs apart, hands on his hips, chin high, Ziegler said: "Edna Kopfstein."

I whipped my head up, breathless. He avoided looking at me.

The other women stared at one another, confused. Edna who? None of us were named that. What was going on? Kopfstein, the lieutenant had said. That was a Jewish name. They rested their cutlery on the table or on the edge of their plate, clasped their fingers over their bellies. Even Elfriede had rested her fork, despite the piece of cake skewered on its tines, but after a brief hesitation, she raised it and stuck it in her mouth, slowly starting to eat again. Her audacity astonished me. She was always like that, Elfriede, always pretending she wasn't afraid, never letting anyone—not even an SS officer—injure her self-respect.

Ziegler let her finish. What kind of game was he playing?

When Elfriede's plate was empty, he repeated: "Edna Kopfstein."

I shot to my feet so brusquely that my chair toppled over.

"Don't steal my spotlight, Berliner," Elfriede said. With this, she walked over to the lieutenant.

"Let's go," he said, and she followed him without turning back.

It was Saturday. That evening we would go home.

THE BUS TOOK off without Elfriede on board.

"Where is she?" Leni asked me. "She wasn't at lunch or dinner."

"She'll tell us all about it tomorrow," I said, trying to calm her.

"Who's Edna Kopfstein? What does she have to do with her?"

"I don't know, Leni. How should I know?"

"Do you think they had to talk about Ernst again?"

"No, I don't think so."

"Why did you jump to your feet like that, Rosa?"

I turned away and Leni gave up. We were all shaken. From time to time, from her row, Augustine tried to catch my eye. She shook her head, as if to say, *It can't be, I can't believe it, a Jew, Rosa, did you know about this?* As if to say, *What do we do now that they've discovered her, do you know what to do?*

The next day, at the spot on the road where Elfriede usually waited for the bus, there wasn't even a cigarette butt.

In the lunchroom, they announced that on Monday the Führer would be leaving town and wouldn't be back for ten days, so for ten days no barracks for us. Neither that night nor the following nights did Ziegler appear at my window. Of Elfriede, no news.

SPEAKING WITH A group of military men she hadn't stopped socializing with—I don't know if Heiner was among them, but by then everyone knew what had happened—Ulla learned that it had been Ernst who said, *Can you believe what she told me? You know what that woman did? She took one of the food tasters to get an abortion from a man who lives hidden in the forest, and nobody knows who the guy is or why he's hiding, maybe he's a deserter or an enemy of the Reich.*

Leni had told him the story. Maybe it had seemed adventurous to her, a way to show off, an attempt to seduce him. She had trusted Ernst.

Ziegler had gone to Heike's house and interrogated her for hours.

When he began to threaten her children, she talked. *In the Goerlitz Forest*, she said, *in the area of Lake Tauchel.*

The man had no documents, but it wasn't difficult for the Sicherheitsdienst to discover that he was a Jewish doctor, one of those barred from practice. He had managed to get by all that time. Elfriede had always known him; he was her father.

The mother, a pureblood German, had asked for a divorce. Elfriede, half Jewish, had chosen not to abandon him, though they didn't live together. Years earlier, when she still lived in Gdańsk, a friend of the family gave her her ID card. Together they bleached some of the writing to change the date of birth, detached the photo and replaced it with another, used a marker to re-create the four stamps, refining the eagle's wings and the ring around the swastika, and Edna Kopfstein had become Elfriede Kuhn.

FOR A YEAR she had managed to fool the SS. They had had an enemy in their midst and every day they served her succulent food, convinced she was one of their own.

She must have lived in a constant state of alert, Elfriede, with every mouthful the fear of being unmasked, with every bus ride a sense of guilt over those who had departed on trains and would never return, over those who hadn't been shrewd enough, hadn't been good enough at lying—not everyone has those talents.

Perhaps after the war she would reclaim her name, her documents, would recall her clandestine period with the dignified composure of someone who's saved herself, even though those years would return to her every night in nightmares. To exorcise them she would tell her grandchildren about it over Passover dinner—or maybe not, maybe she wouldn't say a word about that period, like me.

If she had never been summoned to be a food taster, maybe she would have managed to survive. Instead Elfriede was deported, along with her father.

HERTA WAS THE one who told me. She'd heard it while at the well, the women waiting in line for water had told her. The story about the Jewess who had made fools of the Nazis was spreading all through town. In Gross-Partsch, had they always known about us women and our work?

"Deported," Herta confirmed, and she didn't tuck her upper lip between her teeth, didn't look like a turtle, only a mother. There was only one true source of grief in her life: the loss of Gregor. She couldn't suffer for anyone else.

I left the house, slamming the door. It was evening and Joseph asked me, "Where are you going?" but I wasn't listening to him anymore. I walked off with no destination, with an agitation in my legs that only muscular exertion could ease, or sharpen.

Nests on the utility poles and no storks. They would never return here, to East Prussia. It wasn't a healthy environment, nothing but swamps and the stink of rot. They would change course, forget this plain forever.

I walked without stopping, thought, *Why did you do it, you could have kept quiet, what need was there to avenge Leni, who didn't even want to be avenged?*

It had been suicide—Elfriede hadn't been able to bear it anymore, her survivor guilt. Or maybe it had been a false move, a momentary form of recklessness that had proved fatal for her. The same impulse she hadn't been able to contain with me when she shoved me against the wall with its blackened grout. Only now did I realize she had felt watched, had lived with the anxiety of being found out. That day, in the washroom, had she been testing me? Or was the caged animal, so eager to get out, seeking a reason—any reason—to have the gates opened, even at the risk that they wouldn't be opened in order to set her free? Maybe it was simply the only way for her, entrenched and proud, to establish a closeness with me.

We hadn't been dealt the same fate. I was safe. I had trusted Ziegler and he had betrayed me. It was his job, that's what he would say. After all, every job involves compromises. Every job is a form of slavery—the need to have a role in the world, to advance in a specific direction, to save oneself from derailment, from marginality.

I had worked for Hitler. So had Elfriede, who had ended up in the Wolf's Lair and had hoped to get away with it. I didn't know if she had grown so accustomed to a clandestine lifestyle that she felt safe, safe enough to make a misstep, or if she had delivered herself to a fate she could no longer avoid.

We had all unintentionally ended up in the Wolf's Lair. The Wolf had never seen us. He digested the food we had chewed, had excreted the waste of that food, and had never known anything about us. He stayed curled up in his lair, the Wolfsschanze, the origin of all things. I wanted to penetrate it, to be forever swallowed up in it. Maybe Elfriede was there, locked in a bunker, waiting for them to decide what to do with her.

I wandered down the train tracks through the tall grass that stung my legs, passed the railroad crossing—a slender tree trunk to which two boards painted red and white had been nailed together in an X shape—and continued without once turning back. The rails went straight on, embedded in a tangle of purple flowers. It wasn't the clover in the meadow; there was no beauty that could reawaken me. I advanced like a sleepwalker, with the determination of a sleepwalker I followed my path until the very limit, wanting to cross it, plunge into the beating heart of the forest, be part of it once and for all, as much a part of it as the reinforced concrete of the bunkers, the moss and wood chips in the camouflage plaster, the trees on the rooftops. I wanted to be swallowed up. Perhaps thousands of years later the Wolfsschanze would expel me and I would be nothing more than fertilizer.

A GUNSHOT TORE me out of my stupor. I fell backward.

"Who goes there?" they shouted. I remembered the land mines Ziegler had told me about. Where were the mines? Why hadn't I been blown up? "Hands over your head!" Had I taken a different road, a road that wasn't mined? Where was Ziegler? "Don't move!" A shot into the air, nothing more than a warning, they were being indulgent.

The SS men came over, their weapons trained on me. I raised my arms, was on my knees, uttered my name: "Rosa Sauer, I work for the

Führer, I was walking in the woods, don't hurt me, I'm one of the food tasters."

A rifle aimed at the center of my back, they grabbed hold of me, shouted, I don't remember what, just their angry voices crashing into my ears, their gaping mouths, their hands intruding on me, the fury with which they dragged me away. Maybe they would take me into the Wolfsschanze, lock me up in a bunker too.

Where was Joseph? Was he looking for me? Herta was waiting, sitting in the kitchen, her fingers—her deformed fingers—interlaced. She had been waiting for me, or only for Gregor, her entire life, but night had already fallen, her son wasn't going to return with a hearty appetite, and I was no longer hungry.

They took me to the Krausendorf barracks. How foolish of me to think they would let me enter a place reserved for the Führer's elite. They sat me down at the lunchroom table. I had never been there alone. On that table Leni had lost her virginity. *What was wrong with it?* Ernst must have thought. *Leni seemed consenting, I swear.* We all seemed consenting in Germany. They closed the door. I sat there counting the empty seats, a guard barring the way out into the courtyard.

After half an hour, fifty minutes, Krümel opened the door. "What are you doing here?"

My eyes filled with tears. "What are *you* doing here, Crumbs? Aren't we on vacation?" I was seeking compassion.

"You can't keep out of trouble, can you?"

I smiled at him, my chin trembling.

"Want something to eat?" he said, despite the guard being there.

Before I could reply, Ziegler walked in. They had called him in to solve the unpleasant situation: one of his food tasters had attempted to enter the innermost ring of the bunker city without authorization.

Krümel respectfully greeted the lieutenant, said goodbye to me with a nod of his head. He didn't wink at me like he had when, months and months before, he would gossip with me in the kitchen. Ziegler dismissed the guard and closed the door.

Without sitting down, he told me they would take me home, but next time I wouldn't get off so easily. "Would you mind telling me what it is you were trying to do?" He came over to the table. "Tomorrow I'm going to have to personally answer for what happened. I'll be in trouble because of you. I'll have to convince them you were only going for a walk, that it's all just a misunderstanding, and it won't be easy, you know. After what happened in July anyone could be a traitor, a spy, an infiltrator. . . ."

"Like Elfriede?"

Ziegler fell silent. Then he asked, "Was it her you were looking for?"

"Where is she?"

"We sent her away."

"Where?"

"Where you can imagine."

He held out a slip of paper. "You can write to her," he said. "I did what I could, believe me. She's alive."

I stared at the hand holding the slip of paper. I didn't take it.

Ziegler crumpled it up, threw it onto the table, turned to leave. Maybe he thought my response was a final show of defiance, that if I was alone I would put the address in my pocket. I had no pockets, nor my leather satchel.

"I don't want to write to anyone else who isn't going to write me back."

Ziegler stopped, looked at me with compassion. It was what I had been seeking, but it did nothing to console me.

"They're waiting for you outside."

I got up slowly, wearily. As I passed by him, he said, "I had no choice."

"Did you get a promotion? Or do they still see you as the poor underachiever that you are?"

"Get out." He pushed on the doorknob.

In the hallway I felt like I was walking through water. Ziegler noticed, once again had the instinct to help me, but I pulled away. I would rather have fallen. My ankle didn't buckle. I kept walking.

"It's not my fault," I heard him say as I reached the SS guard waiting at the barracks entrance.

"Yes, it is," I replied without turning around. "It's our fault."

40

THE LOSS OF ELFRIEDE LEFT ME CATATONIC. I COULDN'T HATE LENI, but I couldn't forgive her either. As I saw it, her chagrin was the guilty conscience of a child who's caused mischief—it wasn't enough for me. *You should have thought about it first,* I wanted to tell her, but didn't. I didn't talk to anyone. In the lunchroom the voices were subdued. Though softened, the murmur was unbearable to me. Elfriede deserved a bit of respect, and I needed peace and quiet.

My friends ate with their heads hung low and didn't dare ask what I knew or why I had risen from my chair so quickly that Saturday. I felt their eyes on me, not only those of the Fanatics, who didn't spare me their judgment. If Augustine hadn't held me back one morning I would have slammed Theodora to the ground—Theodora, who during all those months had eaten right next to Elfriede yet wasn't upset about what had happened to her. The Fanatics had seen Elfriede on a daily basis, had risked dying with her and with her had escaped death, but that wasn't enough for them to feel compassion for her. How was it possible? I've asked myself that for years, decades, and I still don't understand.

Heike got sick—seriously, this time. She presented a doctor's note with the word "indisposition" written on it and was absent for weeks. I don't know if they paid her anyway for those days. Discretion kept Beate from going on again about her having children to raise. I hoped Heike would get well not sooner but later, just long enough for my anger to subside—maybe it never would subside. I felt like beating her, punishing her.

How dare I? I was no better than she was. No new woman came to replace Elfriede. Her seat beside Leni remained empty, as did her bed beside mine. Maybe they did it on purpose, so we would remember what happened to those who didn't toe the line. Or maybe the Führer had more important things to think about. Officers in his own army had tried to kill him, it wasn't like he would be concerned about one fewer food taster.

ONE AFTERNOON WHEN I was off work because the Führer had left town again, as I was hanging out the laundry, Herta came over to me. The scent of the soap was blasphemy, as was the sun high in the sky, along with the cool sensation of the damp clothing against my fingers.

Inside the house the radio was on, and through the open window came the voices and music of celebrations for the day of the German mother. That was where the Führer had gone, to award Crosses of Honor to prolific mothers. It was already August 12, I thought, hanging a tablecloth on the line—I had lost track of the days. August 12 would have been the Führer's mother, Klara's, birthday if she hadn't died thirty-seven years earlier, when Adolf wasn't yet a man grown—only a somewhat anxious son who had lost his mother.

Herta stood there stock-still instead of helping me. She seemed to be on the verge of saying something, but said nothing, listened to the radio. The Führer would be awarding a gold Ehrenkreuz to the finest women, those who had managed to churn out at least eight healthy children, never mind if some of them died afterward of hunger or typhus well before they ever grew a beard, well before they ever wore a bra, and never mind if others would die in the war. The important thing was that there were new draftees to send to the front, new females to impregnate. Augustine said the Russians, who were getting close, would leave us all pregnant. Ulla replied, *Better Ivan on your belly than an American over your head.*

I looked up at the sky. No plane, neither from the U.S. nor the USSR, had cut through it. It was shrouded by clouds of gauze, which the sun intermittently shone through. Herta had already explained to me that we would flee to the woods if bombings began, that we would bring food and water and blankets for the night. There weren't any bomb shelters in Gross-Partsch, no bunkers had been built for the villagers, there were no tunnels in which to protect ourselves, and Herta would sleep more peacefully with her cheek resting on the roots of a tree than in the cellar. At the very thought of it she couldn't breathe. *Fine*, I had told her, *we'll do what you want.* I told her that whenever she raised the question, though I planned to stay home, amid the commotion, like my father, to plump my pillow and roll over to face the other way.

The radio, on the other hand, belied our every concern: Why would you think such bad thoughts today, of all days? Today is a holiday, today we celebrate the children of the Reich. Germans, everyone knows, love children, don't you? There were women who had made an effort but hadn't had it in them. Laden with six children, they would receive only a silver cross. It was better off that way—the medal would encourage them to give it their all, so perhaps the following year they would make their way up the charts. One must never give up—that was what the Führer taught us. The other women would have to settle for a bronze cross. They had given birth just four times, could expect nothing more. My mother-in-law, for instance, despite herself, wouldn't have won anything at all—only three pregnancies, two children having died at a tender age and the other one lost. Germans love children, even those who were buried, even those who were missing, and I hadn't had even one.

"How long has it been since your last period?"

I dropped a damp dishcloth into the basin, gripped a clothespin in my fingers.

"I don't know." I thought about it, couldn't remember. I had lost track of the days, of all those days that had engulfed me. I picked up the dishcloth again, hung it on the line, only so I could steady myself on it. "Why?"

"I see it's been a while since you washed your pads. I haven't seen them hanging out to dry."

"I hadn't even noticed."

Herta rested her hand on my belly, felt it.

"What are you doing?" I pulled back. Now detached from the clothesline, I was collapsing.

"You. What are *you* doing? What have you done?"

My lips quivered, my nostrils. Herta was in front of me, arms outstretched, almost as if to contain a big belly that wasn't there, that might grow.

"I haven't done anything."

Was I pregnant with Ziegler's child?

"Why did you pull away from me, then?"

I would have to get rid of the baby. Like Heike. But Elfriede was gone.

"I haven't done anything, Herta."

My mother-in-law didn't reply. I had always wanted a baby, it was Gregor's fault if things had turned out this way. Herta reached out her hand again. And what if I wanted to keep the child?

"What are you asking me?" I shouted.

A second later, Joseph was at the window. "What's going on?" He had switched off the radio.

I waited for his wife to answer, but she gestured for him to let it go. Since Elfriede had gone, I was depressed, had mood swings, didn't he know that? I ran to my room, stayed there until morning, and spent the night awake.

DURING THE MONTHS when Ziegler had been there, I had observed my body as though it were something new. Sitting on the commode, I would inspect the fold of my groin, the flesh of my inner thigh, the skin on my sides, and wouldn't recognize them, they didn't belong to me, they were as intriguing to me as someone else's body. While bathing in the washtub I would check the weight of my breasts, the framework of my bones, the adherence of my feet to the ground, and would sniff my scent, because it was the scent Ziegler smelled—he didn't know it was so similar to my mother's.

We had been entwined all night, sheltered from our personal histories. We had denied all reality, believed we could suspend it. We had been fools. It had never occurred to me that he would make me pregnant. I wanted a child from Gregor. Gregor had vanished, and with him my chance to become a mother.

My breasts were plump, tender. In the darkness I couldn't study my areoles to see if they had changed shape or color, but I could feel my glands, which were hard clusters, knots in ropes. Up until the day before, my kidneys had never bothered me, but now I felt my lower back hot, as though from lashes.

While the whole world was launching bombs and Hitler was building an ever more efficient extermination machine, in the barn Albert and I had clung to each other as though it were sleep, it was like sleeping, a place far from there, a parallel place. We had ended up together for no reason—there never is a reason to love each other. There is no possible reason to embrace a Nazi, not even having given birth to him.

Then the summer of '44 began to wither and I noticed I existed less since he no longer touched me. My body revealed its wretchedness, its unstoppable race toward decay. It had been designed with that end—all bodies are designed with that end. How is it possible to desire them, desire something destined to rot? It's like loving the worms that are to come.

Now, however, that same body began to exist again, and again it was because of Ziegler, though he was gone, though I didn't miss him. I had a child. Why on earth shouldn't I keep it? And if Gregor were to return? Well, then, maybe—*God forgive me*—maybe it was better if he didn't return, maybe I would be better off bartering Gregor's life—*What are you saying?*—for the life of my child. *I have the right to want this child, the right to save it. Do you realize what you've just said?*

When I left the house to go to the barracks, Herta was taking down the laundry. We didn't speak to each other, neither then nor when I returned home from my first shift that day. Then the bus came to pick me up again and Sunday was over. That night I would remain in Krausendorf, would return only on the following Friday.

———

LYING ON THE bed beside the wall, I kept one arm outstretched so it touched Elfriede's mattress. It was empty and I felt my stomach lurch. Leni was sleeping, whereas I was searching for solutions, had searched for them all week long. Tell Ziegler, accept his help. He would find a doctor who could terminate the pregnancy, perhaps one from the headquarters. He would pay him off to keep it a secret, and the man would do what he needed to do in the barracks washroom. *But what if I scream from the pain, if I bleed onto the tiles?* It wasn't the right place. Ziegler would put me in his jeep and sneak me into the Wolfsschanze, bundled in several layers of military blankets hidden in the trunk. The SS would smell my scent through the blankets—they were perfectly trained guard dogs, I would never get away with it. It would be better for the lieutenant to drive the doctor out to the woods, I would wait for them there, my hands on my belly. Like Heike, I would expel my child while clinging to a tree, but I would be alone, because the doctor would have been impatient to leave and Ziegler would have driven him back. I would dig a hole at the foot of a birch tree, would cover it with earth, carve a cross onto the bark, *Without initials—my son has no name, what sense is there in naming him if he's never born?*

Or, against all expectations, Ziegler would want to keep it. *I've bought a house,* he would announce, *a house for us here in Gross-Partsch. But I don't want to stay here in Gross-Partsch, I want to live in Berlin. Here are the keys,* he would say, closing them in my palm, *tonight we'll sleep together. No, tonight I'll sleep in the barracks, like yesterday, and the day before that, and tomorrow. Sooner or later the war will end,* he would reply, and he would seem so foolish to me, with that hope of his. Maybe it was all a trick—he would force me to give birth to the baby and would then take it to Munich, would take it away from me, would have his wife look after it. No, he would never admit to his family, to the SS, that he had fathered a bastard. He would get rid of me. *Deal with it yourself, who can guarantee it's mine?*

I was alone. I couldn't confess it to Herta, to Joseph, to the other women, and in any case no one could do anything about it. That was why I even dreamed of turning to Ziegler. I had lost my mind, felt I was losing my mind. If only Gregor were there, I so needed to talk to him. *It's nothing,* he would say, holding me close, *you were only dreaming.*

My punishment had finally arrived. It wasn't poison, it wasn't death—it was life. *God is so sadistic, Father, that he punishes me with life. He understood my dream, and now He looks down from Heaven above and laughs at me.*

WHEN I GOT back home on Friday, Herta and Joseph had already eaten dinner. They were about to go to bed. She had a cardigan over her shoulders, the air had grown chilly. She forced out a hello. He was kind, as always, and asked nothing about his wife's coldness toward me.

Lying in bed, I felt worse than usual. My kidneys were burning and a needle pierced my left nipple repeatedly, as if someone had decided to stitch it up, seal it off. *You're not going to breastfeed your son— steal milk from Krümel if you really want it to be born.* My head, squeezed between the blades of forceps, was throbbing. I writhed with cramps until finally falling asleep.

In the morning I got out of bed in a daze. Rubbing my eyes, I noticed a dark patch on the bedsheet. My nightgown was stained too. . . . A hemorrhage—I was losing the baby. I sank to my knees, buried my face in the mattress. Ziegler's child, I had lost it. I hugged my belly to hold it back—*Don't go, don't be like the others, stay with me.* I stroked my breasts, they were soft, nothing was sore. Only a faint, barely perceptible ache below, something I had experienced so many other times before.

I had never been pregnant with Ziegler's child.

It can happen, Elfriede would have said. *I'm surprised at you, Berliner. Didn't you know? All it takes is a major disappointment or a body weakened from stress and you skip your period. Hunger would also do it, but you're not hungry, unlike me. I've skipped my period too, down here. We've synchronized, like Leni said.*

My cheek pressed against the mattress, I wept for Elfriede, sobbing, until the sheet was drenched, until I heard the horn blaring. I put on a sanitary pad, fastening it in place with a diaper pin, quickly got dressed, left the red stain on the cotton sheet uncovered so Herta could see it.

On the bus, I rested my temple against the window and continued to weep. For the child I would never have.

41

Beate hadn't been wrong. Things were going badly for the Führer. Not only had he been betrayed by some of his own men in July and risked being killed, but just over a month later he lost half a million men on the Western Front and found himself short on garrisons and cannons, while Paris was liberated. On the opposite front, Stalin had the upper hand; he had conquered Romania, made Finland capitulate, driven Bulgaria to officially withdraw from the war, and trapped fifty German divisions in the Baltic region. Stalin was drawing closer and closer—the generals did nothing but repeat it, and the leading heads of state caught hell for trying to convince him of it, but Hitler wouldn't listen; his troops would continue the battle until the enemy was too tired to fight anymore, as Frederick the Great had said. He would wear them down, keep honor high, there wouldn't be another 1918, not as long as he was still alive—and to seal his vow he would beat his chest with his right hand while his left hand, hidden behind his back, was at the mercy of the now-customary tremor that Morell hadn't yet been able to diagnose. *Enough with all the nonsense that Ivan is at the door,* the Führer screamed, *it's a hoax.*

We didn't know all this, not clearly. It was forbidden to listen to enemy radio, and though Joseph did manage to tune in to the English or French channels from time to time, we understood little to nothing. Nevertheless it was clear to us that, rather than admit it, Hitler was lying. He had lost control, was failing, was dragging us down with him. Many began to detest him at that point. My father had detested him right from the start. We had never been Nazis. No Nazis in my family, except me.

In November I was taken to the former principal's office, this time without any ploy. The guard had summoned me so discreetly that the other women thought I was going to the washroom. I wondered what Ziegler wanted now—we hadn't spoken to each other in three months—and I clenched my fists in anger.

Of course, I had seen him after the night when I had refused to take the slip of paper from him. I had seen him in the hallways and lunchroom, but today he looked different to me. His hairline had slightly receded, his face tough, the skin glistening on the sides of his nose and his chin.

I gripped the doorknob, prepared to walk out.

"You need to save yourself."

Who did I need to save myself from, if I hadn't saved myself from him?

He got up from the desk, stopped two meters away from me, almost as if out of caution, and folded his arms. He said the Soviets were coming, would pillage everything, destroy the houses, it was necessary to leave. Up until the very end the Führer had been opposed to the idea, didn't want to go too far from the Eastern Front—his presence there, he said, was a beacon for the soldiers, but airplanes continued to fly across the skies over the Wolfsschanze, and staying would be madness. In a matter of days Hitler was departing for Berlin with his secretaries, top kitchen staff, and various collaborators, and gradually all the others would be evacuated, though not before blowing up the bunkers and barracks.

"What do you suggest, then? Shall I ask Hitler to give me a ride?"

"Rosa, please, that's enough. Don't you understand? This means total defeat."

The end had come. I had lost a father, mother, brother, husband, Maria, Elfriede, even Mr. Wortmann. I was the only one still unharmed, though the end was right around the corner.

"Hitler is leaving on the twentieth with the Wehrmacht Supreme Command. As for all the others, the civilians who work in the head-quarters, before they leave they'll have to take care of the logistical issues: documents, military supplies. . . . They're going to board a train a few days later. You're going with them."

"Why should they let me?"

"I'll find a way to hide you."

"What tells you I'm willing to hide? What will they do if they discover me?"

"It's the only solution. People will start leaving once they realize they have no choice. You have the chance to leave now, and on a train."

"I'm not getting on any train. Where do you mean to send me, anyway?"

"I told you, to Berlin."

"Why should I trust you? And why should I be saved while the other women stay here? Just because I went to bed with you?"

"Because you're you."

"It's not fair."

"Not everything in life is fair. But that isn't my decision, at least not that."

Not everything is fair, not even love. Some people loved Hitler, loved him unreservedly—a mother, a sister, his niece Geli, Eva Braun. He told her, *You, Eva, are the one who taught me how to kiss.*

I drew in a shallow breath, felt my lips part.

Ziegler moved closer, touched my hand. I jerked it away.

"What about my in-laws?"

"Be reasonable. I can't hide just anyone."

"I'm not leaving without them."

"Stop being so stubborn. Listen to me, for once."

"I've already listened to you once and it didn't end well."

"I just want to help you."

"I can't bear surviving any longer, Albert. Sooner or later I want to live."

"Then go."

I sighed, "Are you leaving too?"

"Yes."

Someone was waiting for him back in Bavaria. In Berlin no one was waiting for me. I would be all alone, without a bed, surrounded by bombs. The pointlessness of that existence offended me. Why so much effort to preserve it? As though it were a responsibility—but to whom did I still owe any responsibility?

It's a biological instinct, no one can avoid it, Gregor would have objected with his typical common sense. *Don't think you're any different from the rest of the species.*

I didn't know whether the rest of the species would rather live a life of misery just to avoid dying, whether they would rather live in deprivation, in solitude, just to avoid jumping into Moy Lake with a stone tied around their neck. Whether they considered war a natural instinct. It's deranged, the human species; its instincts shouldn't be heeded.

JOSEPH AND HERTA didn't ask me who the person powerful enough to sneak me onto a Nazi train was. Maybe they had always known. I wished they would keep me from leaving, *You're staying here, it's time to atone.* Instead Herta stroked my cheek and said, "Be careful, my daughter."

"Come with me, both of you!" Somehow I would convince Ziegler, he would find a way to sneak them aboard too.

"I'm too old," Herta replied.

"If you're not coming, then I'm staying. I'm not leaving you alone," I said. I thought of Franz, of when I used to wake up, terrified, after the Abduction. I would take his hands in mine, and the warmth would calm me. I would slip into his bed, cling to his back. "No, I'm not leaving you alone." Herta and Joseph's house was warm, like my brother.

"You're leaving the first chance you get," Joseph declared with an authoritarian tone I had never heard him use. "It's your duty to save yourself." He was speaking like his son.

"When Gregor comes back," said Herta, "he'll need you."

"He's never coming back!" The words had escaped me, shrilly.

Herta grimaced. She pulled away from me, sank into a chair.

Joseph clenched his jaw and went out the back door despite the temperature.

I didn't rush after him, didn't get up to console Herta. I could feel that we were separated from each other, that we were already alone, each in our own way.

When he reappeared at the door, though, I apologized to them both. Herta didn't look up.

"I'm sorry," I said again. "I've been living here with you for a year, and you're the only family left to me. I'm afraid of losing you. Without you, I'm afraid."

Joseph threw a log onto the fire to feed the flames, then sat down too.

We were still together, all three of us, our faces warmed by the fire, like when we had daydreamed about Gregor's return and planned Christmas dinner.

"You'll come back to visit us, you and my son," said Herta. "Promise me."

I could only nod my head.

Zart leapt onto my lap, arched his back, and stretched his legs. Then, once curled up on my knees, he began purring, as though he were saying goodbye.

THREE MORNINGS LATER the bus didn't show up. Hitler had left. The other women didn't know he was never to return. I didn't say goodbye to Leni or the others. I couldn't have. Over the previous week in Gross-Partsch, using the cold weather as an excuse, I had rarely left the house.

One night, the sound of fingernails on the windowpane awakened me. I lit the oil lamp and went to the window. Ziegler was standing there, very close up. Through a trick of light, in the reflection of the glass I saw my face superimposed on his. I slipped my coat on, went outside. He explained where and when the next day I was to meet a certain Dr. Schweighofer, who knew the whole plan and was a reliable fellow. When he was sure everything was clear to me, he quickly wished me good night, shrugging his shoulders like he used to.

"See you tomorrow, then," I said. "At the station."

He nodded.

The next afternoon, by the front door, Herta squeezed me tight as Joseph shyly stepped forward, rested his hands on our shoulders, and wrapped his arms around both of us. When we let go, my in-laws watched me disappear for the last time around the bend of Gross-Partsch, on foot.

It was late November and I was about to set off for Berlin on Goebbels's train. Goebbels wasn't there, and Albert Ziegler wouldn't be coming.

42

I IMAGINED GOEBBELS'S TRAIN LIKE THE *AMERIKA*—THAT IS, THE *Brandenburg*—which Krümel had told me about. Would Krümel also be leaving that night? Would I run into him on the platform? No, he must have gone with Hitler. Otherwise, who would prepare semolina for him? *The Führer has a stomachache, he always does, and traveling makes him nervous, especially now that he's losing the war . . . but semolina is a cure-all, you'll see, Crumbs will take care of you.*

I showed up for the appointment with Dr. Schweighofer in an anonymous café in Gross-Partsch at six o'clock on the dot, as Ziegler had told me to. There was no one in the café. With one hand the owner was brushing scattered granules of sugar off the bar and collecting them in his other hand. Only when he was finished did he serve me a cup of tea, which I didn't even touch. Ziegler had told me I could recognize the doctor by his mustache, which he wore identical to Hitler's. Once, in the barn, he had told me that they often advised the Führer to shave off his mustache, but he objected, saying he couldn't, that his nose was too big. Schweighofer's nose, on the other hand, was slender, and his mustache light-colored, slightly yellowed, perhaps by cigarette smoke. When he walked in he quickly scanned the empty tables and spotted me. He came over, said my name, I said his, held out my hand, he shook it hurriedly, *Let's go.*

During the drive there he told me that at that hour the person standing guard was someone he trusted, someone who would let me into the Wolfsschanze station without asking for documents. "Once inside, follow me. Don't look around. Walk at a brisk pace, but without looking nervous."

"What if someone stops us?"

"It's dark out and there will be a great deal of confusion. With a bit of luck they won't notice us. If they do, I'll pretend you're one of my nurses."

So that was why Albert wasn't taking me there in person. I had mistaken it for another sign of his cowardice—despite the power provided him by his rank, he was too craven to take his own lover to catch Goebbels's train, too cowardly to demand that she too be allowed to depart with the Wolfsschanze's direct employees, even though she neither lived nor worked there. Speaking with the doctor, though, I realized Ziegler had entrusted me to the man's care because he had a plan: I would pass myself off as part of the medical staff. It might work.

SHIVERING INSIDE HIS post, the guard let us through after only a summary glance. I found myself in the middle of a bustle of men loading wooden crates of various sizes onto the train cars while the SS and soldiers kept watch over them, barking out orders and guarding the goods. The train was ready on the tracks, its snout already pointed elsewhere, as though it had turned its back on the Wolfsschanze. The swastikas on its side were a ridiculous frill, as relics of the losing side always are. It was anxious to go—that's how it seemed to me. Goebbels wasn't there, and the train no longer answered to him, only to its own instinct for self-preservation.

Schweighofer trudged along without looking back to check whether I had fallen behind.

"Where are we going now?" I asked.

"Do you at least have a blanket in that bag?"

In my suitcase I had packed only some sweaters—in a few months I would come back for the rest, I thought, would persuade my in-laws to come with me to Berlin—and a blanket, as Albert had suggested. Herta had also made me some sandwiches, since the journey would last several hours.

"Yes, I have one. Listen, I was wondering, without documents, can I still claim I'm your nurse? What if they ask me for them?"

He didn't reply. He walked quickly. I had a hard time keeping up.

"Where are we going, Doctor? We've reached the end of the cars."

"The passenger cars, yes."

I didn't understand what was going on until he had me climb into a freight car at the end of the train, far from the crowd scrambling around on the platform. He shoved my back with his palms, making me tumble inside, and climbed in behind me. Unconcerned about my bewilderment, he pushed a few crates aside, chose my spot, and pointed at it: a niche behind a stack of trunks.

"They'll shelter you from the cold."

"What are you talking about?"

A fine plan indeed. Hours, days traveling in a freight car, sealed up in the darkness with the risk of freezing to death. I continued to be Ziegler's pawn.

"Doctor, I can't stay in here."

"Do as you please. I've fulfilled my obligation—my agreement with the lieutenant was to take you to safety, and this is all I can possibly offer you. I'm sorry. I can't add you to the list of civilians, the cars are already chock-full. People will travel standing or sitting on the floor. It's not like we can take the whole town with us."

He hopped onto the platform, slapped his hands on his trousers, and was holding them out to me to help me down when a male voice called out to him.

"Hide, quickly," he told me, then turned to the person who had called to him.

"Good evening, Sturmführer. I was here making sure my precious equipment was properly arranged, that nothing's been broken."

"How can you check that? Weren't the crates sealed tight?" The voice was getting clearer and clearer.

"Yes, I know. It was a foolish notion, I admit. However, I couldn't help but come," Schweighofer said. "Knowing they're here, safe and sound, is a comfort." He tried to laugh.

The Sturmführer replied with a short, polite chuckle. I stayed hidden behind the crates as he came closer. What might he do to me if he discovered me there? Whatever it was, I had nothing left to lose. Ziegler had been the one to insist. I didn't want to leave, was tired of trying to save myself. And yet the SS still struck as much fear in me as they had on my first day.

The floor of the train car swayed beneath me when the Sturmführer leapt up into it, and the crates resounded as he slapped them. I held my breath.

"They seem to have done a fine job, Doctor. It's unkind of you to have doubted them."

"What? Why, no, it was just a precaution. . . ."

"Don't worry, everyone knows doctors are unusual people." Another chuckle. "Go get some rest, now. We have a long journey ahead of us. We'll be leaving in just a few hours."

The floor swayed again and the SS officer's soles landed on the platform. I kept my head between my knees, both arms wrapped around them tightly.

All at once a metallic rumble blackened the train car until everything went dark. I shot to my feet, groped around for the exit, searched for a crack through which a trace of light might seep in, staggered, with nothing to cling to, as voiceless as though gripped by an Abduction, then tripped over the crates, fell.

I could have gotten back up, banged into the crated supplies until I found the door, pounded on it with my fists, pounded and shouted, sooner or later someone would hear me, someone would open the door for me, what they would do to me I didn't care, I wanted to die, had wanted to die for months. Instead I lay there, sprawled on the floor. It was apprehension, fear, or only the survival instinct—it never left me. I never had enough of living.

43

THE COMMOTION AWAKENED ME. SOMEONE WAS OPENING THE FREIGHT car door. On all fours, I dragged myself into my nook behind the crates, drew my knees up to my chest. A faint light entered, and one after the other a number of people—I couldn't say how many—climbed into the car, thanked whoever had taken them there, and settled down amid the trunks, murmuring something I couldn't make out. Wondering if they noticed my presence, to summon my courage I clutched the handle of my suitcase. The rumble of the door slamming shut silenced everyone. Who knew what time it was or when the train would set off again? I was hungry, exhaustion had glued my eyes shut. Surrounded by darkness, I had lost all sense of time and space. The cold nipped the base of my neck and lower back, and my bladder was full. I heard the other people whispering but couldn't see them. I drifted in a colorless dream, a reversible coma, bleary isolation. It wasn't solitude, it was as if no one in the world had ever existed, not even me.

I relaxed my bladder and peed on myself. The hot rivulet consoled me. Maybe the urine would trickle across the floor until it touched the feet of the other passengers. . . . No, the crates would block its way. Maybe the smell would drift over to my travel companions, who would think it was from the contents of the trunks, *Who knows what's inside them, it might be the smell of disinfectant.*

My thighs wet, I fell asleep again.

———

THE CRY WAS desperate. I opened my eyes to the darkness. It was a baby's cry. It mingled with the clatter of the moving train, its sobs muffled by the bosom of its mother, who was probably cuddling it against her—I couldn't see—as the father whispered, *What's wrong, that's enough, don't cry, are you hungry?* It sounded like the mother had been trying to feed the baby but it had been no use. In the din, jostled by the rocking of the train, I took out my blanket, threw it over my shoulders. Where were we, how long had I slept, my stomach was empty, I was hungry yet had no will to eat. My body was protecting itself by sleeping. The baby's distress scratched at that viscous drowsiness without piercing it, it was but an indecipherable echo, a mirage. And so, when I began to sing I didn't recognize my own voice. It was like drifting off to sleep or wetting yourself or feeling hunger without the will to eat, a state prior to life, it had neither beginning nor end.

I sang the nursery rhyme I had sung for Ursula at Heike's house, and later for Albert in the barn. In the darkness, amid the child's wails and the groans of the freight car, I spoke to the fox who had stolen the goose, warned it that the hunter would make him pay, and didn't think about the stunned faces of the other passengers, *Who on earth is that?* the father must have said, but I didn't hear him, the mother clasping her child's face to her breast and stroking its tiny head, *Dear little fox, no goose for you,* I sang, *with a little mouse why not make do?* and the baby stopped crying and I repeated the nursery rhyme all over again, *Sing with me, Ursula, by now you know the words.* I repeated it from beneath my blanket and the baby dozed off, or stayed awake but stopped wailing—it had been a vitalistic act, its crying, like every rebellion. Then it too had desisted, had given in.

I fell silent, groped around in my suitcase in search of a sandwich.

"Who's there?" the woman asked.

A faint glow cast a shadow on the floor. I followed it, slowly slipping out of my niche, and peered out from behind the barricade of crates.

The infant was wrapped in layers of blankets. The father had lit a match and in the glow of the tiny flame the mother's face trembled.

———

CHRISTA AND RUDOLPH thanked me for calming their son. *How did you do it?* His name was Thomas, he was only six months old and he didn't want milk, was too agitated.

"Is someone waiting for you in Berlin?" was the first question that came to my mind.

"No, we've never even been there. This was the only way to get out, though," Rudolph said. "We'll come up with something."

I didn't have anyone waiting for me in Berlin either. I could leave that to him, he could come up with something for me too. I asked my travel companions if they wanted to eat. Christa rested the baby on a pallet of folded blankets. He was finally asleep. Rudolph lit another match because the first one had gone out, and we took out what we had brought with us. We laid it out on two dishcloths and together ate what we had, as though it were still possible for human beings to break bread together, even human beings confined to a freight car, huddled in a space meant for goods. That's how friends are made: in confinement.

OF THE JOURNEY I remember little. The stops along the way. There was no hole through which to glimpse the cities, woods, or countryside, we never knew where we were or whether it was day or night. Silence crept over us like snow, and perhaps snow really had fallen, but we couldn't see it. We curled up close to one another to warm ourselves, sighed from boredom, only occasionally from anxiety, I listened to the light breathing of the sleeping baby and thought of Pauline. Who knew where she was, how much she had grown, who knew if I would see her again in Berlin? We shivered beneath the covers, were thirsty, our remaining water dwindling, we touched the rim of the canteen to our lips to moisten them, would make do with that, we counted the matches, *How many are left?* Rudolph lit them just so Christa could change the baby, the cotton diaper with excrement rolled up in a corner, we had gotten used to the stink, chatted in subdued tones in the shelter of the darkness. There was even time for me to play with Thomas and hear him laugh when being tickled, to cradle him in Christa's place when she was exasperated by his crying, cradle him with his head

on my neck, or rub his tummy. Of the journey I remember the sandwiches chewed in the dark, the mouthfuls savored, Christa's tin jar,
in which the urine swished like a beaded necklace being fiddled between one's fingers, the pungent smell reminding me of the shelter in
Budengasse, the dignity with which the three of us held back any other
bodily need until we reached our destination. Shit is proof that God
doesn't exist, Gregor had said, but I thought of how much compassion I felt for my companions' bodies, for their innocent, unavoidable
baseness, and just then that baseness seemed to be the only true reason to love them.

When the train came to a halt at the umpteenth stop we didn't
realize it was the final one, that we were in Berlin, having arrived at
last.

Part
THREE

44

THE STATION IS NOISY AND CROWDED, THE PEOPLE MOVING SO FAST I'M afraid they'll barrel into me, the ones behind me passing me by, those coming in my direction veering to the side only at the last second, dodging me with a twist of their hips—I'm already standing still, a cat caught in the headlights. The weight of my suitcase makes me tilt to the right as I walk, but clutching its handle gives me a sense of security—at least it's something to cling to.

I look for a washroom. I hadn't wanted to use the one on the train, and now I can't hold out any longer. Since the line is short my turn comes quickly. Afterward I look at myself in the mirror. My irises are afloat in the dark basins of the circles around my eyes. It's as though my face has undergone a landslide and my eyes rolled around for a long time before settling where they are now, sunken in. I straighten a barrette at my temple, comb my hair with my fingers, even put on some lipstick—at least a touch of color on this pale face. *You've always been vain*, Herta used to tell me. Today is an important day, though. It's worth it.

The throngs of people disorient me. It's been a long time since I last took a train, and the journey frightened me, but I had to do it, it might be my last chance.

I'm thirsty, though there's a line here too. I get behind the others anyway. A woman says, "Please, ma'am, go ahead of me." She's under thirty, freckles everywhere—her face, her chest, her arms.

Those beside her turn around. "Of course, ma'am," a man says, "go ahead of me too."

"Can we let this woman cut through?" the freckled woman asks, raising her voice a little.

I cling to the handle of my suitcase. "That's not necessary," I say, but she guides me forward, her hand on my back, accompanies me. I have a caved-in face and withered arms—that's how they see me.

After I've drunk from the fountain and thanked them all, I find the exit. The sun is bright. It shines against the picture window so strongly that it cancels out the skyline of the city. I shade my eyes with one hand to cross the threshold, blink repeatedly until I gain a clear view of the square. Who knows where I can find a taxi? The clocks on the corners of the façade, in the niches beside the row of small arches, read one-forty.

It's pretty, the Hannover station.

I GIVE THE taxi driver the address, roll down the window, lean my head back against the headrest, watch the city dart by as the newscast on the radio reminds us that today is the day the Schengen II is being signed, thus opening the borders between West Germany, France, Belgium, Luxembourg, and the Netherlands.

"Where is Schengen?"

"I think it's in Luxembourg," the taxi driver replies. He doesn't say anything else. He doesn't feel like chatting either.

I look at my reflection in the rearview mirror. The line of lipstick is uneven because my lips are chapped. I try to wipe off the imperfection with my fingernail, wanting to look presentable when I see him. On the radio they mention the Italia '90 World Cup. That afternoon in Milan, West Germany is playing against Colombia. I could talk about that, about football. He never cared for football and I know nothing about it, but with the World Cup it's different—everyone watches that. Besides, we need to break the ice with one topic or another.

The taxi pulls up to the curb, the driver gets out, takes my bag from the trunk, gives it to me. Right before walking in, I see my face again in the reflection of the glass door. The red stands out against my pale complexion, the line of lipstick can't decide where my lips end. I take a tissue from my pocket and wipe them until the color is entirely gone.

As soon as the elevator doors open, I recognize Agnes's profile. She's waiting for a hot beverage to come out of the vending machine. She's ten years younger than me and looks even younger than that, despite the curve of her belly, which pulls on the fabric of her blue slacks until its pattern is slightly distorted. But she still has a smooth face, Agnes, a face that hasn't caved. She takes out the cup, blows on it, uses the stirrer to mix in the sugar, and then sees me.

"Rosa! There you are."

I had been standing there holding my suitcase, yet again a cat caught in the headlights.

"Hello, Agnes."

"How nice to have you here. Did you have a good trip?" She hugs me, being careful not to burn me with her piping-hot cup. "How long has it been?"

"I don't know," I reply, pulling back. "Too long."

"Do you want to give me—" She reaches out her free hand.

"No, I'll keep it. It's not heavy. Thanks."

Agnes doesn't show me the way, stands there.

"How are you?" I ask.

"Like people normally are in these circumstances." She looks down for a second. "And you?" She stands there holding the cup, doesn't drink from it. When she notices I'm staring at it she holds it out to me. "Do you want some?" Immediately realizing her mistake, she turns toward the machine. "I mean, do you want something? Are you thirsty, hungry?"

I shake my head. "I'm fine, thanks. Margot and Wiebke?"

"One's gone to pick up her son from school, she'll be here later. The other is working, so she can't come today."

Agnes doesn't drink her beverage. I'm neither thirsty nor hungry.

"And how is he?" I ask after a pause.

She shrugs, smiles, lets her eyes fall to her beverage. I wait in silence for her to finish drinking it. After she's tossed everything into the trash can, she distractedly wipes her hands on her slacks. "Shall we go?" she says.

And I follow her.

HE'S ATTACHED TO an IV, two thin tubes up his nose. His head has been shaved, or maybe he's simply lost all his hair. His eyelids are closed, he's resting. The June light coming in through the window pulverizes his features, but I recognize him.

Agnes has me put my suitcase in a corner, then goes to the bed, leans over. Her belt cuts her tummy into two sections, but she still has smooth hands, the same hands that caress the sheet.

"My love, are you sleeping?"

She calls him her love in front of me. It's not the first time, it's happened before, too many years ago for me to be used to it. She calls him her love and he wakes up. They're blue, his eyes. Rheumy, slightly pale.

Agnes's voice is so sweet as she says, "You have a visitor," and she steps aside so he can see me without needing to rise from his pillow.

His blue eyes lock on to mine and I no longer have anything to cling to. He smiles at me.

"Hello, Gregor."

45

AGNES TOLD HIM SHE WOULD TAKE ADVANTAGE OF MY BEING THERE TO go for a coffee. She had just had one, it was an excuse to leave us alone. I wondered if she did it for me—because she was afraid I was embarrassed—or if it was embarrassing for her to be in the same room with her husband's ex-wife and him, now that he was dying.

Before leaving, she gave him a drink of water. She placed a hand on the back of his neck to raise his head, and Gregor rested his lips on the edge of the glass like a child who hasn't yet learned to drink from one. Water trickled down, dampening his pajamas. Agnes wiped his neck dry with a paper towel torn off a roll resting on the nightstand, straightened his pillows, tucked him in, whispered in his ear something I'll never know, kissed his forehead, adjusted the roller shutters so the sunlight wouldn't bother him, said goodbye to us both, and slipped out the door.

It's strange to see another woman take care of Gregor, not so much because the man was once my husband but because I myself had fed him, bathed him, warmed his body when, a year after the war ended, he returned home.

THE DAY GREGOR reappeared, potatoes were boiling in Anne's kitchen. I was living with her and Pauline. It was summer, like now. Pauline had stayed outside to play hide-and-seek among the rubble of Budengasse while Anne and I, having come home from work, had gone upstairs to cook something. My apartment was still uninhabitable, and Anne—who was also without a husband—had offered to let me stay with them. All three of us slept in the same bed.

I poked one of the potatoes with a fork to see if it was done. As always, my feet were aching. Between home and work it was an hour-and-a-half walk at a good pace, but fortunately after dinner I would share the footbath that Anne prepared every evening. We would sink our blistered feet into the basin together and sigh. Pauline, on the other hand, was never tired, despite spending all day chasing the other children through the ruins of the city while we hauled buckets, pushed wheelbarrows, stacked bricks in exchange for seventy pfennigs an hour and a special ration book.

The potatoes were ready. I put out the flame. From the street Pauline cried, "Rosa!"

I looked out the window. "What is it?"

A frail man was leaning against her. He looked crippled. I didn't recognize him.

Then, with a barely perceptible voice, the man said, "It's me." And my heart broke.

I SIT BESIDE the bed. I weave my fingers together on my belly, rest them on my lap, smooth my skirt out beneath my legs, clasp my hands together again. It's because I don't know where to put them. It's because I don't dare touch him.

"Thank you for coming, Rosa."

He has a frail, broken voice, like the one I heard from Anne's window that evening forty-four years ago. His skin has grown tight, making his nose look larger, the bones of his face protruding.

With my finger I search for a trace of remaining lipstick, not wanting him to see me looking sloppy—it's stupid, but it's true. I was afraid he would ask Agnes, *Who is she, who is that woman standing in my hospital room, her eyes sunken, her face wrinkled?* Instead he had known at once who I was, had smiled at me.

"I really wanted to see you," I say.

"Me too, but I didn't think you would."

"Why not?"

Gregor doesn't reply. I stare at my fingernails, my fingertips—they aren't smudged with lipstick.

"How's it going in Berlin?"

"Everything's fine."

Try as I might, nothing comes to mind to say about Berlin, about my existence there. Gregor is also silent. Then he asks, "And how's Franz doing?"

"These days he's got his hands full with his granddaughters. His son brought them to Germany on vacation, and he keeps them in the shop while he shaves customers or cuts their hair. More out of kindness than interest, his customers ask, 'What's your name, how old are you?' and the girls answer in English. The customers don't understand and Franz gets a real kick out of it. It makes him so proud that his granddaughters speak another language. Since he became a grandfather he's become quite a fool."

"No, your brother has always been strange."

"You think so?"

"Rosa, he didn't write to you for years!"

"Oh, you know, he says he wanted to cut his ties, that Germans were looked down on after '18, that some even changed their last names. . . . Then, when America entered the war, he lived in terror of being interned."

"Yes, yes, I know the story. What was that offensive dish? Hold on. . . ."

"The offensive dish . . . ? Oh, sauerkraut!" I laugh. "They changed its name, called it 'liberty cabbage.' At least that's what Franz says."

"Exactly, sauerkraut." He laughs too.

He coughs. It's a thick, chesty cough that forces him to raise his head. Maybe I should hold it for him, help him. "What should I do?"

Gregor clears his throat and goes on as though it were nothing. "That telegram he sent, do you remember it?"

He's accustomed to coughing and wants to talk—that's all he wants. "How could I forget it?" I say. "'Are any of you still alive?'" That's all that was written, except a phone number and address.

"Exactly. And you called more than anything to make sure it wasn't a joke."

"Yes, that's right! And the moment Franz heard my voice the cat got his tongue."

Gregor laughs again. I didn't think it would be this easy.

"When the girls go back to Pittsburgh at the end of the month, you'll see—he'll go crazy. But then again, he's the one who decided to return to Berlin. Some people, sooner or later, need to return. Who knows why?"

"You returned to Berlin yourself."

"I was forced to leave Gross-Partsch. My case doesn't count."

Gregor falls silent, turns toward the window. Maybe he's thinking about his parents, who died before he could see them again. I never saw them again either.

"I've missed them a lot too," I say, but Gregor doesn't reply.

He's wearing long-sleeved pajamas, and the sheet is pulled halfway up his chest.

"Are you hot?"

He doesn't reply. I sit there on the chair, lace my fingers. I was wrong—this isn't easy.

"If you've come all the way here," he says after a while, "it means I really am about to die."

This time I'm the one who doesn't reply.

Gregor comes to my rescue. "As if I would die now that you've come back."

I smile and my eyes well up.

As if you would die now that you've come back, I would tell him whenever he lost heart. *Dying is no longer an option, sorry, I won't let you.*

He weighed fifteen kilos less than when he had departed. In the prison camp where he'd been held he lived in hunger and came down with pneumonia, had been left with chronic fatigue. His leg was lame—it hadn't been treated properly because he had run away from the hospital in a state of delirium. Since all the cots around him contained only amputees, he was convinced they were going to amputate his leg too. The pain had slowed him, left him easy prey to capture. It didn't seem possible to me that he'd done something so reckless—it wasn't like Gregor.

"But what if I had returned to you an amputee?" he asked me once.

"Your being back would've been enough."

"We were supposed to celebrate Christmas together, Rosa. I didn't keep my promise."

"*Shhh*, get some sleep now. Sleep, because by tomorrow I want you all better."

Perhaps it was from an intestinal infection, or only because his digestive system had been compromised by months of hardship, but he couldn't keep anything down. I would make him meat broth, when I managed to get my hands on any meat, and those four spoonfuls he was able to swallow would be expelled immediately. His excrement was liquid, greenish, and let off an odor I never would have believed could be produced by a human body.

We set him up in Pauline's room and at night I would stay there in a chair beside his bed. At times the little girl would wake up and come looking for me. "Are you coming to sleep with me?"

"Sweetheart, I need to stay with Gregor."

"If you don't, will he die?"

"As long as I'm here with him, I swear to you that he won't die."

Some mornings I would wake up because the sunlight was hitting my eyelids and I would find her curled up on top of him. She wasn't our daughter, but I might still count her breaths as she slept.

Gregor's debilitated body had nothing in common with my husband. His skin had another smell—but Pauline couldn't know that. Keeping that man alive was my only purpose in life. I would tuck him in, wash his face, his arms, his chest, his penis and testicles, his legs, his feet, dipping a cloth into the footbath basin, which Anne only prepared for herself in the evenings, now that I had stopped collecting rubble to avoid leaving him alone. I would trim his nails, shave his beard, cut his hair, accompany him to the bathroom, wipe him. At times he unexpectedly regurgitated, coughed, spat into my hand. I never felt disgust—I loved him, and that was that. Gregor had become my child.

The minute he woke up Pauline would wake up too. In a low voice, so he wouldn't hear her, the little girl would say, "As long as we're here, Rosa, I swear to you that he won't die."

Gregor didn't die. He got better.

"You know, when Agnes told me she'd called you and that you were coming, it reminded me of something that happened during the war. Maybe I already told you about it in a letter."

"I don't think so, Gregor," I say with fake reproach. "You wrote practically nothing to me about the war."

He grasps the fake reproach and laughs. "Still rubbing it in my face. Unbelievable!" And since he laughs, he coughs. The lines on his forehead grow thicker. The dark splotches on his face quiver.

"Do you want some water?" On the nightstand is the glass, still half full.

"We didn't know what we could write. It was dangerous to show you were discouraged, and I was so discouraged. . . ."

"Yes, I know, don't worry. I was joking. What is it you remembered?"

"There were two women. They came looking for their husbands. They'd come I don't know how many kilometers on foot, hundreds of kilometers, in the snow, sleeping out in the cold, just to see them. But once they arrived they discovered their husbands weren't there. You should have seen the looks on their faces."

"So where were they?"

"I have no idea. At another camp, probably. Or they'd been taken to Germany, or maybe they were dead. Who knows? They weren't among our prisoners. The wives walked all the way back, in the same snow and the same cold, without learning anything about them. Can you believe it?"

When he speaks more, he gets breathless. Maybe I should make him not talk, stay here with him in silence, take his hand—if only I dared touch him.

"But why did that come to your mind? It's not like I came here on foot through the snow."

"True."

"Besides, you're not my husband anymore." .

What an unhappy thing I've said. I didn't mean to be rude.

I stand up, walk around the room. There's a locker in which Agnes has probably stored towels, a change of pajamas, everything he needs. Why isn't Agnes back yet?

"Where are you going?" Gregor asks.

"Nowhere, I'm right here."

I trip over his slippers at the foot of the bed before sitting back down.

"Even if you didn't walk through the snow, you took at least a three-and-a-half-hour trip to come say goodbye to me."

"Well, yes."

"Why do you think people need to say goodbye?"

"What do you mean?"

"You came all the way to Hannover to do it. You must know the reason why."

"Well . . . maybe people need nothing to be left hanging. I think."

"So you came here to tie up the loose ends?"

The question catches me off guard.

"Rosa. We've been left hanging since '40, you and I."

WE LEFT EACH other by mutual consent, and it was very painful. People normally say, "We decided by mutual consent," to mean they didn't suffer from it, or that they suffered less, but it's not true. Sure, it's possible to suffer more, if one of the two can't come to terms with it, if they hurt the other intentionally, but separation is inevitably a painful experience. Especially in cases where the people have been given a second chance, against all odds. The two of us had lost each other, and after the war we had found each other again.

It lasted three years, then we split up. I don't understand those who say, *It had been over for a long time.* It's impossible to establish the precise moment when a marriage ends, because a marriage ends when the spouses decide it's over, or at least one of the two decides it is. Marriage is a fluctuating system—it moves in waves, it can always end and always begin again, it has no linear progression, nor does it follow logical paths. The lowest point in a marriage doesn't necessarily mean it's over; one day you're in the pits and the next day you're soaring again without knowing how it happened, and you can't remember a reason, not a single one, why you should separate. It's not even a question of pros and cons, of pluses and minuses. Everything considered, all marriages are destined to end and each marriage has the right—the duty—to survive.

Ours held together for a while out of gratitude. We had received a miracle, we couldn't squander it. We were the chosen ones, were destined to be. With time, even the enthusiasm of a miracle dampens. We had thrown ourselves headfirst into rebuilding our marriage because that was the word on everyone's lips back then: rebuilding. Leaving the past behind, forgetting. But I never forgot, and neither did Gregor. *If only we had shared our memories,* I told myself at times. We couldn't. To us it would have seemed like squandering our miracle. Instead we tried to protect it, to protect each other. For the rest of those years we were trying so hard to protect each other that we ended up with nothing but that: barricades.

"Hi, Dad."

In walks a young woman with long, straight hair parted down the middle, a light-colored linen dress with shoulder straps, sandals on her feet.

"Hello," she says, seeing me.

I stand up.

"Margot," Gregor says.

The young woman comes over to me and I'm just about to introduce myself when Agnes comes back. "Oh, honey, you're here? And the boy?"

"I left him at my mother-in-law's." She looks out of breath, Gregor's daughter, a veneer of perspiration on her forehead.

"This is Rosa," Agnes says.

"Welcome." Margot offers me her hand. I shake it. She has Gregor's eyes.

"Thank you. I'm happy to meet you," I say, smiling. "I saw you in a photograph. You'd just been born."

"So you sent around pictures of me without my permission, huh?" she said to her father, grinning and giving him a kiss.

GREGOR SENT ME pictures of his baby girl and hadn't thought it might hurt my feelings—he just wanted to make me still feel part of his life. It was an affectionate gesture—not protective, but affectionate. He wasn't protecting me any longer, had forgotten how it was done. He had married Agnes, I had gone to their wedding, had wished them all the best and done so sincerely. Never mind that I felt sad on the train back to Berlin. The fact that he wasn't alone anymore didn't make me feel any less lonely.

Wolfsburg, they announced over the loudspeaker on the way back, *Wolfsburg station.* I started. How had I not noticed it on the way there? Maybe I'd been sleeping. I had passed through the town of the wolf to separate myself once and for all from my husband.

"I BROUGHT YOU a present, Dad."

Margot takes a folded sheet of grid-ruled paper out of her purse and hands it to Gregor.

"Wait," Agnes says, "I'll open it for you."

It's a crayon drawing. There's a bald man lying in a bed beneath a sky of pink clouds. Growing between the legs of the bed are flowers with petals in a rainbow of colors.

"It's from your grandson," Margot says.

I'm there beside them. I can't help but read what's written on it. It says: *GRANDPA, I MISS YOU. GET WELL SOON.*

"Do you like it?" Margot asks.

Gregor doesn't reply.

"Think we can hang it up, Mom? Should we hang it up?"

"Hmm. . . . We'd need a pushpin, or some tape . . ."

"Dad, aren't you going to say anything?"

He's too touched to reply, it's clear to see, and I feel out of place right now, with this family that isn't mine. I move away, go to the window, look out at the courtyard between the slats of the rolling shutters. There are patients in wheelchairs, nurses pushing them along. There are people sitting on benches; it's hard to say whether they're sick or healthy.

THE FIRST TIME Gregor tried to make love to me again, after all that time, I withdrew. I didn't say no, didn't make an excuse, I simply tensed. Gregor stroked me sweetly, believing it was shyness—we hadn't touched each other for too long a time. Contact with his body was a habit, I handled it with experience, with practicality. The war had given back to me the body of a veteran, and I had enough youth and energy to take care of him. But we hadn't touched each other with desire—desire was a feeling I had forgotten. We had to learn it all over again, slowly but surely, with gradual practice—that was what Gregor believed. I thought it was desire that brought about intimacy, and immediately, like a sudden jerk, but maybe the opposite was also possible—starting with intimacy, reappropriating it until grasping desire, like when you wake up and try to grasp a dream you've just had, but it's already vanished; you remember the atmosphere but not a single image. Sure, it might be possible, certainly other wives had succeeded. How they managed to, I have no idea. Maybe ours hadn't been the right approach.

46

THE DOCTOR DOESN'T WEAR GLASSES. WHEN HE COMES IN I CHECK MY watch. It's already late afternoon. Agnes and Margot chat with him, talking about the World Cup, then about Margot's son, whom the doctor must have met at some point in this room. He's very friendly, has an athletic build and a baritone voice. I'm not introduced and he doesn't take notice of me. He asks us to step outside, he needs to check on Gregor.

In the hallway, Agnes asks me, "Are you staying over at our place, then?"

"Thanks, I've booked a hotel."

"I don't see why, Rosa, there's plenty of room. Besides, you'd be keeping me company."

Yes, we could keep each other company, but I'm accustomed to living alone, I don't want to share anyone else's space.

"I'd rather not be a bother, really. Anyway, I've already booked, it's a little hotel here in the area. It's convenient."

"Well, remember: if you change your mind at any time, just call me and I'll come pick you up."

"If you don't want to be alone, Mom, you can sleep at our place."

Why is Margot saying that? To make me feel at fault?

The doctor joins us. He's finished. Agnes asks for an update on Gregor's condition. Margot listens carefully and then asks her own question. I'm not part of the family so I go back into the room.

GREGOR IS TRYING to roll down his left sleeve. His right arm is bare, its sleeve raised to allow the IV needles to penetrate his vein. The other, instead, is covered with blue cotton. Blue must be Agnes's favorite color. Maybe Gregor rolled it up to scratch himself. He has dry skin streaked with white lines left behind by his fingernails.

"We weren't left hanging," I tell him without sitting down. "We moved on."

Gregor keeps trying but can't roll the sleeve down. I don't help him, don't dare touch him.

"You came back, I took care of you, you got better, we reopened the office, we rebuilt the house, we moved on."

"Is that what you came here to tell me?" He gives up, lets go of his pajama sleeve. "Is this your goodbye?" His voice is raw, hoarse.

"Don't you agree?"

He sighs. "We weren't the same as before."

"But who was the same as before, Gregor? Who managed that?"

"Some people did."

"Are you trying to tell me other people were better than us, than me? I already knew that."

"I never made it an issue of better or worse."

"And you were wrong to."

"Did you come here to tell me I was wrong, Rosa?"

"I didn't come here to tell you anything, Gregor."

"Then why are you here?"

"If you didn't want me here you could have said so! You could've had your wife tell me over the phone!" I mustn't get angry. It's pathetic, an old woman getting angry.

Here she comes, his wife. She rushes in, looking alarmed.

"Rosa," she says, as though my name contained all the questions.

She goes over to Gregor, rolls down his pajama sleeve. "Everything okay?" she asks him.

Then she turns to me. "I heard you two shouting."

I'm the only one who shouted. Gregor wouldn't be able to, not with those lungs. It's me Agnes heard.

"I don't want you to get tired," she tells her husband. She's talking to me—I'm the one tiring him.

"Excuse me," I say, and walk out.

I pass by the doctor and Margot, don't say anything to them, walk down the hall, don't know where I'm going. The neon lights are giving me a headache. On the stairs I feel like I'm falling, but instead of clinging to the handrail I grab the chain tucked beneath my shirt collar, pull it out, clutch it in my fist. The metal is cold and hard. Only when I reach the end of the stairs do I open my hand. On my palm, the wedding band attached to the chain has left behind two circles.

I HAD NEVER been to her house before. All I had to do was push on the door to enter a dark room—there was a single, narrow window—with a table and a small sofa. The chairs had been knocked over amid broken dishes and glasses, the credenza drawers yanked out and dumped onto the floor. In the half-light, the gaps in which they had once been inserted looked like burial recesses waiting to be occupied.

The SS had turned everything upside down. So that was how it happened, how someone was uprooted. I was left with objects, the need to touch what had belonged to Elfriede now that she was gone.

Taking a deep breath, I stepped forward until I reached a curtain. Hesitantly I pushed it aside, a feeling of trespassing. In the bedroom, linens and clothes were piled on the wooden flooring. Torn off the mattress, the sheets were a heap of rags, perched atop it a pillow ripped apart at the seams.

The world had broken down once Elfriede was gone, and I had been left in that world without even a body to grieve over, yet again.

I knelt on top of the clothes, stroked them. I had never touched her stony face, her cheekbones, or even those bruises on her legs that I had been the cause of. *I'll stay by your side,* I had sworn to her in the barracks washroom. And at that moment we had ceased to be as giggly as schoolgirls.

Stretching out on the floor, I scooped up the clothing around me, gathered it beneath my neck, my face pressed against the floor. They didn't have a scent, not hers, or I had already forgotten it.

When you lose someone, the pain you feel is for yourself, the pain that you'll never see them again, never hear their voice again, that without them, you think, you'll never make it. Pain is selfish. That was what made me angry.

But as I lay there amid her clothes, the vastness of that tragic end revealed itself in its entirety. It was such a huge, unbearable event that it drowned out the pain, engulfed it, expanded until it occupied every centimeter of the universe, became proof of what mankind was capable of.

I had learned the dark color of Elfriede's blood just to avoid seeing my own. *The sight of someone else's blood is okay, is it?* she had asked me.

All at once I was hungry for air. I rose to my feet and, almost to calm myself, began to pick up the articles of clothing one by one, shaking them out to smooth the wrinkles, hanging them in their place. How absurd, tidying up, as though there were any need to, as though she might return. I folded the linens, stored them in the wardrobe drawers, pulled the sheets back onto the mattress and tucked them in, to then take care of the torn pillow.

It was when I slid my arm into the pillowcase to smooth down the stuffing that I found it—something cold and hard. I pulled it free from the rough wool and saw it. A gold ring: a wedding band.

At the sight of it, I flinched. Was Elfriede married too? Who was the man she loved? Why hadn't she ever told me?

So many things we had hidden from each other. Is it possible to love each other amid deceit?

I stared at the ring for a long time, then dropped it into an empty jewelry box on the bedside table. Sticking out of an open drawer was a metal case. A cigarette case. I opened it. There was one left, the last cigarette she hadn't smoked. I took it out.

Looking at it between my fingers—the ring finger clad in the wedding band Gregor had given me one day five years earlier—I remembered Elfriede's hand drawing a cigarette to her lips, her pointer and middle fingers letting go for a second, spreading like scissors, to then collect it again during the hour-long waits in the courtyard, or the day I hid in the washroom with her. I remembered her hand with ringless fingers.

My hunger for air became unbearable, I had to get out. On impulse I grabbed Elfriede's wedding ring, clenched it in my fist, and ran away.

47

ON MY RETURN I FIND GREGOR ALONE AGAIN, HIS EYES CLOSED. I SIT down beside him, like I used to at night in Pauline's room. Without opening his eyes he says, "Forgive me, I didn't mean to make you angry."

How could he tell I was the one who had come in?

"Don't mind me, I'm a little emotional today."

"You came to visit me, you wanted a moment of peace between us, but it's not easy to know my time is running out."

"I'm so sorry, Gregor."

All I want is to touch him. To cover his hand with mine. He would feel the warmth, and that would be enough.

Gregor opens his eyes, turns. He's serious, or lost, or desperate—I can't read him anymore.

"You shut yourself off, you know?" He smiles with all the sweetness he can muster. "It's hard to live with someone who shuts herself off."

I dig my nails into my palms, clench my teeth.

I once read in a novel that there's no place where people are so abysmally silent as in German families. After the end of the war I couldn't let it be known that I had worked for Hitler; I would have paid the price, might not have survived. I didn't even tell Gregor, not because I didn't trust him—of course I trusted him. But I couldn't have told him about the lunchroom in Krausendorf without telling him about who had eaten with me every day: a girl with blotchy skin, a woman with broad shoulders and a sharp tongue, one who had had an abortion, and another who believed she was a witch, a young woman obsessed with movie stars, and a Jew. I would have to tell him about Elfriede, my sin. The one that outdid all the others in my inventory of sins and secrets. I couldn't confess to him that I had trusted in a Nazi lieutenant, the very man who sent her to a camp, the very man I loved. I never said anything and never will. I never tried to contact any of them either. The past doesn't go away, but there's no need to dredge it up; you can try to let it rest, hold your peace. The one thing I've learned from life is survival.

"The more I told you that you were shutting yourself off, the more you closed up on me. You're doing it right now." Gregor coughs again.

"Please drink something."

I pick up the glass, hold it to his mouth, and remember when I would do it in Pauline's room, remember the frightened look on his face. Gregor rests his lips against the glass and focuses on the act, as though it takes great effort, while I hold his head up. I've never touched his head without hair before. For so many years I haven't touched my husband.

The water dribbles down his chin and he pushes the glass away.

"You don't want any more?"

"I'm not thirsty." He wipes his lips with his hand.

I take the tissue out of my pocket, dab his chin dry. At first he flinches, then lets me do it. The tissue is spotted with red, and Gregor notices. He looks at me with unbearable tenderness.

48

THE DINNER CART FILLS THE HALLWAY WITH NOISE AND AROMAS. THE attendants enter, Agnes is behind them. They give her the tray, she puts it on the nightstand and thanks them. When they move to the next room, she tells me, "Rosa, we couldn't find you. Everything all right?"

"Yes, I have a slight headache, that's all."

"Margot wanted to say goodbye to you, she had to run. In any case they're going to send us all home pretty soon."

She tears off a paper towel, tucks it into the collar of his blue pajamas like a napkin, sits down very close to the bed, and feeds Gregor, slowly. From time to time she puts the spoon down to wipe his mouth. He sucks down the broth, smacking his lips, at times sinks his head into the pillow to rest—even eating tires him. Agnes minces the chicken into tiny pieces, I sit on the other side, across from her.

Gregor gestures, letting Agnes know he's full, and she says, "I'm going to go wash my hands in the bathroom."

"All right."

"After that I'm going home. Are you sure you don't want to come, at least to have something to eat?"

"I'm not hungry, thanks."

"Well, if you get hungry later on, there's the hospital cafeteria. The doctors and nurses eat there, but also the patients' families. It doesn't cost much and the food is decent."

"Maybe you could show me where it is."

I'm left alone with Gregor. I'm exhausted.

Outside, the sky is shifting. Sunset takes all the time it needs, then speeds up, collapses.

"If I had died in the war," he says, "our love would have survived."

I know it's not true.

"As if love were even the point."

"Then what is, Rosa?"

"I don't know, but I know you've just said something foolish. Old age doesn't agree with you."

It sounds like he's coughing, but he's laughing. It makes me laugh too.

"We gave it all we got, but we didn't make it through."

"We spent a few years together—that's not bad. And afterward you had the chance to have a family." I smile. "You did good to stay alive."

"But you're alone. For such a long time, Rosa."

I caress his cheek. He has skin like crepe paper—rough. Or maybe my fingertips are. I've never caressed my husband's cheek as an old woman, have never known what it feels like.

I slide two fingers over his lips, trace them delicately, then stop in the center and press gently, very gently. Gregor opens his mouth, parts it slightly, and kisses them.

THE SELECTION IN the hospital cafeteria is quite wide. There are steamed vegetables—carrots, potatoes, string beans, spinach—and sautéed vegetables, like zucchini. There are peas with bacon and stewed beans. There's pork shank and also grilled chicken breast. Soup and breaded flounder fillets, perhaps with mashed potatoes. Fruit salad, yogurt, even a pastry with raisins, though I never ate raisins again.

A dish of string beans, some mineral water, and an apple are all I order. I'm not hungry. At the cashier's, along with cutlery they give me two slices of whole wheat bread and a prepackaged pat of butter. I look for a free place. There are many. Walking around the tables of faded turquoise Formica—empty, greasy, or covered with crumbs— are men and women wearing white jackets, shuffling their rubber clogs, trays in hand. Before choosing a place, I want to figure out where they're going to sit. I find a relatively clean table that's relatively far away from them.

I steal glances at the other people sitting in the room, though from this distance I can't see very well. Who knows if someone else is eating what I'm eating tonight? I peek at everyone's trays and finally spot her. A young brunette woman, her hair gathered in a ponytail, is savoring a serving of string beans. I raise a forkful from my plate, taste it, and feel my heartbeat slowing. Modest bites, one after the other, until my stomach pulls. A slight nausea—nothing, really. Resting my hands on my belly to warm it, I sit there, motionless. Almost no one's around, only a soft murmur to be heard. I wait awhile, perhaps an hour, then get up.

Notes and Acknowledgments

In September 2014, I read a short Italian newspaper article about Margot Wölk, Hitler's last living food taster. Frau Wölk had never told anyone about her experience, but at the age of ninety-six she decided to make it public. At once, I was eager to learn more about her and her experience. A few months later, when I tracked down her address in Berlin with the intention of sending her a letter to ask to meet her, I learned that she had recently passed away. I would never be able to talk to her, nor tell her story. I could, however, try to discover why it had struck me so deeply. And so I wrote this novel.

I thank Tommaso Speccher for his supervision on historical facts.

Thanks to Ilaria Santoriello, Mimmo Summa, Francesco D'Ammando, and Benedetto Farina for their scientific advice.

Without Vicki Satlow's support this novel would never have been written. I dedicate it to her. And to Dorle Blunck and Simona Nasi, who helped me right from the start. Finally, I dedicate it to Severino Cesari, who had read everything I had ever written, but wasn't fated to read this novel.

Recommend

At the
WOLF'S TABLE

---

for your next book club!
Reading Group Guide available at
www.readinggroupgold.com